FAR AHEAD A SOUND PIERCED THE NIGHT

"Aiiee!"

Remo knew that sound. It was Chiun's familiar cry of anguish, only it had a weird, horror-struck quality now.

Clutching the briefcase, Remo broke into a run. His feet floated across the sand and into brush. From there he sprinted through the trees. He had no eyes for anything along the way, counting on his ears to take him to the site of the anguished wail.

Whatever it was, Chiun was in trouble.

Deep trouble.

Created by
WARREN MURPHY
and RICHARD SAPIR

THE Destroyer™

ENGINES OF DESTRUCTION

A GOLD EAGLE BOOK FROM
WORLDWIDE®

TORONTO • NEW YORK • LONDON
AMSTERDAM • PARIS • SYDNEY • HAMBURG
STOCKHOLM • ATHENS • TOKYO • MILAN
MADRID • WARSAW • BUDAPEST • AUCKLAND

First edition July 1996
ISBN 0-373-63218-5

Special thanks and acknowledgment to
Will Murray for his contribution to this work.

ENGINES OF DESTRUCTION

Printed in U.S.A.

For Marque Shields, who rides a decidedly
different kind of bike.

And for the Glorious House of Sinanju,
P.O. Box 2505, Quincy, MA 02269
[E-mail: Willray@cambridge.village.com]

1

Nobody knew when it all started, because it had been going on since the days of Casey Jones. Nobody thought it unusual, because it was as common as a caboose. No one knew when it would end, because as long as man set hurtling engines on ribbons of steel rail, derailments were inevitable. And no one saw a sinister pattern emerge in the waves of rail accidents, because from the earliest days of steam locomotives there had always been rail accidents. Some years there were more. Some years less.

For three unrelenting years there were more. Many more.

Rail fans, train crews and transportation experts alike said the nation's aging rail system was approaching critical mass.

The National Transportation Safety Board blamed engineers on drugs, aging and downgraded tracks, poor maintenance and just plain dumb-ass bad luck.

Everyone agreed that Amtrak was experiencing the worst of the rash of derailments. In three grim years more than one hundred Amtrak passengers had died—more combined fatalities than the nation's passenger rail service had suffered since its inception twenty-five years before.

The fact that Amtrak's cars were filled with passengers, while freight handlers hauled inert commodities, was ignored. As was the fact that the average passenger train hauled a lot more passengers that the average passenger jet. Naturally a train wreck could be more deadly than a plane crash. But they never were. More people walked away from train crashes than died. Nobody could say the same when a 747 cratered. Yet whenever an Amtrak train careened off its rails, it made the front page, not the third section. They weren't hauling cabbages, after all.

The experts all agreed that if you took Amtrak out of the statistical loop, rail traffic was as safe as it ever had been.

Which, if you knew the history of rail, had a lot to do with where you sat.

TY HURLEY SAT in the cab of a new Southern Pacific MK5000C freight hauler, his left hand on the throttle, his right goosing the independent brake as he chased the twin uncatchable gleams of starlight racing ahead of him along a curving stretch of rail approaching Big Sandy, Texas.

The cab vibrated to the deep baritone thunder of the twenty-five-ton Caterpillar 3612 diesel while Ty watched the brake pressure and RPM readouts seesaw on the liquid-crystal display screen buried in the cream-colored molded plastic of the instrument panel. Not twenty feet at his back, under four toiling, yellow-bladed exhaust fans, five thousand horses galloped in concert, but it felt wrong. All wrong.

Ty Hurley hadn't become an engineer to sit in climate-controlled comfort, sucking down polyurethane smell, insulated from the big four-stroke monster-block V-12 prime mover he controlled through a careful balancing of power and braking. This was not railroading. This was not his dream.

He missed the industrial black control panel of his old SD40-2 diesel, with its analog dials and ineffective wall fan laboring to circulate the stale cab air. That was railroading. Ty might as well have been flying the space shuttle as this overengineered appliance. But most of all, he was going to miss being an SP hogger. Southern Pacific had been absorbed by Union Pacific, and his red-nosed gray MK5000C would soon wear UP Cascade green livery. It was the end of an era.

The only things that remained the same were the two uncatchable gleams on the matched steel rails.

Ty had been chasing those gleams all his life, man and boy. Ever since he'd first heard the lonesome wail of a thundering redball freight as it raced toward destinations far, far from Texas.

It had been a good, satisfying life for a man who had never seen the big cities of the East or done much to distinguish himself. He hadn't ever "wiped the throttle"—floored an engine—but he hadn't torn up any track or spilled a load, either. Not on a dozen years on the SP. It was something to brag about, especially these days.

As he adjusted the brake pressure, coming to the big truss-and-timber-pile bridge that crossed the Sabine River, Ty tried counting his blessings.

He was thirty-six and in good health. He had a job. It was the job he'd always wanted. True, the work wasn't exactly how Ty had envisioned it back in the small town of Wichita Falls, but it paid well, and the fringe benefits kept the little wife content and the twins in Nintendo and Snickers bars.

He would probably get used to the MK5000C in time. Maybe, Ty reflected, he would haul freight long enough to see the day when it, too, would become outmoded. Hell, already they were saying the next thing big was AC. An AC monster block wouldn't birds-nest if you ran it flat out by mistake. Ty had never birds-nested an engine, either. Another blessing on the tote board of life.

Most of all, Ty wasn't his poor daddy. His father had worked the SP before him. A good man, now creased of face and broken of heart and spirit.

One day Luther Hurley was highballing down the main line when a bright yellow school bus had trundled crossways onto a crossing and got hung up on the track. Tearing around a long bend in the line, trying to make up time, Luther had seen the stalled bus only at the last. He threw the brake too late. But he could have thrown it five miles back and it would have been too late. Luther Hurley had been pulling seventy double-stacked flatcars rattling behind his bicentennial-liveried MP15 diesel. He couldn't have stopped that hurtling dragon of steel in time if he'd found a way to throw it onto its side like a Brahma bull.

The brake key broke in his hand as, screaming, Luther had plowed smack into the school bus, dragging it squealing and sparking for over a mile along unforgiving tracks.

He was the only one to survive—if you could call the way Luther Hurley lived after that awful day a life. The rescue boys had to pry his hand off the blaring horn, and when they finally did, they realized he had been screaming all along.

Ty Hurley never heard the story directly from his father, who went home that day, never to ride the rails again. A railroad man's pension kept him in beer and Sominex. Ty had read all about it in the newspapers the next day. The report had quoted some expert as saying a freight engine hitting a stalled bus was the equivalent of that same bus hitting a stationary Coke can. There was flat out no survivability factor.

That pithy fact impressed Ty more than the body count, which he had long ago forgotten. It still made him shudder to think about it. And when he came up on a crossing gate, both ends of his digestive system clenched involuntarily.

No, at least he was not his father, who was strong enough to resist falling into hard drink after his working life ended but was never much good for anything else.

From where Ty sat, train travel was the safest thing going. As long as you stayed on the train. Get in the train's path and you were track ballast. Ty knew the statistics. In the worst year less than fifty train passengers died en route. Every year at least five hundred died trying to beat hurtling diesel monsters to crossings or trespassing on tracks and hump yards.

Somewhere past midnight Ty came out of a bend just shy of Big Sandy and grabbed his horn. In town they raised a big old rumpus whenever he did that. Said he woke up the entire town. They never understood it was for their own good. Never connected the warning blast with a twenty-year-old newspaper clipping yellowing in Ty's drawer with his socks and fresh underwear.

For as long as he had any say, Ty would sound his air horn good and loud when approaching a crossing.

And damn anyone who complained. It wasn't just their lives. It was Ty Hurley's, too.

The MK5000C air horn assaulted the Texas night, sounding muffled inside the new cab. Just to be safe, Ty gave it another hoot.

He saw the bone white sport utility vehicle bump and jounce toward the diamond of crossing tracks where the former Southern Pacific line intersected Union Pacific iron, and his heart thumped like a drum, making the big veins in his hands pulse and his tongue go dry.

"Oh, dear Lord, please don't...." he muttered thickly. He hit the horn again.

In response the sport vehicle surged ahead.

"No, you dad-burn fool. No, you can't win. Back away, back away!" Ty screamed in the soundproof womb of the big hauler, knowing he couldn't be heard by anyone but his savior.

The lights of the sport vehicle were two mothy fans making the crossing glow spectrally. The gates began dropping in response to the automatic signal. A bell commenced clanging.

And Ty changed his tune.

"Hurry up. Damn it, hurry up! You can do it. Floor that sucker."

The gates were winning, and Ty's heart started to drop down his gullet.

It mounted again when the sport vehicle suddenly accelerated and smashed into the gate.

Ty watched it with eyes growing wide.

The sport machine bounced its front tires over the rails and, when its rear set hit iron, it stopped dead.

"Get out! Get out!" Ty screamed, one fist punishing the plastic moulding until it cracked like an egg.

The bone white door flew open, and a figure stepped out. Pinned by the glare of MK5000C's big cyclops headlight, he looked like a little bug. His actions were not buglike.

He had what looked like a long stick in his hands. He jammed it into a tie. It quivered upright like a bug's feeler.

Turning, he climbed awkwardly to the car's roof, reached down and plucked up his stick. Then he stood up. He just stood there facing the onrushing gray monster diesel with its blunt scarlet nose.

"Jesus Loving Christ!" Ty moaned, shifting the reverser key into neutral. Simultaneously he hauled back on the throttle, initiating dynamic braking. Instantly the traction motors were transformed. They became individual generators, straining to inhibit thousands of tons of headlong inertia.

Ty knew it was too late. He knew it was in the hands of God Almighty. All he could do was clutch his controls and stare at the unavoidable disaster in which he would be an unwilling and impotent participant.

He had heard of people committing suicide by lying down on the rails. It happened back East once or twice. They still talked about a Connecticut Yankee who just laid his idiot head down on CSX tracks and let the cruel steel trucks do for him what he hadn't the nerve to do with a bullet.

But this—

The man stood against the night, all in black. That was all Ty could make out. He wore black. Even his face looked black. Not the black of a black man but the ebony of a beetle's wings. It was as if Ty Hurley's worst nightmare had taken the shape of a man stepped out of Hell to bedevil him.

Before Ty's eyes he grew and grew, and despite the revulsion climbing his gorge, even with the image of a crushed-flat Coke can searing his imagination, Ty looked deep into that black face, into the eyes he could not see, trying to make out the features that would any second be smashed beyond recognition, wondering if that was what his poor silver-haired daddy had done. Wondering if he had seen the fear-stunned little faces, the whites of their small round eyes in that awful protracted moment before the bus was busted open like a loaf of Wonder bread, scattering childish bodies like so much sunflower seed.

Suddenly the man lifted his arms. His hands were together, holding his stick. In the blackness Ty Hurley could not make out what it was, but the image that jumped into his mind was of a sword lifted high and defiant, as if the man in black were some fearless warrior of old determined to defeat a modern freight train with a thin blade of steel.

In that heart-stopping instant of time, Ty Hurley prayed for the man. Prayed because he knew that of the two of them, only Ty would survive.

As the baritone-voiced beast bored toward him, the man laid the sword across one shoulder and seemed to be taking practice swings, like a ball player. He was real casual about it.

At the last possible second, the man cocked and let fly. The blade caught a sliver of moonlight, and Ty saw it, too, was black. Leaving his hands, it pin-wheeled up as if in slow motion. Ty's eyes went to it even as his brain said, *He's chickened out. He's gonna jump clear. Thank God. Thank God Almighty.*

Then the whirling blade was coming at his wind-screen like a furious helicopter blade, and below his line of sight the fragile utility vehicle exploded in a fireball that instantly scorched the blunt Action red nose black. And without any shudder of contact or any loss of momentum, the thirty-car freight slammed the broken thing along.

A few miles down the line, it got so twisted up it just fell apart. The pieces that were not flung aside were flattened into the track.

Ty Hurley saw and heard none of that. His hands were frozen—one on the reverser key, the other on the air horn.

His eyes were open and they were looking up, blinking uncomprehendingly. He was staring at a work boot. He didn't know whose boot it was, but it looked familiar, very familiar. It looked just like the boot he had laced up this morning, as a matter of fact.

Then the train leaned into a turn. Ty's head rolled slightly, and he could see the boot was his own. He could see himself sitting firm and unshakable at the controls of the monster hauler, and in the final moments before the darkness closed in, he wondered if he were having some kind of out-of-body experience.

For he saw that his uniform collar was very red, and where his head should have been was a curious kind of void in which arterial red blood fountained.

He had a curious thought, too: *If I'm up there, what are my eyeballs doing on the floor?*

That was the exact moment the blood finished draining out of his brain, and all life oozed away from his severed head, extinguishing that final, ridiculous, unanswered thought.

Without a conscious brain at the controls, the big MK5000C roared on through the night, swaying through the turns, blind and unstoppable, the heavy work boot of its dead engineer holding down the deadman pedal. Microprocessor controls kept the power from exceeding load-hauling tolerances. It rattled through Big Sandy, Texas, and on up to Texarkana, where it naturally ran out of track and piled into the big steel bumpers at the end of the line, with predictable results.

WHEN NTSB INVESTIGATOR Melvis Cupper reached the scene, the yard-crew foreman had one word for him.

"Birds-nested."

"So why didn't the engineer just brake that sucker?"

"I wasn't referring to the engine. We haven't cracked the damn cowl yet. I meant the engineer. He's the birds-nested one."

When he climbed into the big MK5000C cab, now lying on its side like a fallen war elephant in the mess that had been the freight yard, Melvis understood what they meant.

The damn engineer was all over the cab. The impact had flung him every which way, including apart. Fingers had snapped off. One leg was twisted all the way around and jammed up behind one shoulder. The opposite leg looked normal at first. The foot was pointed in the correct direction, but the exposed calf above it had been wrenched around at least three times. It looked like a twist of white taffy.

Worst off all, his head had been torn off his neck.

"Jesus," Melvis muttered.

"Looks like flying glass lopped it clean off."

Melvis speared his flashlight ray all around. "I don't see much loose glass."

"Well, there must be some. Feller's decapitated, ain't he?"

"That's a fact," Melvis admitted.

But the only glass present in the cab were a few splinters from the spiderwebbed window ports, the biggest of which was smaller than a fingernail.

"It's possible the big hunk of glass that got him broke apart in the crash," Melvis allowed.

"Which crash? The one back at Big Sandy or this mess right here?"

"Gotta be this one here. He only hit a Nishitsu Ninja. Damn flimsy little Jap jeep ain't no match for a roaring juggernaut like the MK5000C. Hell, the tallest part of the radio aerial wouldn't even reach up to the headlight."

"Reckon that makes sense, when you put it like that."

It was the only thing that did make sense.

Then the foreman had a thought. "If busted glass didn't get him on impact, why the hell did he ride her all the way in like he did? He had near to *fifty* damn miles to brake."

Melvis shrugged. "Maybe he froze at the controls. It happens."

"Nobody freezes for fifty miles and then plows into the freight yard, full tilt like he done."

"Well, it's for sure he didn't lose his head at the crossing," Melvis grunted. "Plumb contrary to nature is what that notion is."

But when they backtracked to the initial impact site, they found a solitary sliver of glass that looked as if it had come off an MK5000C.

Melvis ordered the window glass reassembled, and the sliver fit exactly. There was no getting around it. The engineer had been decapitated at the crossing.

"His foot should have slipped off the deadman pedal," the yard foreman said. "How do you explain it?"

"Dope," said Melvis Cupper.

"You NTSB boys are all the time sayin' dope when you can't find a reasonable explanation."

"Dope," Melvis said flatly.

It went into his preliminary report as drugs, and the report was dutifully logged into an NTSB computer in Washington, D.C., where it was archived for access by NTSB offices nationwide.

The clerk typist who performed that simple action did more to facilitate a serious investigation of the mystery of the Texarkana disaster than any field investigator. No one suspected this—any more than they suspected the three-year reign of rail terror was no string of coincidences or run of bad luck.

There was a pattern. But no one could discern it.

2

His name was Remo and he was test-driving his new wheels under battlefield conditions.

Traffic flowed all around him. Lead-footed drivers jockeyed in and out of busy lanes in a violent rush. Strangely, most of the flow was sideways, not forward. Drivers struggled to get out of their lane and into another one. Then without bothering to signal, they slid back into lanes they had just slipped out of. It was very ritualistic. A space would open up, and everyone would make a dash for it. Bumpers clashed. Horns blared. Pungent curses lifted above the din. The winner hardly ever spent more than a quarter mile occupying the hard-won slot. As soon as he saw another, he had to have it. The concept of yielding to traffic was as alien as obeying the speed limit.

Remo had a long time ago thought he'd figured out the Boston driving mentality. Every Bostonian firmly believed the common courtesies of the road applied to everyone except himself. So each driver ignored them, serene in the mistaken assumption that the other guy would dutifully observe the rules of the road. But hardly anyone ever did.

Boston drivers were always running late, as well. They were perfectly willing to risk life and limb to shave six or seven seconds off a trip. And they changed lanes as fast and erratically as most people changed their minds.

It had gotten so insane Remo had stopped driving in the city. Instead, he took cabs or the subway.

Remo couldn't find the right car to handle Boston traffic so he had demanded his employer come up with something appropriate. After all, if Remo were to die in a car crash, his employer would be out millions of dollars in training expenses—not to mention one of the two greatest assassins on the market today.

His employer had balked. At first.

"Absolutely not."

"Look, Smitty," Remo had told him. "They pour money into training fighter pilots, and when the jets go down they move heaven and earth until they rescue them even though the big loss is the plane. Right?"

"That is true," Dr. Harold W. Smith admitted slowly.

"So, you've poured tons of money into my training, and since I'm stuck living in this madhouse—"

"Boston is not a madhouse."

"Boston traffic is like playing bumper cars in Sherman tanks against homicidal maniacs. These people are okay on foot, but put them behind the wheel of a car, and they fall right off the evolutionary ladder."

Smith cleared his throat. "I am sure you are exaggerating."

"Last time I tried driving from the airport, three people did their best to run over my car because I stopped for a pedestrian at a freaking crosswalk."

"Unlikely."

"Once I was head of the line at a red light when it turned green. I didn't start up instantly, and some idiot behind me leans on his horn and calls me every name in the book."

"He must have been in a hurry."

"He was—to get to the hospital after I dislocated his tongue."

Smith made an uncomfortable noise in his throat.

"Put it in my contract," Remo said. "I want a car that will stand up to Boston traffic. And it's gotta be red."

"Why red?"

"Why not?" countered Remo.

And since good assassins were hard to find, Dr. Smith had done that. Eventually. It had taken longer than Remo expected. There were a few rejects. The first car was a Bonneville. Remo took it around the block for a test drive and was promptly sideswiped by a newspaper-delivery boy on a bicycle.

Remo got out and asked the boy if he were all right. The boy threw the afternoon paper at him and threatened to sue.

"You cut *me* off," Remo pointed out, relieved that the boy's pitching arm was unhurt.

"You should look where you're going, asshole!" the boy screamed, his nose ring shaking under his dilated nostrils.

"Does your mother know you talk that way?"

"My mother taught me to talk this way when I talk to assholes. This is a brand-new bike. Now look at it."

Remo looked. The bike had lost a fleck of electric green paint. Otherwise it was unscathed.

"I just got this car," Remo had countered, pointing to his scratched front fender.

"Will your mother beat the living crap out of you for scratching it up?"

"I didn't scratch it up. You did. And watch what you say about my mother. I never knew her."

"You're lucky. My mother's going to rip me a new cake-hole."

"Remind her for me to wash out every other orifice with soap, too."

"I could sue you, you know. My father sues people all the time."

"He should start with your mother for dropping a blivot like you into the world," Remo screamed.

"You can't talk to me like that," the newspaper boy screamed back.

"If I were your father, I'd demand my sperm back," yelled Remo, warming to the subject.

At that, the boy stalked over to Remo's new Bonneville and licked the wounded front fender with his tongue. Remo thought it was a new variation on paint sniffing until the boy straightened and Remo saw the fresh scratch that exactly matched the one made by the collision. The boy then stuck out his tongue at Remo, revealing the silver stud bolted through it.

Whereupon Remo dismantled the ten-speed with his bare hands, reassembling it into a vertical bird cage with the boy caught inside. Remo left him cawing like a crow.

The Bonneville went back to the dealer.

The second car was a Chevy Blazer. It survived the first trip around the block and even got as far as Route 128 and back when Remo happened to park it in front of a supermarket, where a Mercedes SL backed into it.

The woman driver got out from behind the wheel, took one look at the Blazer's damaged front end, her nicked bumper, and turned on Remo.

"You're supposed to watch where you're going!" she shrieked.

"I was parked," Remo declared, reasonable of tone because by this time he suspected all Boston drivers were mentally unstable.

"It's your word against mine," she flung back, flouncing past him.

"You're supposed to exchange papers at the scene of an accident," Remo called after her. "State law."

"I didn't have an accident. You did. Exchange them with yourself."

Remo waited until the woman had entered the store and then kicked her tires. He did this casually, going from tire to tire. His leather loafers bounced off the hard rubber. Each time the tire gave a low pop, and air began hissing.

When Remo reclaimed his battered Blazer, the woman's car had settled onto its rims.

Remo sent the Blazer back, too.

His employer had then complained that Remo was obviously driving in an unsafe manner.

Remo suggested that the only safe way to operate a motor vehicle in greater Boston was to lash weather balloons to the chassis and float over traffic.

"Try again," he told Smith.

The latest vehicle had arrived just that morning. Remo took one look at it, rubbed his hands together and said, "I can hardly wait."

And he had made a beeline for the Neponset River Bridge and the wild joys of Boston traffic.

So far it was everything he had asked for. But mostly it was red. Red flake, to be precise. Remo didn't know they made red-flake auto-body paint anymore. He remembered seeing it on customized hot rods as a kid, when owning a bicycle was beyond his financial reach.

Remo was tooling along the Southeast Expressway—better known as the Southeast Distressway during rush hour, or the Green Monster on good days—trying her out. It was a long, congested ribbon of elevated highway that ran through Boston proper like a torpid boa constrictor. They were going to be tearing it down soon to make way for the depressed Central Artery. Remo hoped they had the good sense to drive a stake through its heart, too.

The July sun blazed down and made his vehicle burn like a hot coal. He could be seen for miles. That was a big plus. Boston drivers had trouble seeing anything smaller than the Hancock Tower.

As he approached the Roxbury-Mass Ave. off ramp, a man in a black Ford Ranger Bigfoot tried to cut in front of him, horn blaring, oversize wheels clawing asphalt.

In the past Remo would have gotten upset or angry. Instead, he grinned from ear to ear.

Remo fed the engine gas and accelerated, cutting him off.

Recovering just in time, the man gave Remo the finger. So Remo gave his wheel a gentle nudge. His vehicle eased over into the other lane. The Bigfoot driver tried to crowd him back. It was no contest. The other driver only had a jacked-up sport utility vehicle with Bozo the Clown tires. Remo was driving a fourteen-ton armored personnel carrier.

Remo ran him over into the breakdown lane and, not satisfied with that, crowded him against the guardrail.

The Ranger shed sparks and paint for over a mile before the cursing driver finally stopped yanking the wheel toward Remo in a futile attempt to run him off the road. He just ground to a halt, one tire resembling blackened Shredded Wheat.

"I like it," Remo said as he put the mauled Ranger behind him.

"You are insane," said Dr. Harold W. Smith, gray face turning white, from the passenger seat. He clutched his briefcase before his chest. His gray eyes were stark behind his rimless glasses. He had come to Boston to personally hand over the keys and special papers that made the APC street legal. Remo had talked him into coming along for the test drive. Smith obviously regretted it.

"That was defensive driving," Remo protested. "You saw him cut me off. Don't deny it."

Coming up on the Neponset-Quincy exit, Remo eased carefully into the exit lane.

Two nuns in a metallic silver Honda hatchback suddenly overhauled him, cut over hard and almost sent him into the rail. Only Remo's superhuman reflexes avoided high-speed disaster.

Dropping in behind the hatchback, Remo gave them a blast of his horn.

The nun who wasn't driving leaned out of the open hatchback and threw her black rosary at him. It bounced off the red flake armor, scattering beads everywhere.

"See!" Remo said. "This is what I'm talking about. Even the nuns go batty when they're on the road."

"Incredible."

"Boston drivers. They are the absolute worst."

"And you have become one of them," Smith said tightly.

"What!"

"You are enjoying this, Remo."

"I'm enjoying having the upper hand in traffic," Remo said heatedly. "I'm enjoying not taking my life into my hands when I pop down the street for a sack of rice. I'm enjoying the fact that no matter how crazy the other guy is, no matter what he's driving, I'm bigger, harder and more impervious than he is."

"Then you will accept this vehicle?"

"With bells on. It have a name, by any chance?"

"It is called a Dragoon."

"I can hardly wait to tell Chiun I am the proud owner of a fully loaded Dragoon."

"Actually," Smith said, "I had the offensive weaponry removed."

"Too bad. Around here they would make great scofflaw discouragers."

"Less weight means better fuel economy," Smith said tightly.

"Good thinking. How many miles to the gallon does this beast get anyway?"

"Three," said Harold Smith, director of CURE, the supersecret government agency that had no official existence.

WHEN THEY PULLED into the parking lot of his private apartment complex in the seaside city of Quincy, the Master of Sinanju was waiting for them.

He stood only five feet tall, his wispy body tented in a teal silk kimono, but the wisdom of the ages seemed to have been inscribed on his parchment features. He was Korean. Bald. Hazel eyed. Long nailed. There was a little hair over each ear, and a wind-troubled wisp that passed for a beard. His voice was a querulous squeak.

"How fares the mighty dragon?" he called out.

"Dragoon," Remo corrected.

"I care not how the word is pronounced in this contentious province," said Chiun, who did not look remotely like one of the two most dangerous assassins of the twentieth century. "It is the official conveyance of the Master of Sinanju. Therefore, it will properly and respectfully be addressed as the Sinanju Dragon."

"Dragoon," said Remo. "Tell him, Smitty."

The Master of Sinanju looked up at the man he called Emperor. Smith was climbing out of the Dragoon. He was a thin, spare man past retirement age. Everything about him was gray. Hair, eyes, unhealthy skin color. A man like Smith could have benefited from careful color coordination of his wardrobe selection. Instead, Smith habitually dressed in gray three-piece suits that enabled him to blend into almost any situation like some colorless chameleon.

"Call it what you will," he said. "I must be going."

Chiun's sparse eyebrows lifted, making his hairless scalp wrinkle up. "So soon? But you have only this day arrived, Emperor. I had planned a feast in your honor."

"I really must be going."

Chiun inclined his aged head. "Great is our disappointment, but we will endure it heroically, swallowing our bitter tears, for we understand that we are but servants, mere tools to be employed at will and if necessary disposed of like a sword that has lost its edge. I do not blame you, O discerning one. For our dullness stands exposed before your all-seeing orbs."

And the Master of Sinanju bestowed the withering regard of his hazel eyes upon Remo's hands.

Smith followed Chiun's gaze.

"He's still at it," Remo said, holding up his hands. They looked like ordinary hands. His wrists were freakishly thick, but the hands might have belonged to anyone. The fingers were on the long side, but no one would mistake them for the digits of a concert pianist. The nails were neat and carefully trimmed.

Shying from the horrible sight, Chiun threw a teal sleeve across his eyes. "No, I cannot bear to look upon those maimed things. Look away, O Emperor. Remo, hide them, lest you offend Smith the Tolerant for all time."

"Where do I hide my hands?" Remo asked, lifting his arms to show off his white T-shirt and tight tan chinos.

"You have pockets."

"There's nothing wrong with my hands."

"You have the nails of a sloth, and you say that!" Chiun whirled. "Smith, a boon. Surgeons have changed Remo's face in the past. Can anything be done for his retarded fingernails?"

"I have never heard of cuticle implants," Smith said with no humor whatsoever.

Chiun's spare shoulders sagged. "Then it is hopeless. When I pass into the Void, I will be the last of my line with nails of the correct length."

With that, the Master of Sinanju lifted his hands and stared at them, his parchment features a mask of regret. His nails curved out a good inch beyond his bony fingertips. They looked like ivory daggers and could slice a human throat open with a casual flick.

"He's still trying to get me to grow Fu Manchu fingernails," Remo undertoned to Smith.

"Resist," Smith whispered back.

"Yes!" Chiun cried. "Resist these Western urges, Remo. Do as Smith commands. Let your fingers flower and grow. Unleash the deadliness that lurks within. There is nothing to fear. I will teach you proper nail cultivation. Do this one thing, and your training will be complete. I will ask nothing more of you."

Remo shook his head firmly. "No soap, Chiun. Once I cave in on the nails, you'll be fitting me for a fighting kimono."

"You should be on bended knee begging for a respectable kimono. You look like a scarecrow in those hideous pantaloons."

"Trousers," said Remo.

"Remo needs to blend in with our society," Smith said firmly.

"Let your society know him for a Sinanju assassin! What is this mania for secrecy?"

Remo and Smith exchanged glances. Neither man spoke, but their weary expressions all but said, *You explain it to him this time.*

"I must go," Smith said in his lemoniest tone of voice.

"Need a lift to the airport?" asked Remo.

"No. I came by train."

"Train?"

"Yes, it was the most economical option. Also I wished to observe the Amtrak system firsthand."

"Why's that?"

Smith lowered his voice. "That is an operational matter."

"Checking out Amtrak involves national security?"

Chiun piped up, his wrinkled face suddenly stern, "Remo! Do you not read your newspapers? The insurgent Amtraks are at the forefront of the rebellions in the far western provinces. Even as we stand here, unsuspecting, they are sowing sedition and advocating the overthrow of the Eagle Throne, which we are pledged to protect."

Smith adjusted his Dartmouth tie uncomfortably. "If you do not mind, I must be going," he muttered.

Chiun inclined his head in a stiff semibow. "Though you take the very sun with you, we will press on, unbowed, living for the day that you call upon us to do your bidding, O generous one," he cried.

"Er, yes," Smith said. He hurried up the street to the subway station as if being hectored by bullies.

"Do you always have to do that?" Remo asked Chiun.

"It is better than suffering that man's tiresome company all evening," Chiun sniffed.

"Smitty's not so bad."

"He eats his rice with a fork," Chiun spat, and then promptly kicked all four oversize tires on the Dragoon.

"Why are you doing that?" Remo asked.

"Because you neglected to."

Remo patted the hull. "So how do you like it?"

Chiun regarded the gleaming monster of steel plate critically and asked, "Why is it scarlet?"

"So the maniacs will see me coming and get the hell out of my way," Remo explained. "And you haven't answered my question."

Chiun wrinkled up his tiny nose. "It lacks dragons."

"I like it the way it is. Without dragons."

"It is half mine. There will be a dragon painted upon my half. See that it is finished by morning."

"If it's *your* half, why do *I* have to paint it?"

"Because if you do not, I will insist upon dual matching dragons, not to mention front and rear phoenixes."

Remo sighed. "What color dragon?"

"Gold and green are good dragon colors. But I leave this to you."

"You know, I haven't painted anything since kindergarten."

Chiun shrugged. "You are still young and have all night to learn your craft."

With that, the Master of Sinanju bustled back into the fieldstone building they shared. In past times it had been a church, a Sikh temple and possibly had seen other, more secular incarnations. Now it was a nondenominational condominium. Converted back in the eighties, it had never been offered to the public. Instead, Harold Smith had bought it at auction, turning it over to the Master of Sinanju as part of a previous contract settlement. Chiun had promptly dubbed it Castle Sinanju, and they had moved in. Remo occupied one wing and Chiun the other. They shared the low, crenellated bell tower. It was to this tower Chiun had repaired, Remo knew. Ostensibly to meditate but in reality to watch as Remo once again did his bidding.

There were times in the past when Remo would have fought Chiun's dragon. But theirs was now a long association, and Remo had learned to get along. So what if he had to paint a dragon? It was a small thing to do for the man who had transformed Remo Williams from a still-breathing dead man to the sole heir to the House of Sinanju.

It had been so long ago Remo had forgotten the year. He no longer thought in years anyway. That was Western. Remo wasn't completely Eastern, but a subtle blend of East and West.

In the days when he had been Remo Williams, Newark beat cop, all Remo knew about the East was soaked up during a tour in Vietnam. Turning in his Marine fatigues for city-cop blues, Remo had settled down to the perfectly ordinary life of a police officer.

The day the stony-faced detectives arrested him changed all that. He was charged with the beating death of a pusher—another name he had forgotten. Faster than he could absorb events, Remo was tried, convicted and given the seat of dishonor in the Death House.

He woke up, not dead but in a place called Folcroft Sanitarium in Rye, New York. He was soon to discover it was the cover for CURE, the organization that had framed him. Just as he was slowly realizing the electric chair had been rigged to deliver a non-lethal charge.

They put him in the hands of Chiun, the last Master of Sinanju. He wasn't given a choice. Since he was already dead and buried in the eyes of the world, finishing the job was just a matter of plunging a charged needle in his arm and dumping him into the still-fresh grave with his name on it.

Remo had never heard of Sinanju before that day so long ago. He learned that Sinanju was the name of a tiny fishing village in North Korea, which in turn became the seat of the House of Sinanju, a line of assassins that stretched back some five thousand years. But most of all, Sinanju was the name of the martial-arts discipline practiced by the Masters of Sinanju—village and house.

Remo had been selected to be the first Westerner to be taught the secrets of Sinanju. It sounded cool when Remo had first had it explained to him.

"Is this like kung fu?" Remo asked Chiun.

"What do you know of kung fu?" Chiun snapped.

"Bruce Lee does it in movies. Five guys jump him, and he sends them flying in all directions."

Chiun's bright hazel eyes had narrowed in a look Remo would learn to fear. "You enjoy seeing men fly in all directions?"

"Sure."

And getting up from his lotus position on the Folcroft gym floor, Chiun had obliged Remo. By throwing him in all directions.

A half hour of being bounced off assorted walls taught Remo a very valuable lesson.

One, do not piss off Chiun.

Two, never mention Bruce Lee or kung fu ever again.

The first eye-opening lessons. It made Remo almost nostalgic thinking about them.

Remo soon learned that kung fu, not to mention karate, judo and aikido were all lifted without benefit of payment or credit from Sinanju, which was the sun source of the martial arts.

He then learned what to put into his mouth and what not to put into his mouth. He learned to breathe correctly, from the stomach, not through the lungs exclusively. He learned the first exercises that seemed pointless, and he ate tons of bitter kimchi to purge the fats and sugars that had poisoned his system.

It was long and painful, and Remo never realized he had sloughed off the first outer scales of his Western skin until long after it had happened. By then there was no turning back for either of them.

It was so long ago. An American President had seen his nation fragment into unweldable pieces. Because the title of his stationery said President of the United States of America, he felt obliged to put the country back together.

CURE was created. Secret, funded by hidden budget money, unknown to all except the chief executive, its director, Harold Smith, and later Remo and Chiun, it was the unofficial instrument for correcting America's many ills.

Ills that, by the time the President had perished by an assassin's hand, had grown unchecked and seemingly uncheckable.

Harold Smith had turned to the East to save the greatest nation of the New World. He turned to

Chiun, ancient, childless, pupilless—the fading fragment of a former glory.

The East thought Sinanju passed into memory. The West knew nothing of it. It was the perfect solution. America needed an assassin. Sinanju required continuity. A bargain was struck. A dead man would be trained in the forbidden art that was soon to die. No face was lost on either side. All was secret.

And Remo had learned, becoming an assassin and, in time, much more. He became Sinanju, capable of feats of strength, skill and reflex ordinary mortals were only capable of in rare moments of crisis. For Sinanju opened up the entire brain to its full potential. An awakened brain in turn unleashed the dull muscles and inhibited senses.

If a human being could accomplish it, Remo could surpass it. He saw more clearly and much farther than other men. His reflexes were as sharp as those of many predators. His strength and agility exceeded human tolerances.

All this, Chiun had done for him. And if, so many years into their relationship, he had to have a dragon on his side of the family APC, Remo was going to give it to him.

The trouble was, there was nothing in the discipline of Sinanju that imparted artistic skills. Oh, Chiun had tried to teach Remo the slashing ideographic characters used by the ancient Sinanju Masters to record their mighty deeds. But he had failed. Remo proved more adept at the relatively modern Hangul alphabet, which Chiun considered crude and inexpressive.

But if Chiun wanted a dragon, Remo would give him one. For he loved the Master of Sinanju with all his heart.

And above all, he was absolutely, positively not growing talons.

3

Dr. Harold W. Smith stood by the automatic glass doors at Boston's South Station waiting room, expecting his train to be called. He had already figured out the track. An Amtrak train had pulled into track 7. It was the only silver train with the red-and-white-and-blue Amtrak stripe running down its length in the station. The other trains were all emblazoned with the hideous purple-and-yellow MBTA livery—local commuter trains. People were glancing up at the big electronic departure board anxiously, waiting for the track to be posted. That information was abundantly self evident. Yet they loitered by the big board while Smith hovered by the doors. It would be just a matter of being one of the first out the door.

That way, Smith was assured of a seat. He had to have a seat. It was a four-hour trip back, and he couldn't afford to waste the time.

It was surprising how crowded the train had been coming up. People actually stood in the aisles. It wasn't a holiday or weekend. It was just an ordinary Tuesday in midsummer.

Smith himself had to stand until New Haven, where the train stopped as the electric engine was switched for a diesel. He understood that once the Northeast

Corridor was fully electrified, the fifteen-minute delay would be a thing of the past.

As soon as the *Yankee Clipper* emptied out at New Haven, Smith had dropped into a vacant seat. Just in time. The train had filled up again within minutes and remained packed all the way to Boston.

Smith was taking no chances on the return trip. His arthritic knee was acting up again. And if he stood, he could not work. Harold Smith detested idleness, a reflection of his cheerless New England upbringing.

When the announcer finally called, "All Aboard for the *Merchant's Limited*," Smith made an unseemly dash for the door. The doors parted, and he hurried down the track to duck into a no-smoking car.

Selecting a comfortable window seat, he settled in, his well-worn briefcase balanced tightly in his lap. By habit, he took the seat next to one of the emergency window exits. Harold Smith never took undue chances with his life. If he died, CURE would have to shut down. America could not afford that just yet.

The coach soon filled up.

A large black woman in a purple print dress waddled up the aisle and stopped at Smith's row.

"Is this the catbird seat?" she demanded, pointing at the empty seat next to Smith.

"What?"

"I'm looking for the catbird seat."

"I do not know what you are talking about," Smith protested.

"Looks to me like the catbird seat, so I might as well take it."

The woman dropped into the empty seat beside him and by way of introduction dug a meaty elbow into Smith's lathlike ribs.

"Excuse me," Smith said, squirming in his seat.

"You're excused," the woman said, unperturbed. "What did you do anyway?"

"I did nothing."

"Then why'd you excuse yourself?"

"Your elbow is in my side," Smith said uncomfortably.

"Is that supposed to be a dig?"

"Excuse me?"

"There you go again. *Now* what's wrong?"

"Your elbow is still in my side."

"I can stand to lose a few pounds. I will be the first to admit it. But these train people don't make the seats big enough to accommodate those of us of the ample persuasion. If you take my meaning. Ain't nothing can be done about it, honey. I tried dieting I tried not eating. Oprah I ain't."

Smith looked around for another seat. But there was none. Craning his head, he tried to see into the cars behind him. People were coming down the aisles, wearing that worried look that told him there were no seats to be had.

"Now who's squirming?" the woman asked.

"Sorry," said Smith.

"That's better. You settle down now, and we'll get along fine. Like the man say, you got to go along to get along."

The train lurched into motion, and Harold Smith watched the station fall away. Gathering speed, the *Merchant's Limited* rattled past an iron monstrosity of a bridge that looked as if it had been built by medieval ironworkers. There was a brief stop at Back Bay Station. As the suburbs of Boston began clicking by, the train picked up speed.

Smith waited until the conductor had collected his ticket before trying to open his briefcase.

"Need help with that?" his seatmate asked.

"I can manage."

"Just 'cause I'm a woman don't mean I ain't strong. You look like you could use a hand."

"I am fine."

"You don't look, sound or act like it," the woman said doubtfully.

Smith turned the briefcase sideways, then the long way, but given the way the woman in the adjoining seat was spilling over into his seat, it was impossible to move his arms usefully.

Smith had to be careful. The briefcase was booby-trapped. If unlocked incorrectly, explosive charges would detonate, destroying its contents. Not to mention Smith and anyone in a ten-foot radius.

"You gonna stop fussing any time soon?" Smith's fellow passenger said thinly.

Smith sighed. "Yes. I am done."

"Good. But it still ain't open."

"I changed my mind."

"I don't blame you for giving up. I'm that way about childproof caps myself. You know, I think the companies got it all backward. They should sell medicine in chocolate boxes and chocolate in childproof bottles. If they did that, my life would be a whole lot tidier, and I'd fit into this damn seat to boot."

Smith stared out the window, watching the familiar undulating stone fences and granite outcroppings of New England pass by. They reminded him of his upbringing. Only Harold Smith could be moved to quiet nostalgia by the sight of hard, unromantic granite. But that was the kind of person he was.

At Providence, Smith waited patiently. Hardly anyone got off, but several people got on, all looking disappointed at the lack of empty seats.

"I know that look you wearing," the woman beside him said.

"What is that?"

"You were hoping I was getting off here. Well, I ain't. So you can just get over it."

"I do not know what you are talking about," Smith said stiffly.

"You ain't hardly spoke to me all this time. You ignoring me. That's fine. I been ignored before. It won't hurt me. But this ain't my stop, so don't get all hopeful-faced on me."

The train started up again. It rolled out of the station and into the light of day, diesel engine laboring.

Smith cleared his throat. His Adam's apple bobbed like a yo-yo.

The woman eyed him skeptically. "Something on your mind?"

"No."

"The next stop ain't my stop, either. If this is the catbird seat, like I hope it is, I ain't getting off until the accident."

Smith blinked. "What accident?"

"The accident what's gonna happen."

"How do you know an accident is going to happen?" Smith asked sharply.

"Because one always does on these things. Don't you read the newspapers?"

"Yes. But the accidents are entirely random. There is no predicting them."

"Well, it can't be random enough to suit me. I just want to have my accident and stop riding these damn rattletrap things."

Smith thin jaw sagged. "You *want* an accident?"

"As God is my copilot."

"Why?"

"For the insurance money, why else? You think I *like* riding these stuffy old coaches? Hah! Not likely. Once I file my claim, I fly first-class all the rest of my days. No more having my insides shook up in one of these rattlers."

"And if there is no accident?"

The woman shrugged. "Then I guess I ride this damn thing all the way back and start saving up for the next run."

"Madam," said Harold Smith.

"Yeah?"

"You are a fool."

"Maybe. But I'm in the catbird seat, and so are you. Just hope you got the strength in your skinny old body to open that window exit."

Smith said nothing. He was thinking.

For a year now he had been tracking the rash of rail disasters plaguing the nation's railroad system, attempting to glean a pattern or purpose to the unusual surge of derailments and train wrecks.

His computers had found nothing significant, other than the statistical quirk of so many incidents over such a long time.

Smith was a student of statistics, going back to his pre-CURE days at the CIA, where he'd been a data analyst. He understood probabilities, coincidences, cluster effects and other statistical phenomena that the superstitious attributed to everything from bad astrological conjunctions to sunspots.

He understood it was possible that these disasters were simply a run of bad luck aggravated by the declining state of the nation's web of rails.

But Smith also understood the longer the phenomenon persisted, the less likely mere happenstance could be blamed. The longer the list of statistics grew, the less likely the reasons were purely statistical.

Smith had been close to sending Remo and Chiun into the field to look into the problem, when abruptly the string of disasters had stopped. It was a hopeful sign. It had lasted three months so far. If it continued, it meant the worst was over.

Now Smith found himself seated next to a woman who was expecting an accident.

"What makes you think there will be an accident on this particular line?" Smith asked carefully.

"'Cause one ain't happened yet."

"I beg your pardon?"

"I said, one ain't happened on this stretch yet. They been happening elsewhere but not here. So I figure to ride this line until I get lucky. Something bad's bound to happen."

Smith swallowed hard. "If you are referring to the rash of derailments, they appear to have stopped."

"They didn't stop in Texas."

"Texas?"

"There was a big train wreck in Texas last night. Ain't you heard?"

Smith blinked. He had not. He began every day scanning AP wire-service feeds off his computer links. There had been no derailment reported in the morning feeds.

"Are you certain of your facts?" he asked the woman.

"I got eyes. I can read. A freight train slammed into the yards at Texarkana. Made a damn mess, too. Saw it all on the TV."

"Pardon me," said Smith, wriggling in his seat.

Carefully he undid the catches and opened the briefcase, exposing his portable computer system with its satellite phone uplink to the big mainframes housed in the basement of Folcroft Sanitarium, the headquarters for CURE.

"What's that?"

"My laptop," Smith said brusquely.

"I think you need more lap than you got."

Initializing the system, Smith dialed up his mainframes and, that done, called up the AP wire.

It was the first item.

Freight Accident—Texarkana, Texas (AP)
A Southern Pacific freight train crashed into a sport jeep stalled at a crossing grade in Big Sandy, Texas, destroying it. Out of control, the train barreled on east to the Texarkana freight yards for some fifty miles, where it crashed. The engineer was decapitated in the crash. National Transportation Safety Board officials are investigating the cause of the accident.

Smith's prim, bloodless mouth thinned. Loss of life was minimal, he was pleased to see. Oddly there was no word of the driver of the demolished utility jeep. Presumably he had survived.

By all accounts it was a man-made tragedy. A driver had caused it by his reckless attempt to beat a freight train. It was a mistake so common that when Smith analyzed past train accidents he factored those out as statistically meaningless.

"They'll never replace papers," the woman said suddenly.

Smith looked up. "I did not catch that," he said thinly.

"I say, that thing will never replace the newspapers. I don't care how many trees gotta die. Newspapers don't need batteries. Mark my words. The information superhighway is gonna end up sprouting weeds from every crack."

"I see," said Smith, slipping back into thought.

The conductor was coming down the aisle calling out the next stop.

"Mystic. Mystic next! Exit to the rear. Mystic, Connecticut—five minutes."

The train had been humming along the track, doing 120 miles per hour. There was none of the familiar clickety-clack of the trucks on the rail sections. This was CWR track—continuous welded rail. The coach shook and shimmied monotonously.

Glancing out the window, Smith saw Long Island Sound shimmering under a summer sun. The water was lapping at the rail bed up ahead.

As the train rattled and swayed into a long turn, he could see the diesel engine pulling the long silver snake of the train behind it.

The train gave out a low, mournful sound. It was repeated, a more protracted note this time.

There was no warning. Smith was taking in the ocean view, his mind a blank, not thinking of anything in particular when the train shuddered. They were running through an area of salt marsh where cattails waved in a gentle sea breeze.

Then came a boom. A jolt. The car seemed to buck. Smith's eyes flew back to the car interior. He caught the startled looks on faces jerking up from reading material and Amtrak tray meals.

That shared moment of uncertainty seemed to last forever. In reality it was a split second broken by a string of dull detonations.

Boom-boom-boom-boom—

And the coach was suddenly hurtling in a direction that was contrary to the tracks below.

Harold Smith clutched his briefcase and held on firmly.

It did him no good. He was pitched from his seat, thrown unceremoniously into the aisle. The last thing he saw were the flying bodies of his fellow passengers.

The strange thing was that nobody screamed. Not one living soul emitted the tiniest bleat of surprise even as the shriek and scream of tortured steel filled the universe of chaos that had violently taken hold of their lives.

Remo was preparing to conjure up a dragon.

He had stripped off his summer white T-shirt and stood on the passenger side of the big scarlet Dragoon APC. At his feet were an assortment of spray cans. He had bought them at a local hardware store, buying two of every color because it was easier than thinking the color scheme through ahead of time.

If he was going to paint his first dragon, it was going to be a spontaneous dragon. It was going to be a dragon never before seen. It would be a dragon among dragons.

The problem was, what kind of a dragon would it be?

There were dragons and there were dragons, Remo knew.

Some dragons were Chinese. Others Korean, Japanese and even English. There were probably Welsh dragons, too. Maybe even French dragons.

As Remo stood by the blank red canvas that was the Dragoon's armor, he tried to summon up in his mind the exact properties of Korean dragons.

There was only one hitch. Remo had never paid much attention to dragons before this. He was not a dragon aficionado. Or whatever dragon fanciers were called.

Feeling the pressure of eyes on the back of his head, Remo looked back and up.

At the bell-tower window facing the street, he saw the troubled visage of the Master of Sinanju abruptly pull back. Chiun had moved so fast Remo wasn't sure if he actually saw his true face or some kind of after-image lingering in the void where he had been. But he had been there. No question.

Remo called up. "Hey, Little Father!"

No answer came.

"Hey, Chiun."

The face returned to the window, looking placid and innocent.

The window was heaved up.

"Did you call, Remo?" said Chiun, his voice all innocence and surprise.

Remo let the old fraud's imposture pass. "You still got that black kimono with the golden dragons?"

"Possibly," Chiun said thinly.

"Can I borrow it a sec?"

"Why do you wish it?"

Remo made his face placid. "Could be I want to try it on for size."

"Design your own dragon, plagiarist," Chiun said, snapping the window shut.

"So much for cunning," muttered Remo, eyes returning to the blank expanse of red.

Feeling eyes on him again, Remo got his inspiration.

Walking to the nose of the Dragoon, he stabbed out his right index fingernail. It looked as ordinary as he did. But the index nail was cut slightly longer than the rest. Remo did that purposefully, because while he had no use for long fingernails, the fingernail could be a potent weapon. Especially if one had been trained to use it correctly.

Touching the hard plate with the nail, Remo closed his eyes.

The problem was he still sometimes thought like a Westerner. A Westerner would sketch his dragon on paper first, transferring it to the canvas as a tracing. From that, the final drawing would be done and paint applied.

Remo was going to devise his dragon Eastern style. No tracing for him. Chiun wanted a dragon. He was going to get his dragon. And it was going to be whatever kind of dragon lurked in the red steel, waiting to be discovered.

Shutting his eyes, Remo stepped backward. One pace. Two. Then three. The nail screeched against the plate, making a shriek. A thin wire of scarlet peeled and curled away as Remo's nail—the product of long years of diet, exercise and training—scored the hard, complaining metal.

A long, undulating wave drew itself from nose to stern. When he reached the end, Remo allowed himself to peek.

Not bad. It had a dragonlike back. Repositioning his nail, he started forward.

The metal squealed a different tone going in this direction. He worked quickly, surely, instinctively. This was the Sinanju way. Remo had never done anything like this before, but Sinanju opened the mind, and the mind revealed all manner of hidden talents when it was open.

Hopefully it also revealed dragons.

Reaching the front, Remo stopped and peeked through one eye.

He was back at the point where he had begun. And now he had a long undulating form outlined in silver thread against red. Was it a dragon? Well, it wasn't *not* a dragon. It was a start. So, emboldened, Remo sketched in legs.

These he did with his eyes open. He made a front talon and a back claw. The tail was already there, so he edged it with short triangular spines. Yes, it was starting to look like a dragon, all right.

Now the head. That was trickiest. The front part of the dragon shape didn't really look like a head. He looked back. Actually the tail looked more like a head, and the head might pass as a tail. But if he switched ends, what were those barbs on the current tail?

Remo regarded his silver-thread dragon from every angle before he was seized by a brilliant inspiration.

Attacking the head, he made eyes and added teeth. Then he went to the back and performed a few operations there. Finally he added a curling, batlike wing.

Then, stepping back, Remo took it in in all its etched splendor.

It was bloodred—a good dragon color—outlined in silver. Silver went well with red.

Yes, it was a dragon. No doubt about it. And best of all, he had created it without resorting to messy spray paints.

As he took it in, Remo continued to feel a dull pressure on the back of his head that might mean a sniper was zeroing in on him but usually meant Chiun was watching.

He turned, grinned and said, "What do you think?"

Chiun was not there.

"Hey, Little Father. I know you're up there."

The window remained closed.

"Chiun. It's done."

Abruptly the front door was flung open, and out stepped the Master of Sinanju like a fussy teal hen. His face was bunched up like a yellow raisin.

Bustling up, he stopped, regarded the side of the Dragoon vehicle and cocked his head this way and that, eyes thinning to walnut slits.

"What do you think?" Remo asked proudly.

"Why does it have two heads?"

"The back is the head and the front is the tail."

"Why it is backward then?"

"It's *not* backward. It's supposed to be facing that way."

"It faces away from danger?"

"It's a decorative dragon, not a battle dragon."

"It is a cowardly dragon." Chiun squinted. "Its eyes are Western."

"You're imagining things. I drew it Eastern style."

"And its tail is English. I will not have an English dragon on my chariot."

"I don't know what you're talking about. It's a perfectly respectable dragon."

"And I detect Japanese influences in the scales."

"Those are barbs."

"Hah. Definitely Japanese. Erase it. For it offends my eyes."

"I can't erase that. I scored it with my own fingernails."

"It is no wonder then. Would you paint a seascape with a brush that lacks bristles?"

"That's not a good comparison."

"Erase it."

"It can't be erased. It's an etching."

"Then browbeat Smith into purchasing a new Dragon. I will not ride in this monstrosity. I would be shamed before all."

With that, the Master of Sinanju flounced back into the house, pointedly locking the door after him to signify that if Remo ever desired entry to Castle Sinanju again, he would have to mend his ways.

Picking up a spray can, Remo decided he would have to start all over again.

"Maybe I'd be better off letting my nails grow, after all," he grumbled, applying scarlet to his dragon.

AN HOUR AND TEN CANS of scarlet and metallic gold later, Remo's Dragoon looked as if it had been defaced by drunken graffiti artists. He had switched to Western style. The result—no dragon. Nothing that looked remotely like a dragon. Nothing that looked remotely like anything.

Seeing that his hands were flecked with paint droplets, Remo decided to call it a day. Maybe tomorrow was the day a dragon would come.

Reaching the door, Remo found it locked.

"Uh-oh."

No sense breaking in the door. Chiun would never let him hear the end of it.

Remo walked around the building. It was a hot summer day, so certain windows would be open for ventilation.

He found one at the far end, high up just under the eaves.

Remo looked around. No cars on the streets. No nosy people walking by. Perfect.

Taking hold of the fieldstone side, he let his fingertips sense the surface, absorbing its imperfections. It looked smooth to the eyes, but in fact was very rough. Crooking his fingers, Remo found tiny purchase points. He lifted. A bystander watching him would have said he was trying to pull the building down into its own cellar. In fact, that was the technique. Remo was not trying to climb the building. That would not work, strangely enough. But by attempting to drag the building down so the open window reached Remo's head height, a miracle happened.

From Remo's point of view, the building actually sank.

In reality, Remo was scaling the building using his fingers and toes.

His head came up to the open casement window, and he stuck his head in.

A stern face greeted him. "If you have bespattered my fine castle with paint, I will never forgive you," said Chiun in his squeakiest register.

And because Remo knew the next step might be slamming the window in his face, he sprang sideways to the next window, rolled in, snapped to his feet and faded off to one side while the Master of Sinanju pulled the other pane shut with a hard bang.

"Too late," Remo said.

Chiun whirled. For an instant Remo believed he had outsmarted his teacher, but Chiun pretended otherwise. He grasped his wrists with his long-nailed hands and the sleeves of his silken teal kimono met, concealing them from view.

"Your hands are filthy. Wash them this instant."

"My plan exactly," Remo said agreeably. "And while I'm at it, my nails look like they could use a good trimming."

Chiun's eyes narrowed to crafty slits, but he made no protest.

Going to the nearest bathroom—there were more than a dozen strategically placed throughout the sixteen-unit complex—Remo closed the door and gave his hands a good scrubbing with pumice soap. That took off the worst of the paint. The rest was ingrained into his skin.

Remo had a technique for that, too. Human skin consisted of a dead outer layer that sloughed and scaled off in the course of normal living. So Remo, after drying his hands, started dry-washing them vigorously.

His hands blurred. They even smoked a little. And into the washbowl tiny flecks of black material began precipitating. It was paint, turned black by the same friction that burned it off the skin of his fingers.

Hands clean, Remo rinsed them under cold tap water, then examined his nails. They were not very long, but could stand a trimming anyway. No sense encouraging Chiun's hopes by being lax.

Reaching into the medicine cabinet, Remo found a pair of nail clippers. They were extra-heavy-duty and custom-made out of drop-forged titanium. Since he now possessed fingernails that could score steel, Remo needed something tougher than the kind of clippers one could buy at K mart.

Carefully Remo began clipping his nails, starting with the smaller, easier ones. He worked from pinkie to thumb on his left hand. Switching hands, he naturally took the heavy clipper in his left hand and started with the thumb, then jumped to the pinkie and worked back from there. By the time he reached the nail he always saved for last—the extrahard, longish right index nail—he had a tiny pile of shavings on the porcelain sink counter that, if swallowed, would kill a rhinoceros.

The long nail was the tough one. If Remo cut it too short, he risked disarming a useful weapon. Through the years Remo had learned to enter locked buildings by scoring window glass with his right index nail. It was a handy tool to have, even if he would never admit this to the master of Sinanju.

Once Remo had inadvertently cut the nail too short, and for a solid month felt as if he had chopped off his right index finger to the knuckle. That was how much that nail was a part of him.

So Remo carefully trimmed the nail back, leaving enough to be useful. The titanium blade sounded like a tiny bolt cutter at work.

The nail came off in a perfect half-moon sliver and joined the tiny pile.

An impatient knock came at the door.

"You are hogging the bathroom," complained Chiun.

"There's others," Remo called back.

The door hammered under an angry fist. "I wish to use that one."

"All right, all right. I'm done," said Remo, sweeping the nail clippings into a wastebasket.

Opening the door, Remo stepped back as the Master of Sinanju hurried in. His eyes went to Remo's hands.

"Show me your hands. Are they clean?"

"Oh, get off it."

Chiun snapped his palms together. "Show me."

Dutifully Remo offered his hands for inspection.

"I feel like I'm back at the orphanage," he grumbled as the Master of Sinanju turned his hands palm up, then down again, scrutinizing the pale skin for paint flecks and under the nails for stubborn grime.

He flinched at what he saw.

"You have cut them!" Chiun squeaked.

"Sue me."

"It is a wonder you do not chop off your fingertips, you pare the nails so cruelly."

"They say if you cut back its branches, a tree will flourish."

"You are not a tree."

"And you are not my father. Get off my nails."

Relinquishing Remo's hands, the Master of Sinanju made a frowning face.

"You are beyond redemption. Now go. I will clean up here."

"I didn't leave a mess. There's nothing to clean up."

"Go, go," said Chiun, shooing Remo from the room.

More than happy to get off so lightly, Remo walked the mazelike corridors of the place that had been home almost as long as any other place in his vagabond existence.

Well, it wasn't so bad sometimes, he thought as he headed down to the first-floor kitchen, where the fresh scent of rice steaming wafted up. He and Chiun had come a long way from the days when, as part of his contract with Harold Smith, the Master of Sinanju was obligated to liquidate Remo should CURE be compromised. Now they were as close as father and son and, while they had their arguments, both loved and respected each other—Remo Chiun more than Chiun Remo. Remo didn't care how long the Master of Sinanju grew his nails. Or how flamboyant the kimono of the day was. All Remo wanted was to be left alone, to dress as he wished. A clean T-shirt and chinos were just fine with him, day in and day out. What he saved in wardrobe he put in shoes—expensive Italian loafers and no socks, thank you very much.

It was a simple life, Remo thought as he walked down the hall, picking up a universal TV remote from a small table. As he passed open doors, he used it to turn on the TV sets that were a fixture in almost every room, one by one.

This way he caught the news as made his way to the kitchen and the alluring scent of rice. Chiun could turn them off later.

Remo reached the stairs when something said by a network newscaster made him stop.

"Amtrak officials say the cause of the deadly derailment is unknown at this time."

He ducked into the room.

"More after this," the newscaster said.

Before the picture faded, Remo noticed the graphic floating beside the anchor's head. It said Amtrak Derailment. There was a digitized picture of a flopped-over Amtrak train in the box.

"Damn," said Remo.

He switched channels. NBC was still in its precommercial opening segments.

"At this hour rescue operations are still underway in the Connecticut seaport town of Mystic, but with darkness closing in, officials say that recovery and rescue will only become more difficult."

"What train?" said Remo.

"Now this," said the anchor.

Remo flicked stations again and got a gourmet-cat-food commercial featuring a dancing Siamese in a tux waltzing with a fully grown woman in a floor-length dress. It looked like a public-service announcement for human-feline interspecies romance.

Further up the channels, Remo caught live CNN footage of a big yellow crane at the scene of the rail accident. The tracks were twisted all out of shape. There were cars on the track bed, cars in the water and the live remote newswoman was saying that this was the worst passenger accident since Bayou Canot—whatever that was.

"At this hour the *Merchant's Limited* death toll stands at sixty-six and bodies are still being pulled from the water. The ten-coach train left Boston's South Station at 7:00 p.m. and was two hours into its run to Washington when it encountered catastrophe."

"Oh, man," said Remo, grabbing a telephone. He thumbed the 1 button, and the call, after rerouting through three states to foil tracing, rang the contact telephone on Harold Smith's desk at Folcroft Sanitarium. The line ran and rang and rang, and Remo knew by the eighth ring that wherever Harold W. Smith was, he was either dead or unconscious. For the foolproof code line also rang his briefcase cellular, which, if Remo knew Smith, nestled under his pillow when he slept.

Harold Smith never failed to answer the CURE line.

Something was very wrong.

5

The Master of Sinanju wore his sweet parchment face like a mask of mourning as Remo tore south down Route 95 into Connecticut.

"We must contact the puppet President," he was saying as Remo leaned on the horn and barreled through frightened traffic.

"We don't know he's dead," Remo snapped.

"Technically we are under contract to Smith, not the puppet regime," Chiun continued. "It may be that our present contract will require an adjustment—in our favor, of course."

"The President of the United States is not a puppet. He's really in charge."

"Now, yes. And since true power is conferred upon him by Smith's untimely death, we must hasten to his side to guarantee the proper succession."

"Not until we know that Smith is dead for sure," Remo said testily.

"He did not answer your telephone call. Nor did he answer mine. He is dead. The man is incapable of not answering telephones."

"He could be unconscious somewhere."

"A ringing telephone would rouse him from any state of consciousness less than the complete destruction of his stubborn brain," Chiun insisted.

"He could be under the knife, being operated on."

"He would hear the telephone through his stupor, and his blind, groping hand would instantly clutch for the telephone."

"Not through anesthetic."

Chiun's thin mouth pursed unhappily. "He is dead. The most generous emperor the House has ever known, cut down cruelly in the prime of his magnificent generosity. Woe is us."

"You couldn't wait to get rid of him a few hours ago."

Chiun gasped. "Remo! Repeat this canard never again. Smith was a giant among dwarfs, a prince of emperors. Pharaohs there were, shoguns, maharajahs and deys, but none so generous as Smith. Emperors showered gold in the past, but their largess was but brass dribblings compared to Smith the Golden."

"Smith the Golden?"

"His every pronouncement enriched the universe," said Chiun, closing his eyes at the sublime memory.

Remo frowned. "*Your universe,* and for the last time he's not dead."

"Let us pray that this is true, but of course it is not. Remo, you may pay brief respects at the site of the catastrophe, but merely slow down. Do not stop. We must reach the city of Washington before the President of Vice attempts to unseat the puppet he secretly loathes."

"It's not like that," Remo said in a tight, tired voice.

"Then there is the scheming queen. Not an hour will pass between her learning of this calamity ere she will attempt to weld her ambitious skirts to the Eagle

Throne. Those people are worse than Corvinus the Unjust.''

"Who?"

"A Magyar—a Hungarian to you—ruler the House was forced to serve during a difficult era."

"Why was he 'the Unjust'?"

The Master of Sinanju lowered his voice. "He was elected."

"Tsk-tsk."

"It was a Balkan scandal," Chiun confided. "Such things were not done in those days."

Noticing the flashing blue lights in his side mirror, Remo saw that a Connecticut State Police cruiser was bearing down on him.

"I don't have time for this," he said tightly.

"What?" asked Chiun, turning in his seat.

"State trooper on our case."

Chiun shrugged. "He will follow until one of us runs out of fuel."

"That will be us," Remo said, glancing at the fuel gauge.

"Then I suggest you stop. For we are Sinanju, who do not fear Smokies."

Sighing, Remo pulled over and rolled down the window as the trooper emerged from his cruiser, striding toward them.

"We do not have time for this," Chiun said.

"I said that."

"So, back up."

"If we back up, he'll only call for his backup. Then we'll have the entire Connecticut barracks chasing us."

"Not if you squash his radio, too."

"It's a thought," said Remo, who abruptly backed up.

The Dragoon jumped into reverse, and its right balloon tires started climbing the cruiser's hood. The weight was too much for the cruiser's radials. They bloated up and one after the other popped as Remo crushed the windscreen, flattened the roof, demolished the strobing light bar and bumped down off the collapsing trunk until the APC was back on level ground again.

The state trooper took great offense to this display of overwhelming vehicular superiority. He took out his service pistol and emptied it into the APC's side, which lost a few specks of red paint but not much else.

The trooper was reloading and trying to empty his second clip when Remo got underway again.

"He will think twice about challenging us again," Chiun said confidently as rounds spanged harmlessly off the APC's rear deck.

"Are you kidding? By midnight there will be an APB on us from here to New Rochelle."

"As long as we are in Washington by then," said Chiun.

As HE WADED through the salt marsh, Amtrak conductor Don Burris was grateful for one thing.

At least there were no alligators.

There had been alligators during the Bayou Canot derailment. But that was an Alabama bayou. A wayward tugboat had struck a train trestle, weakening it. So when the *Sunset Limited* rolled over it, seven cars tumbled into the water, spilling diesel fuel and human passengers into the gator-infested bayou waters.

It had been bad. Real bad. Forty-seven died. But it could have been worse.

Burris had been a conductor on that run. He was one of the lucky ones. His coach had stayed on the rails.

This was bad. No shit, it was bad.

The *Merchant's Limited* had slammed into a bull-dozer straddling the track. What a bulldozer was do-ing on the rail bed didn't matter now. Saving the living was all that counted. And recovering the dead.

As he waded through tidal rushes and cattails, wearing a fisherman's high rubber wading pants, feeling for bodies with his boots, Burris had another comforting thought. At least this wasn't the era of steam. Back then, when there was a big wreck, the wooden coaches splintered like kindling. If it was winter, the coal stoves set the kindling alight, and the maimed and helpless lay howling as they were con-sumed. Yes, things could have been worse.

Then Burris's foot encountered a soft, heavy weight that gave slightly.

Reaching down with both hands, he started feeling about. His heart was pounding now. This was grisly work, but it had to be done now. Before the bodies got washed out to sea irretrievably or bloated up and were nibbled on by crabs. Bodies in the water turned horrible pretty fast, and folks naturally preferred open-casket wakes for their loved ones.

Burris's fingers swished and gurgled in the water, groping until what felt like seaweed threaded be-tween his splayed fingers. He clamped down, both hands, and knew because they weren't slimy or slick that he had captured human hair.

Taking a deep breath, he pulled.

A little girl's head broke the surface, and her china blue eyes were wide open, her face a ghastly blue-gray. Burris just wanted to bawl like a baby. But he didn't. He gathered up the sopping form and lifted his voice. A frog that he didn't know was lurking in his throat tangled up the words. He cleared it, tried again.

"Body!" he called.

Two rescue workers came sloshing down off the bank and took the body tenderly from his arms. Swallowing hard, Burris resumed wading.

It was bad, yeah, he told himself. But it could have been worse. It could have been the dead of winter. In the dead of winter the water would have been too cold for efficient rescue operations, and the little girl with the innocent blue eyes would have spent the entire night down there. Maybe two. She had suffered enough. No one should lie unclaimed in the cold, cold water even if he or she was dead and beyond all pain and feeling.

Yeah, it could have been worse. But it was bad. It was real bad.

THE ACCIDENT SITE WAS under floodlights when Remo pulled off the road and got out.

Orange Coast Guard Jayhawk helicopters were traveling back and forth, targeting their spotlights on the purly water, where two cars lay half-submerged in the rainbow stink of diesel fuel. Fireboats bobbed in the darkness like ducks in profile.

"Looks bad," Remo said quietly.

Chiun said nothing. They worked their way toward the crash site.

A temporary morgue had been set up on dry ground, where noisy gas generators powered ground lights. The pup tents were stark pyramids in their back-glow. EMTs were rushing in and out, clutching plasma bottles, a besieged urgency in their faces.

Remo grabbed one on the fly. "We need to find out about a friend."

"Tent 3 has the casualty list," the man said breathlessly.

"Thanks," said Remo, moving on.

At tent 3 a harried nurse was working a cell phone and checking off names on a handwritten list.

"A friend was on the train," Remo told her.

The nurse looked up. "Name?"

"Smith."

"Hold on a second," she told the person the other end. Glancing at her list, she said. "No Smith on my list."

"What's that mean?"

"Anything. Body not recovered. Body not identified."

"What if he's injured, not missing?"

"That's the only list I have. Sorry. Try the morgue. A service rep will point you in the right direction." Into the phone she said, "Hello? Sorry. Listen, do you have any more AB negative?"

Returning to the busy night, Remo said, "Guess we try the morgue."

"Yes, it is what we should do. After we are finished here."

The Master of Sinanju was looking into an openflapped pup tent where two bodies lay on cots, sheeted and still.

They entered. Chiun lifted first one sheet and then the other. Neither was Harold Smith.

Going to the next tent, they found a tangle of arms and legs shrouded by a plastic tarp big enough to floor a room. When Chiun raised one end of the sheet, he found only feet. Going to the other, he got the same display.

Whipping the entire sheet away, he discovered that it was no single body. Only parts. No heads. Chiun replaced the sheet, his wrinkled face stiff.

"Let's check the water," suggested Remo.

Chiun nodded grimly.

An Amtrak cop tried to shoo them back from the water. But Remo said, "No time." Taking his shoulder, Remo spun him around.

The cop spun in place like a top and went whirling and staggering away. When he got himself organized again, Remo and Chiun had slipped into the dark water.

Searchlights cutting into the water made the marshy cove weird, as if something monstrous lurked under the oily water, ready to pounce into the world of oxygen.

The water closed over their heads, and they found themselves swimming through slow-moving tunnels of vertical light. They could see the submerged cars lying on their sides in silt, undercarriage fans turning lazily.

One coach was completely underwater and filled like an aquarium. Inside, dim faces were pressed to the window glass, some with their eyes closed as if napping while leaning against the glass. Others wore twisted expressions, their open mouths full of brine. A tiny fish was pecking at the exposed teeth of a black man with only the bloodshot whites of his eyes showing.

Releasing carbon dioxide bubbles slowly from their mouths, Remo and Chiun floated from window to window, trying to see inside. None of the faces was familiar. Most looked ordinary. Just ordinary people, Remo thought. Ordinary people on their ordinary way to homes or vacations or businesses. Now they were dead, drowned in a steel cage from which their weak bodies could not escape.

Remo wanted to let them out, but attracting attention was against Smith's highest directive. Remo was normally ready to violate that directive whenever it suited him. Now, thinking Smith dead, he felt like respecting it.

Noticing a flutter like a stingray, Remo saw that Chiun was at a door. He got it open. A blooping bubble of air came wobbling out and floated upward. Chiun slipped inside.

Remo followed.

They swam the length of the car, using their eyes to the fullest and taking advantage of the crisscrossing searchlights. Where it was too dark to make out faces, they used their sensitive fingertips, visualizing the cold facial planes they encountered.

Harold Smith's patrician features were not among the dead in this coach, they concluded when they reached its end. Swimming back, they left the dead in peace. Others would redeem them.

Bobbing to the surface, they treaded water, facing one another.

"Guess we try the city morgue," said Remo.

Chiun nodded.

After wading back to shore, they walked the twisted tracks to the engine that had slammed into a tangle of yellow metal with catastrophic results.

"Looks like a bulldozer," said Remo.

Chiun examined the twisted tangle critically.

"What does this contraption do?"

"It's used to push dirt and move it someplace else."

Chiun frowned. "What was it doing on the rails?"

"Search me. Maybe it was crossing."

"We are by the water. There is no crossing here."

"Good point," said Remo. "Let's go."

"Hold," said Chiun. Kneeling, he picked up a bent twist of metal. He brought this up to the light. There was a name on it. And a company emblem—four disks in a circle.

"Looks like a nameplate," Remo said.

"It is Japanese. It says Hideo."

"So? It's a Japanese bulldozer."

"What is a Japanese bulldozer doing on these rails?" Chiun said thinly.

"It doesn't matter that it's Japanese. Come on. Let's check out the morgue."

The nameplate disappeared up Chiun's wide kimono sleeve, and Remo started to object but decided the nameplate wouldn't matter to the investigation.

AT THE MYSTIC MORGUE they were told they were too late.

"What do you mean, too late?" Remo demanded.

"The deceased Smith was claimed," the attendant said distractedly as he walked down a line of sheeted bodies, checking toe tags.

"By whom?" asked Chiun.

"Another Smith. Who else?"

"Where'd they take the body?"

"Not my problem. I have a morgue full of unclaimed corpses. I don't ask where the claimed go."

Drawing Chiun aside, Remo said, "Maybe Mrs. Smith claimed it—I mean him."

"We must be certain," Chiun hissed.

Remo addressed the morgue attendant. "Was Smith's first name Harold?"

"That sounds about right."

"We need to be sure."

"Yeah, Howard."

"I said Harold."

"Harold. Howard. Talk to the relatives. I'm up to my ass in body parts."

"One last thing," said Remo.

"Yeah?"

"Where were the injured taken?"

"St. Mary's."

AT ST. MARY'S HOSPITAL they were told the injured did not include a Harold Smith.

"You sure?" Remo asked the admitting nurse.

"No Smiths," the admitting nurse said. "Try the morgue."

"We did."

"They're still dredging up bodies. It may go on all night."

"Thanks," said Remo dispiritedly.

Outside, with the moon up and the summer stars twinkling, Remo and Chiun stood in silence for a long time.

"Hard to believe he's gone," Remo said after a long while.

"Yes."

"Now what?"

"Washington trembles. We must soothe it with our awesome quelling presence."

"We should pay our respects to Mrs. Smith."

Chiun nodded. "Yes, this is permitted."

Remo looked up at the summer constellations. "I just can't believe he's gone."

Chiun's hazel eyes became austere gemstones. "I understand, Remo. Losing one's first emperor is very hard."

"No, it's just that Smith always seems too tough to die."

"All men die."

"It just doesn't seem real."

"Death is the ultimate reality," intoned the Master of Sinanju.

They padded away.

6

Dr. Harold W. Smith couldn't believe he was still alive. His pinched nostrils were clogged. His lungs felt like bloated wineskins. Every time he coughed, tea-colored salt water came out of his nostrils. Every joint throbbed. His eyes, when he opened them, received the light like needlelike daggers, forcing them shut again.

And if that wasn't bad enough, some idiot was pronouncing him DOA.

"Tag him and ship him to the morgue," an emotionless voice was saying.

Smith tried to protest. All that came out of his mouth was a weak dribble of water.

"He moved," a woman's voice gasped.

"Reflex action," the emotionless voice said dismissively.

"But—"

"I'm a doctor. Don't contradict me, nurse. Tag his toe and get him out of here. The salvageables are backing up."

"Yes, Doctor," the unseen nurse said weakly.

Footsteps went away. They sounded mushy. The man was walking away over soft ground or in sopping shoes.

Smith tried to cough again, but nothing came. His head spun. His eyes were closed, and all he saw was ebony blackness—yet that world of darkness spun and spun.

When everything stopped spinning, Smith had no energy left. And the memories started flooding back.

He remembered the *boom-boom-boom* of the train going off the rails. The startled faces of his fellow passengers, frozen in shock, then coming apart in fear as they were flung from their seats like rag dolls.

The lights went out, and the coach was plunged into darkness. The first scream of surprise was voiced. Shrill, inarticulate, it was cut off as if the throat had been guillotined.

After that, Smith experienced the abrupt sensation of the coach traveling sideways, followed by a sickening dropping sensation.

All sound went away. The tortured screaming of metal suddenly stopped like a fire had been quenched.

Harold Smith realized even as he was slammed into a seat that was inexplicably disoriented that the sound was gone because the coach was now underwater.

With a final jolt, it settled.

Smith flung his arms and legs about, seeking the familiar. The seat armrest was pointed at a weird angle. Smith found the release button as the seat back hit him in the head. He saw stars. But when they cleared, the cobwebs in his brain were dispelled.

Smith groped for the window glass. He found a hard metal lever. He couldn't tell if it was the upper lever or the lower one. He yanked it out, and the rubber O-ring seal peeled away in his hands.

Step one.

Smith tried to visualize what to do next when a heavy hand clutched at him.

"Help me!"

Smith recognized the thick voice. His traveling companion. The black woman.

"Let go," Smith said tightly. "I am trying to open the emergency exit."

"Well, what you waiting on?"

But the woman wouldn't let go. A second hand grabbed his leg.

"What's that gurgling?" she demanded.

"Water," Smith snapped.

The unseen voice lifted and went skittering into panic. "Where's it coming from?"

"We are in the water," Smith said tightly. "There is only a little time. Release me at once."

The panicky woman clung more tightly.

One-handed, Smith found the lower lever. He flipped it.

The window hit him with the force of the inrushing water, and again he saw stars.

He had the presence of mind to kick with both feet. His shoes came off. He hardly noticed. The water was cold and embraced him like a clammy shroud. He lost all orientation. There was no telling where he was. He felt cushions, hands and baggage bump against him, and he struggled, mouth pinched shut to conserve the oxygen in his lungs as he tried to fight his way back to the open window.

The current of water beating at him lessened, then slowed, and Smith swam toward it.

His fingers found the open window frame. He grasped them and began levering himself out. With a stab of fear, he found he could not.

Something was holding him back.

Twisting, Smith reached back and around. He found thick fingers and knew even in the dark that the woman was still holding on for dear life, holding on with the unbreakable grip of a two-armed octopus.

Smith kicked wildly, to no avail. Then, knowing he had no choice, he grabbed for the woman's face, found an ear, twisted it like a key and with a hard finger poked her in the eye.

Abruptly her death clutch let go. Smith kicked, got clear of the coach and frog-kicked until his head broke the surface.

Gasping, panting, he trod water, his eyes wide and full of horror. His teeth chattered. Then, recharging his lungs, he dived back down.

Smith found the open window almost at once. He reached in, encountered a limply flailing arm and pulled at it.

Whoever it was came out like a big balloon. Smith felt the body float past.

Smith kicked clear and reached in again.

This time it was like reaching into some cold, watery hell where the damned huddled awaiting redemption.

What felt like two dozen grasping hands reached out to him. Smith took one, but even as he touched it, it went limp. He let go. It was too cold, too dead. He found another—or rather, it found him. Yanking again, Smith extracted another victim. And the person lashed the water, all arms and kicking feet.

There was time to save one more. Smith reached in with one hand. Two hands grasped his thin wrist. He heaved, and his lungs expelled oxygen. The strain was too great, the person too heavy. He tried to pull free, but the hands refused to release him. And when he stuck his other hand in, it was also grasped by frantic, clawing fingers.

The entire world went black for Harold Smith. Then red. His ears filled with a roaring. It sounded red. Everything was red. Everything was the screaming color of blood.

This is it, he remembered thinking. *I am to lose my life because I tried to save my fellow man.*

A weird darkness ate the roaring redness, and Harold Smith knew nothing more until he heard the emotionless voice pronouncing him DOA.

Smith could feel the water in his lungs. They were not full, but neither were they functioning properly. His body was trying to inhale. But his lungs had no elasticity.

He tried to call out, but without air to force through his voice box, no sounds could be made. He forced his stomach to cough, and brackish water bubbled up from his mouth, only to slide back again. It was a cold, ugly sensation.

Smith knew that he had to get over on his stomach. He turned.

"Doctor," the nurse's voice said, shrill and high, "I think this man is moving."

"Help me with this other one," the doctor snapped.

"But, Doctor—"

"Stat! Nurse!"

"Screw you," the nurse said in a small voice, and rolled Harold Smith over onto his stomach. A sudden pressure in his back became a hard pumping that made Smith's ribs creak and groan and his lungs rebel.

Smith began vomiting water from mouth and nostrils and, as terrible as the bitter marsh water tasted, he knew it meant life. He began coughing. He kept coughing. He coughed long after the coughing reflex subsided.

"He's alive," the nurse was saying.

"Then he doesn't need your help. I need you here, nurse."

The nurse dug in with all her strength, and the last of the lung water rushed out.

Smith hacked and coughed on his stomach, eyes pinched shut, his brain pounding with each explosion of air like a tormented sponge recoiling in pain.

When he was again breathing normally, Harold Smith opened his eyes.

The hovering face was very pale. A wide woman's face, the fleshy ridges contorted with concern.

"Please do not move." The voice was that of the conscientious nurse who had saved his life.

"Doctor's . . . name . . ." Smith croaked.

"What?"

"What is the doctor's name?"

"Dr. Skelton," the nurse said. She lowered her voice. "He thinks God planted his feet on the planet personally."

"Thank you . . ." Smith said weakly.

"You just rest. They'll take you to St. Mary's as soon as an empty ambulance is available."

The nurse disappeared. Only then did Smith remember that he had forgotten to ask her name. On second thought, he decided, it was unimportant. She was just doing her duty as she should. On the other hand, the doctor had been derelict. He would pay for that.

Smith waited until he had the strength to get up before he dared move off the cot.

He stood swaying on his stocking feet. The harsh lights burned through his retina. He took hold of the cot to steady himself. It upset. He landed on his face in the mud, only to climb to his feet with a cold purpose.

With difficulty Smith stumbled out into the night. The panorama of the crash lay spread out before him. A crane was trying to lift a coach from the water. Smith had a sickening thought it was his coach but couldn't be sure.

Passing a pup tent, Smith spied the nurse working over a woman who was naked to the waist. A black woman. A flat-faced doctor was applying two round defibrillator paddles to her chest. "Clear!" he called, not giving the nurse enough time to react. She jumped back just as the body convulsed. This was done three times until the doctor stepped back, dragged his shirtsleeve across his sweating brow and said, "Cover the body."

Smith recognized the dead woman's purple print dress. It was his erstwhile seatmate. He never got her name.

Smith moved on, feet making ugly sucking sounds in the mud. Rescue workers hurried back and forth. No one paid him any mind.

Coast Guard helicopters were patrolling the night sky like impotent dragonflies. Fireboats bobbed offshore, blue beacon lights rotating monotonously. Khaki-clad Connecticut State troopers stood watch over the operation. All was a kind of controlled chaos.

The soft mud under his feet squished with each step. Smith felt awful, unclear, without purpose. Dimly he understood that his briefcase had been lost. It was not waterproof. That meant its contents would be useless if found. But if anyone attempted to open it, they would be killed or maimed by the explosive charges.

Grimly Smith realized that was his highest priority.

Stumbling toward high ground, he found a road that led through thick trees to an area where police sawhorses held back the morbidly curious. Reporters and TV crews were pacing impatiently, waiting for permission to come forward. They were getting little cooperation if the bitter complaints reaching Smith's ears meant anything.

Working his way around, Smith happened to notice the fireman in the cattails.

Instinctively Smith ducked so as not to be seen. The fireman was not looking in his direction. He was wading through the cattails, wading out from shore.

Smith noticed two very strange things about the fireman.

The first was that the cattails surrounding him were still. Eerily still. As he moved through them, they failed utterly to respond to the ripples and waves he was making.

Smith had lost his glasses in the wreck, so his eyes were not at their best. Maybe it was a combination of that, the darkness and his deep fatigue, he thought.

Yet something was very strange. The cattails were photograph still as the fireman waded through them. The moonlight was strong here, and it showed the play of eddies in the water. A fish splashed, making a quivering ring. Moonlight danced on its dark surface.

But where the fireman was wading purposely out to sea, there was no disturbance of the surface. No ripples. No splashing.

And most strangely of all, no sound of splash or gurgle.

Smith felt a chill that had nothing to do with his ordeal.

His eyes may deceive him, but his hearing was perfectly reliable.

The fireman was moving through cattails that ignored him, water that failed to eddy or gurgle in response to his progress.

Crouching low, Smith watched the man.

He wasn't searching. He was moving in a direct line, toward open water. The back of his black slicker shone. The back of his black fireman's helmet, with its scoop-shaped brim, reflected the shine of moonlight normally.

Nothing else about him was normal.

As Smith watched, mesmerized for reasons he could not process logically, the black shoulders were swallowed by the black water and still the man waded on.

The waterline crept up to the back of his neck, then the helmet brim, then the crown, and yet the fireman continued, unconcerned.

The top of the helmet became a black dome that traveled on, and Smith could see clearly that no bubbles of escaping air were breaking the surface.

The water failed to purl or corkscrew when the shrinking dome of the helmet was lost to sight.

"It should have purled," Smith muttered. "It did not."

His voice in the darkness was thin and hollow.

Smith watched for bubbles. There should be bubbles. If the man were drowning, his lungs should give up expelled gases. If he wore an oxygen mask, there would be bubbles.

There were no bubbles. There was just the placid water that had swallowed a wading fireman with complete and total soundlessness.

Harold Smith was a very logical man. It was his logic that spoke next.

"I do not believe in apparitions," said Smith in a voice that was firm yet troubled and held a hollow ring that only his wife would recognize as doubt.

Smith tore his eyes from the spot and continued on his way. Entering the water was out of the question. He had not the strength to rescue the fireman.

But he moved down to the waterline to examine the soft mud for footprints. He found a set moving toward the black lapping water, but they disappeared well short of where they should. The tracks simply stopped dead. Watching, Smith saw that the tide was going out. If it were coming in, the lapping wavelets would explain the erasure of tracks. But the water was receding, so there was no explanation.

Eyes lifting, Smith watched the water. A fish struck at something, then vanished. He saw no other bubbles of any kind.

Moving on, Harold Smith was hit by a sudden thought. Fire fighters wore fluorescent bands on their slickers. That man had none. Normally they carried bright yellow oxygen tanks slung over their backs. Smith had seen no oxygen tank.

Coming to a spray of light at the edge of the police line, Smith found a pair of taxis waiting for fares.

He opened the rear door of one and levered himself onto the cushions. All strength seemed to drain from him then.

"I would like to go to Rye, New York," he said.

"That's gonna cost, pal," the cabby said.

"Quote me a rate."

The cabbie pretended to think and said, "Seventy-five bucks. Tax and tip extra."

"What tax?"

"Actually there ain't one. That was just my way of saying, 'Don't forget him what brung ya.' "

And Harold Smith was so drained of strength that instead of bargaining, he nodded yes just before dropping off to sleep.

WHEN THE CABBIE said, "Rye coming up," Smith struggled back to consciousness.

"This next exit," he said, squinting at his surroundings. His head pounded, and his tongue tasted like dead fish.

The cabbie leaned into the offramp.

"Folcroft Sanitarium," Smith murmured. "Follow the third left all the way to the end."

He managed to stay awake until the cab slithered between the stone lion heads that guarded the Folcroft gate.

"That'll be seventy-five bucks," the cabbie told him. "Tip not included."

Only then did Smith realize that someone had picked his pocket back at the wreck. His wallet was gone. And so was his red plastic change holder.

But he stopped caring almost at once, because he fainted, slumping to the floorboards like a gray bundle of wet kindling.

7

Remo was climbing behind the wheel of the APC when he remembered something important.

He snapped his fingers. "Smith's briefcase!"

Chiun made a face. "He is dead. His possessions do not matter."

"It's got his portable computer inside."

"It matters not."

"It's rigged to blow if someone opens it."

"Unimportant," said Chiun, settling into his seat.

"No, you don't understand. If a rescue worker tries to open it, he'll be killed."

Chiun was unmoved. "That is his fault for trifling with the emperor's possessions."

"We gotta find that briefcase before someone else does."

"Washington, then the briefcase."

"The briefcase, then Washington."

Chiun's voice grew still and chilly. "I am Reigning Master. My authority is supreme."

"Fine," said Remo, getting out and slamming the driver's-side door. "You drive to Washington. I'll catch up."

Chiun slid behind the wheel and keyed the ignition. He pressed his sandaled foot to the gas pedal.

The big engine roared. He pressed it again, harder this time. It raced, making ominous sounds of warning.

But still Remo continued to walk away.

The Master of Sinanju hesitated. To go or to give in? If he left, it would be that much more difficult to converse with the puppet President. The man barely spoke acceptable English. Remo would have to function as interpreter. If he remained, it would mean caving in to his pupil's childish whims. Then again, sometimes children had to be humored. Even adult children.

In the end Chiun compromised. He waited until Remo had vanished from sight before leaving the APC. When he exited the big vehicle, he shut the door with the smoothness of two velvet ropes knocking together. No click sounded.

That way, Remo would not know Chiun followed.

The Master of Sinanju decided to follow at a discreet distance. Let Remo wonder. Fretting would be good for him. And it was his turn to fret. Chiun was tired of fretting over Remo. Let Remo fret over Chiun. It was only proper and just that the child come to know the frustrations of the parent.

As he padded along, making no sound and leaving no footprint because he knew exactly how to place his sandals in the correct spots so as not to leave spoor, the Master of Sinanju reflected that it was different now that Remo understood they were of the same blood.

Different yet not as good. It was easier in the past. When Remo misbehaved, it was possible to bring him into line by casting aspersions on his unknown white parentage. When Remo became too full of himself, calling him a pale piece of pig's ear was all that was necessary to rankle him.

Now it was very different. Remo knew he had Korean blood in him, a gift from his father who, while of American Indian descent, had in his veins the noble blood of Korea. And Remo had accepted this. Chiun knew that Remo was descended from the bloodline of Sinanju. Descended indirectly, with much pollution and dilution of the good blood, but there was no denying Remo's essential Koreanness.

As he walked along, face tight in thought, a sea breeze toying with his thin, wispy beard, Chiun sighed faintly.

In some ways the old days were better. In some ways Remo was easier to control. He seemed more content now. Knowing who his parents were and what he was.

This was not good. A contented assassin was a complacent assassin. Chiun had never been content. Chiun the Elder had never been content. Yui, his grandfather, had never known a contented day and he had lived nearly forty thousand days.

Why should Remo, who was, after all, only partly Korean—although admittedly fully Sinanju—experience wanton contentment?

Chiun would have to find a way to reintroduce discontent into Remo's life.

It was the only way to preserve it.

A few hundred yards ahead, beyond a clump of evergreens, the Master of Sinanju heard the gurgle of a body disturbing water.

His mouth thinned.

Remo, no doubt. It was utter carelessness. To enter the water so as to make it complain!

Hurrying ahead, Chiun slipped down to the water to remonstrate with his inattentive pupil. The death of an emperor was no excuse for carelessness. Emperors died in their time. But Masters of Sinanju were not allowed that luxury. Remo could not expose himself to danger as long as the House depended upon his living. When Remo had trained his own pupil, he would be allowed to die at his convenience.

There was no sign of Remo Williams when the Master of Sinanju reached the shoreline.

The water lay still, regathering at one spot. Chiun drifted down and noticed footprints.

Momentarily he frowned. This was inexcusable. Leaving tracks. Even in loose sand, it was not permitted.

Then Chiun noticed the footprints were pointed in the wrong direction.

Whoever had made them had come out of the water.

Eyes narrowing, he examined them briefly.

The prints lacked heels but were sharply outlined. Shod feet. Not Remo's footprints. He insisted upon Western shoes with heels.

The prints were wet. But just barely.

A person had emerged from the sea. He should have dripped pools of water. There was no sign of such drippings. Only the footprints, which were hollows clotted with shadow.

Turning in place, the Master of Sinanju studied the line of prints. His face frowned, wrinkles bunching.

"Sandal prints," he hissed.

Curiously he followed them with his eyes.

They led into the evergreens. Chiun followed them. Remo could fend for himself. For now.

The trail of shod tracks led into a wild forest, where old trees stood naked and dead, their bark long gone, their knobby boles hard and dry to the touch. They might have been the skeletons of trees, but trees did not have skeletons. Only dead old wood that insects riddled for shelter.

The footprints led into the carpet of fir needles, and Chiun followed them.

They passed a fir tree that was scarred by a fresh notch. Sap was seeping from it. Chiun studied the notch. His face frowned more deeply.

Emboldened, he followed the prints, hands tight to his waist, sandaled feet padding softly. As he walked, he stepped into the very imprints he followed. His sandals fit, nearly perfect. His natural gait followed smoothly. This told him that he pursued a man of roughly his own height and leg length. This made his eyes narrow in quiet anticipation.

Chiun quickened his pace.

Moonlight filtering through interlacing branches made webby patterns on the ground. Chiun avoided the light where he could. It was as instinctive as breathing.

The figure ahead of him made no such effort, Chiun saw as he closed in on it.

The figure was short and thick, his body black and shiny. As he moved, square plates of black material shook and flapped with every step. A helmet covered his squat head, flaring at the back to cover the nape of the neck.

The man strode on with an arrogant purposefulness that the Master of Sinanju recognized.

Chiun decided the proper course of action.

Lifting his voice, he cried, *"Nihonjin!"*

The figure whirled, setting its black skin plates flapping.

In its hand was a long ebony sword. And under its black helmet, his face lay in deep shadow. Even Chiun's keen vision, amplifying the moonbeams, could not make out the hidden features.

"Chosenjin!" the figure hissed back.

And taking the haft of his sword in both hands, he struck a defensive position, blade held before his face.

Confidently the Master of Sinanju advanced, fists opening, fingernails splaying.

One blade against ten. A sword forged by man against the Knives of Eternity that grew from the deadliest fingers on earth.

It would be no contest.

The sword started forward. It turned to the right, the wrists twisting. A Wheel Stroke. Easily parried.

"Come meet your doom, *Nihonjinwa,*" Chiun hissed.

The sword descended, and the Master of Sinanju stepped in to parry it.

The blade sliced down in a choppling stroke. Chiun's index nail rose to meet it. They clashed, metal encountering horn.

The big black blade was arrested.

His adversary, grunting in surprise and anger, exerted all his strength to force downward the frail-looking nail with its thin supporting finger.

Calmly Chiun lifted his finger as if toying with a great black feather, and the sword, clasped in trembling hands, was forced to relent.

An explosive curse came from the helmeted one.

"You may relinquish your blade when you wish, *ronin,*" Chiun said without concern.

At that, the armored figure jerked back, reclaiming his sword. The blade lifted and swooped down again. It hummed in the air as a fine blade should. But midway though its fall, it went silent.

Chiun's keen ears detected this even as his fingernail rose to block the slicing thrust.

Blade met nail—*and passed through!*

Chiun recoiled from the contact. It was pure instinct. He feared no blade that he could see. The blade had not been forged that could not be deflected by Sinanju nail.

In that split second of contact, his senses told him this blade had sliced through his nail.

Recoiling, he spun, shifted left, then right, putting distance between his foe and himself.

And lifting his out-thrust finger to the moonlight, he saw that his nail was whole.

It was impossible.

With his own eyes he had seen the blade bite into his precious nail.

But it was whole. Lifting his eyes, Chiun saw that the opponent's blade, too, was whole.

Chiun made a tight face. "Who are you, *ronin?*"

The foe said nothing.

As he zeroed in on the apparition with all of his senses, the Master of Sinanju realized that his opponent's heart wasn't beating. There was no sound coming from him. No labor of lungs. No gurgle of blood.

Was this a phantom?

Chiun decided to find out.

Placing the toe of one black sandal behind him, he made as if to retreat.

The black-plated warrior advanced, naturally assuming timidity on the part of the Master of Sinanju.

Then with a twist of his firmly planted ankle, Chiun sent his silken skirts spinning. His body whirled up in slow spirals whose speed was deceptive.

The retreating toe snapped forward, seeking the helmeted head.

And passed through!

Landing awkwardly because he had anticipated using the recoil of the death blow to land correctly, the Master of Sinanju ducked, feinted and neither felt nor heard the swish of the descending blade.

But the blade did descend.

He saw it as he spun around, hands coming up in a defensive posture. One hand made a fist. The other was crooked like a hawk's talons. He stood ready for anything.

The foe assumed another fighting stance. Chiun recognized that a disemboweling thrust was contemplated. But if the blade had no bite, how could it disembowel?

Chiun struck first.

Tucking his elbow in his ribs, he expelled a gusty breath of air and a perfect punch simultaneously.

The blow drove in true, landing on the chest of the *ronin*. The defending blade was too slow to parry it. The fist sank into the blackness of the breastplate, and Chiun followed it through, as if through a black-beaded curtain and not a solid man.

Stepping around on the other side of his foe, the Master of Sinanju whirled to see him slashing empty air with furious strokes. He attacked the spot where his slow senses were telling him the Master of Sinanju should have stood—but where he stood no longer.

Chiun kicked high. His sandals touched but air. He aimed for the boots. They moved, oblivious to his blows. He struck for the backs of the knees to collapse the legs. First the right, then the left, so quickly the blows would land as one.

The foe felt those blows not, and a cold unease grew in the Master of Sinanju's determined breast.

Here was a foe unlike any other. He was a foe Sinanju couldn't vanquish.

Chiun retreated three steps.

The black figure hunkered down to peer all about. His movements were clumsy, for every inch of his body was armored. But he wasn't slow. The speed of his ghostly blade spoke that fact loudly.

"I am here, *ronin,*" Chiun taunted.

His foe turned, one foot following the other.

The head tilted back, and the face was exposed.

Chiun almost gasped. There was no face under the samurai helmet. Only a black void in which it seemed alien stars twinkled. The face was flat and featureless and gleamed like polished obsidian.

"I challenged you to a fair fight, *ronin,*" proclaimed the Master of Sinanju.

The adversary seemed to understand. Two-handed, he drew back his ebony blade, cocking it so that the blade lay across his right shoulder. It was a preliminary movement Chiun didn't recognize. The *ronin* swung it outward once, twice, slowly, with a measured confidence.

Did he expect Chiun to walk into a swinging two-handed blow? Even if his blade possessed no bite?

Chiun waited warily.

Abruptly the armored arms swung forward. The blade left the mailed fingers. It sailed toward the Master of Sinanju, moving silently, neither cleaving the air nor displacing it.

"You seek to frighten me with your ghost tricks, *ronin*," said Chiun, calmly lifting his index finger to block the blow with his nail just in case.

The blade turned twice in the air as it spiraled toward him. Chiun saw it as if in slow motion. There was no threat in this ghostly blade. It held no more substance than a moonbeam.

The blade swung into its third silent arc and intersected with Chiun's upraised nail.

He felt no bite, no impact, no resistance. It would not even be necessary to duck this harmless blade, he told himself.

Just as it passed without cutting through his nail, Chiun sensed an abrupt change.

And in the firred forest of darkness, he screamed in unexpected pain.

8

It was easier than Remo thought it would be.

He drifted along the shoreline until he came to the rescue site. Everyone was busy. No one had any time for a casually dressed man whose slim form seemed to melt into the shadows while avoiding the sweeping searchlights as if designed to repel all illumination.

They had a big yellow crane at the water's edge, where workmen were lashing lines to the last submerged car. The crane strained upward, and with a sucking sound the coach came up out of the water, gushing noisy strings of water from every joint and broken window.

They let it hang over the water until it finished draining. All eyes were on this scene. Lights were directed onto the coach, and it was possible to see the interior through the windows. See the tangle of humanity that floated in the sinking water as in a fishbowl that was leaking.

As the water level fell, the bodies settled down to the bottom, moving aimlessly and involuntarily like clumps of dead jellyfish.

Remo checked through the salvage debris that was stacked here and there. Piles of it lay unattended. Baggage. Briefcases. Purses. Knapsacks. Articles of clothing. Even toys.

Remo found Harold Smith's briefcase in the second pile he picked through. There was no mistaking it. Once it had been tan, but decades of wear had aged the skin and darkened it to the hue of an old saddle.

Remo claimed it, looked around to make sure he wasn't seen and, satisfied, started back for the Dragoon.

The case sloshed in his hands, drooling malodorous water. It was heavier than normal but grew lighter with each step.

Far ahead a sound pierced the night.

"Aiiee!"

Remo knew that sound. It was Chiun's familiar cry of anguish, only it had a weird, horror-struck quality now.

Clutching the briefcase, Remo broke into a run. His feet floated across the sand and into brush. From there, he sprinted through the trees. He had no eyes for anything along the way, counting on his ears to take him to the site of the anguished wail.

Whatever it was, Chiun was in trouble.

Deep trouble.

CHIUN BURST OUT of the trees before Remo could reach the exact spot.

The Master of Sinanju clutched one hand. It was wrapped tightly in the wide sleeve of his kimono as if injured.

"Chiun! What is it? What's going on?"

"I am wounded," he said in a thin, disbelieving voice.

Remo dropped the briefcase. "What!"

Chiun danced in place. "I am maimed. I am undone."

"Let me see it. Let me see it."

Chiun recoiled, one hand clutching his muffled wrist. "No, Remo. It is too horrible. The sight will drive you mad."

"I can take it, Chiun. Just let me see it."

Visions of a bleeding wrist stump jumped into Remo's head.

Chiun looked down at his feet. "Where is it?"

"Where is what?"

"We must find it. Perhaps the surgeons of this land can reattach it."

"God, no," said Remo, hearing his worst fears confirmed.

"Do not stand there like a dunderhead. Help me find it."

"Okay. Okay. Where did it fall?"

"Back there." Chiun pointed into the forest with his uninjured hand. The indicating nail gleamed like a blade of polished bone.

Remo swept past the Master of Sinanju, eyes scanning the fir needles. He spotted footprints that looked like Chiun's, but that couldn't be. The Master of Sinanju didn't leave footprints.

"I don't see it here," Remo called back anxiously.

"Be careful where you step. Do not break it."

"Your hand?"

Chiun's voice grew querulous. "Hand? What are you babbling about, Remo?"

Remo looked up. "I'm looking for your hand—aren't I?"

"No. My hand is still attached to my wrist, as it should be."

And with a nervous flourish Chiun shook off the silk sleeve, exposing his right hand.

Remo looked. Chiun's right hand was a tense fist like a bony mallet carved from aged ivory.

"I don't get it. What happened to you?"

Chiun's face stiffened to a waxen mask. "I cannot bring myself to say."

"Come on," Remo said, approaching. "It can't be that bad. Let me see."

Chiun averted his face, offering his tightly closed fist to his pupil.

Remo took it carefully. He counted the fingers. All four looked intact. The thumb was still there, too.

Carefully Remo unbent them, opening the Master of Sinanju's fist.

"Tell me it is not as bad as it seemed in the first anguished moment of pain," Chiun moaned.

"I don't see anything," Remo said slowly.

"The longest finger. Tell me it is whole."

"It is."

"And the nail?"

"Yeah, it's— Wait a minute. It's gone."

Chiun threw a thin wrist across his forehead. "I am undone. I am shamed. I have been humiliated."

"What the hell happened?"

Chiun dragged his eyes back to his hand. They fell on the stump that was his fingernail. It projected slightly past the finger's tip, but at a slanting angle, not tapered to a point like the rest.

"It will take years to renew," he wailed.

"Well, months anyway," said Remo. "But what happened, Chiun?"

"I cannot say."

"Why not?"

"My humiliation is too great. Do not force the words from my lips. Just find the member that was once part of me."

"Okay," Remo said, relaxing slightly now that he knew Chiun hadn't really been maimed. "Give me a sec."

He found the nail easily enough now that he knew what he was looking for. It lay on the ground, clearly visible to Remo's Sinanju-trained eyes. In the moonlight it looked strangely white, as if dead.

Remo brought it back to the Master of Sinanju, cupped in one hand.

"Now what?" he asked.

"Wrap in it warm milk," said Chiun.

"That only works with teeth," Remo said.

Chiun hovered over the cupped artifact. "Is there no hope for it, then?"

"Maybe it can be welded back on, but I doubt it."

"I cannot bear the sight of it, detached as it is."

"Maybe Super Glue would work," said Remo.

"I will not stoop to artificial nails to hide my shame. Remo, do the necessary duty for me. I beseech you."

"Do what?"

"Bury the poor thing."

"Bury a *fingernail?*"

"It is the only correct thing to do."

"We can do that later. Mind explaining how you managed to break this nail?"

"It is a sign that I am growing old and infirm. My Knives of Eternity have grown fragile. Never has this happened before. There is no other explanation. Not even a *ronin* could accomplish this on his own."

"A what?"

"If you had listened to me, this would not have happened."

"Don't blame this on me. I had to recover Smith's briefcase, okay? I didn't want a maimed rescue worker on my conscience."

"A maimed teacher is acceptable, however?"

"I didn't maim you."

"I told you Japanese were behind this tragedy, but you did not listen."

"Japanese! Where do you get that?"

In the distance a familiar rumble and growling shook the darkness.

Remo turned. "Isn't that—?"

Chiun puffed out his cheeks. "The fiend! To add insult to injury, he is stealing my dragon!"

Remo flashed toward the sound. He broke from the trees in time to see the scarlet Dragoon APC rumbling down the road.

He started after it but Chiun's voice stopped him like a cracking whip. "Remo. Come back. You do not know what you face."

"A car thief. Big freaking deal," said Remo.

Abruptly the Master of Sinanju was in front of him. He blocked the way, his face stiff and cold. "I will not risk your humiliation, too. Your honor must be unsullied if mine is to be avenged."

"What are you talking about?"

The Dragoon continued rumbling away. Remo tensed.

"Stay. I will explain."

His fists clenched tight, Remo wavered between obedience and pursuit. Ultimately obedience won. He let the air escape his lungs and followed Chiun's beckoning finger back into the dense forest of fir trees.

"You see these tracks?" Chiun said coldly.

"Looks like sandal prints."

"They are not," snapped Chiun, who then led him to a scarred fir tree.

"See this?" he asked, indicating a raw notch in the bark.

"Somebody chopped a hunk from that tree."

"It is the unmistakable bite of a *katana*. Study it well, Remo. For you have never before encountered its like."

In the darkness Remo looked at it from a couple of angles. "Looks like a sword chop."

"Yes. Some might call it a sword. But it is correctly called a *katana*."

Remo's brow furrowed. "I don't know that word."

"Do you know the word *ronin?*"

"No."

"You are abysmally ignorant."

"Sue me."

"Sit."

Reluctantly Remo sat down on the fir needles, which were dry and odorless. A freshening breeze came off Long Island Sound, smelling of rank salt grass and dredged-up muck.

"A foe unlike any I have ever before encountered challenged me with his *katana* blade," said Chiun.

"Right."

"His first blow I parried successfully."

"Of course. You're you."

"His second passed through me harmlessly."

Remo frowned. "Okay. . . ."

"We fought. Blows were struck. None landed. He was as mist. While I was as hard as bone. Yet no harm was done to either combatant."

"You were fighting a ghost?"

"A *ronin.*"

Remo made a face. "I don't know that word."

Chiun lifted a hand, his left. The right lay in his lap, tightly fisted so the embarrassing absence of nail didn't show.

"I am not yet finished with my tale."

Remo subsided.

"Blows rained. Then the blade of doom was descending. But I feared it not, for it failed to swish and flutter the air it sliced through as a true blade should."

Remo nodded. Chiun had taught him years ago that striking swords made distinctive warning sounds.

"As this hateful blade had no substance, I failed to shrink from it." Chiun hung his aged head. "My error, which I will eternally regret."

"Oh, for crying out loud! It's only a nail."

Chiun clapped his hands in Remo's face. "My honor has been besmirched. The honor of the House has been besmirched. Thus, your honor has been sullied, as well."

"I don't feel besmirched or sullied," Remo countered. "Unless you count the fact that you let him run off with my new Dragoon."

Chiun regarded Remo with cold hazel eyes. "I have heard this story from my grandfather, who swore me to secrecy. My father never revealed it. Nor did the Master who trained me. But it is true nonetheless."

Remo had sense enough to close his mouth. Chiun's normally squeaky voice had deepened to the ringing tone he used to relate accounts of past Masters. There was no dissuading him from launching into whatever he was about to recount, so Remo mentally kissed his scarlet Dragoon goodbye and assumed an attentive mien.

"You know of shoguns?"

Remo nodded. "Sure. Old-time Japanese warlords."

"Once during a turbulent time in Japan, the shoguns were at war with one another. All Japan was in chaos. Terrible was the slaughter. Wonderful was the gold to be earned by a cunning Master who was prepared to play shogun against shogun."

An owl hooted. Without taking his eyes off Remo's face, Chiun picked up a stone and flung it. The owl squawked in midhoot and vacated the area in a frantic shivering of wings.

"The Master in those days was Kang. He was a very busy Master. There was no work from Egypt. There was no contact with Persia. The Khanates were quiet. But Japan called for his skills time and time again. Now in these days Kang would betake himself to Japan to succor this shogun or that shogun. He cared not which side of a duel he found himself. For one Japanese was the same as another in Kang's eyes." Chiun lifted a precautionary finger. "His mistake.

"A shogun sent a message to the village of Sinanju, which was peaceful and contented in the days of which I tell. For the gold flowed directly from Japan and into the bellies of the people of Sinanju. And this shogun summoned Kang to come to his keep to treat with him. The message was signed with the crest of a shogun Kang had never met but of whom he had heard.

"So Kang went as asked. He came to this keep, which lay on the Kanja Plain. And coming to this keep, he found it impregnable. No voice responded to his knock. His shouts went unanswered.

"Standing on the ground before the shogun's gate, Kang called up time and again, 'I am the Master of Sinanju, come to treat with the shogun who dwells within.'

"But only songbirds answered him, Remo.

"Thinking the shogun away in battle, Kang studied the keep well, and though it was thought impregnable, he discovered a way in. He breached this impregnable keep and as soon as he was within, a host of samurai fell upon him.

"Well the Master fought. Though every hand was against him, he gave no quarter, showed no mercy. Steel blade broke asunder against his mighty blows. Samurai spilled their innards as their own blades were turned upon them—for the blade has never been forged that could whelm a Master of Sinanju."

Chiun's voice grew hushed. He looked at his tightly clenched fist. A wince of pain troubled his wrinkled countenance. He went on. "When at last the shogun's samurai were exhausted, the Master went to his chambers and presented himself, his voice full of righteous wrath and thunderings.

"'Why have you summoned me into a trap, shogun? Speak, before I remove your head from its ignominious perch!'

"And in a voice that told Kang the shogun considered himself already dead, the defeated one said, 'I summoned you not. Why would I summon one whom the winds whisper had been hired to vanquish me?'

"Hearing these bitter words, the Master understood. He asked but one question. 'Who is your most bitter enemy, shogun?'

"And absorbing the name Nishi, the Master quitted the keep of the doomed shogun."

An understanding light came into Remo's eyes. Seeing this, Chiun nodded with quiet satisfaction, then continued his story.

"Journeying to the castle of the shogun who was called Nishi, Kang announced himself with these words, 'I am the Master of Sinanju, just come from the keep of your most bitter enemy.'

"'He is dead?' asked the shogun called Nishi in the manner of one who already suspected the answer and was pleased by it.

"'No, only his samurai,' said Kang.

"And down from the ramparts of Nishi's castle came a single lump of gold—not even enough to pay for the food the Master had consumed along the way to Japan.

"Kang repaired into the forest for the night, Remo. With the dawn he saw the forces of Nishi array themselves about the keep of the first shogun, whom the Master had deprived of all protection.

"The armies of Nishi consisted of bowmen, swordsmen and spearmen. Some rode fine horses. Others marched on foot. Quickly they surrounded the defenseless keep. The moment of doom had come for the helpless shogun.

"Seated upon his stool far behind his lines where he could watch the coming battle, Nishi gave the order to attack.

"They came in crane formation. They moved in rolling-wheel formation, encircling the untrained servants of the doomed shogun. All this Kang saw from a place of secrecy.

"The battle lasted all day, not because the forces of Nishi met with resistance but because they delighted in slaughter. As the piteous cries and moans of the dying smote Kang's ears, he stared into his palm, where lay the lump of gold that would not carry his stomach back to his home.

"At last, when it was over, Nishi stood up from his stool and rejoiced in his great victory, purchased at so little cost to him, that from that day on all of Japan would tremble at the sound of his name. The pennants of his clan fluttered over all that was formerly his defeated foe's.

"That night Nishi slept in the fine bed of the dead shogun, with the unseeing head of the defeated one standing guard at the door to the bedchamber.

"But when his retinue came to wake him the next morning, they were struck dumb with horror. For perched on a spear pike at the very door sat the unseeing head of Nishi the Cunning. And on the bed where he had slept his last lay his dead body. But on the pillow, Remo, lay the correct head. The head of the shogun who had *not* summoned the Master of Sinanju."

Chiun leaned back.

"Nice story," admitted Remo.

Chiun inclined his head. "Thank you."

"But what does it have to do with anything?"

"Did I say the story was over?"

"No, but you acted like it was."

"You are easily deceived. A trait you will have to overcome if you are to rectify the besmirchment of our House."

"I'm all ears," Remo said wearily.

"You are all nose and feet, but that is another story. Listen well.

"Unseen and unsuspected, Kang returned to his village, bearing no gold but having avenged a grievous insult. There to await another summons from Japan, whose gold and blood continued to flow for years to come.

"Now it was the custom in those feudal times that when a shogun died without heir, his samurai were released. They became masterless samurai, otherwise called *ronin*."

"Ah-hah."

"It was a shameful thing to be a *ronin*, Remo. A *ronin* had no clan, no liege, and no loyalty. Only his *katana* and his meager skills. Some *ronin* offered their services to any who would pay. Even lowly farmers. Others turned to banditry. Some fell into more-evil habits, such as politics. For in those times there were more samurai than there were shogun in need of warriors. Thus, the blight of itinerant *ronin*."

"Kinda like Fuller brush salesmen today?"

"There is no comparison!" Chiun flared. "Now, sit quietly as I relate of my tale the portion that concerns us."

Chiun made his voice hollow. "A time came when Master Kang was at peace in his village. This was several years later. And word came that a peasant in a nearby village had been slain by an itinerant Japanese samurai.

"Now, since the slain one was not of our village—'' Chiun paused to make certain Remo absorbed the word *our* ''—Kang gave this matter no mind. Samurai in Korea were rare, but if the business of the samurai concerned Sinanju, the samurai would come to Sinanju.''

''I'll bet he did,'' said Remo.

''He did. Exactly. A morning came when this samurai trudged into the village, hollow of eye, lean of cheek, his bedraggled body encased in once-fine armor that was as black as onyx. He came to the House of the Masters on the hill, where he took up a pitiful stance. And his voice lifted.

'' 'I am Edo, a samurai made masterless by the Master of Sinanju.'

''Hearing this, Kang stepped into the morning sunlight. 'What shogun did you call master?' demanded Kang of the pitiful *ronin*.

'' 'Nishi the Brave.'

'' 'Nishi the Miserly,' spit Kang, 'For he tricked the House and so sealed his doom.'

'' 'You have made me a *ronin,* and I have come to avenge this curse.' And out from its sheath purred his black *katana*.

'' 'Better that you plunge the blade you now draw into your own belly than point it at the Master of Sinanju, *ronin,*' Kang intoned.

''And without another word, the *ronin* laid the flat of his blade across his outstretched wrist in a manner Kang recognized as a threatening stance.''

''I can tell you exactly what happened after that,'' Remo said.

''You cannot. Listen well. The *ronin* bared his teeth like a wounded animal, all the hate he harbored in his heart leaped into his beady eyes like malevolent fires.

Suddenly he lifted the blade, and *swack!* Down it came, chopping off the first finger of the *ronin*'s right hand. The digit fell to the dirt. Bending, he lifted it up and with a snarl flung it into the face of the Master, who of course dodged it with ease.

"Then without waiting, the *ronin* dropped to the ground—whereupon he opened his belly with his own blade."

Remo nodded. "Hara-kiri."

"No, seppuku! Hara-kiri is what ignorant whites call it. You are not white, although you are sometimes ignorant. The ritual suicide is called seppuku."

Remo sighed. "So the samurai died?"

"Do not dignify the wretch with that honorable term. He was but a *ronin*. And yes, he died, but not before leaving Master Kang in his debt."

Remo looked puzzled. "When did that happen?"

"The removal of the finger and the flinging of it, this is very Japanese, Remo. It signifies that the *ronin* acknowledged his powerlessness to avenge the insult against his person. Loss of the finger meant he challenged Kang to redress the wrong done to him. But the seppuku denied Kang that opportunity forever. Thus, the *ronin* died. Thus Kang lived with an unpaid debt hanging over his head."

Chiun leaned back. Remo waited, watching carefully. Was Chiun done? He looked done. But he had seemed done before. Remo wasn't about to be mousetrapped again.

"What have you to say, Remo?"

"You done?"

"Of course I am done!" Chiun flared. "Now, what have you to say?"

"It's a heck of a story?"

Taking his cloudy puffs of hair in hand, Chiun wrenched at them as if driven to utter distraction. "No!"

"Don't get upset. Don't get upset. Okay, the *ronin* chopped off his finger. Now, someone chopped off your fingernail. They connect, right?"

"Correct. They connect."

"Okay, I see where this goes. A descendent of the defingered *ronin* is after you."

"No. It is the same *ronin*. He has come back."

"From the grave?"

"Wherever it is that *ronin* come back from. I do not know. I am no *Nihonjin*." Seeing Remo's blank look, Chiun added, "A *Nihonjin* is a man from Nihon, which the English call Japan."

"You're telling me that a ghost samurai chopped off your fingernail?"

"Not a samurai—a *ronin*. He had no substance except when he wished. He had no face. He was not of this world. Therefore, he is of the next. For what other worlds are there?"

Remo looked Chiun square in the eye. "A dead *ronin* has my APC?"

"Yes. But he will not be satisfied until he has purchased redress."

"He got your fingernail. What more does he want? I mean, isn't that enough? A finger for a fingernail?"

"No. He desires my life. Possibly yours. My Master is dead, so he cannot take that from me. Therefore, he will make you, the next in line, masterless, thus doubly depriving me."

"This is all over fingers?"

"No. This is about face. Have you not been listening? Kang was deprived of face."

"That meant the *ronin* won. Shouldn't Kang be chasing *him* through the Void?"

"Is this white logic I hear? Are you flinging white logic in my face?"

"Has this guy ever bothered the House before? Since he died way back when, I mean?"

"No. That is why the story was not handed down. It was believed that he sought no revenge other than the unpayable debt. But now he is back."

"That doesn't make sense. Where has he been all this time? Where did he come from?"

"He came from the water. I heard him emerge, at first making sounds but later none and wielding a *katana* that had no substance yet bit like steel."

"You saying he walked all the way from Korea?"

"Yes."

"Wouldn't it have been easier to walk across the Bering Strait and take the land route via Canada? I mean, if you were a ghost, why would you take the long way? The poor SOB had to walk all the way across Asia and Europe, then cross the freaking Atlantic. Lot quicker to just walk the Pacific, don't you think?"

"Are you inflicting more white logic upon me?"

"No, just common sense."

"The answer to your idiotic question is as simple as it is obvious. The *ronin* became lost in his wanderings and came the wrong way. This explains why he was so many centuries before haunting us."

"I don't buy it."

"There is more." And Chiun extracted from his wide kimono sleeve the mangled manufacturer's plate from the Japanese bulldozer struck by the *Merchant's Limited*. "Behold. The crest of the four moons. This, Remo, is the crest of the Nishi clan."

"How do you know those are moons?" asked Remo.

"I know because I know moons."

Remo rolled his eyes moonward. "So in addition to walking the entire Atlantic seafloor, he dragged along the clan bulldozer?"

"I did not say that," Chiun flared.

"Okay, let's say to avoid an argument we have a phantom *ronin* on our tailbones. What do we do about it?"

"We must return to Sinanju."

"What!"

"Because to return to Sinanju means that he will have to follow. To follow means a Pacific crossing if he is wise, an Atlantic crossing if not. Either way, by the time the *ronin* catches up with us, I will be long dead and one of your descendants will head the House."

"I'm not hiding from any ghost *ronin*. Besides, we're under contract to America."

"A Master buries the sword of his emperor. Do you remember that lesson, Remo?"

"Yeah. The emperor dies, the contract's void. Unless other arrangements are made. We're on the way to Washington to do just that, last I heard."

Chiun shook his head somberly. "No longer. We are on the way to Sinanju." Chiun stood up. "Come. We will return to Castle Sinanju, there to pack and prepare for your journey home."

Remo climbed to his feet. He towered over the Master of Sinanju. They stood regarding one another in the moonlight, Chiun gazing up, Remo looking down.

Remo spoke first. "As future Reigning Master, I have some say in this."

Chiun inclined his head politely. "You do."

Remo folded his lean, hairless arms across his chest. "Good."

"When you are Reigning Master and I am retired or dwelling in the Void. On this night you will obey Chiun your teacher so that the House continues."

"One step at a time is all I'm promising."

At that, Chiun flung himself out of the woods like a silken wraith, Remo padding after him, thinking, *Won't my life ever settle down?*

9

Connecticut State Trooper Francis X. Slattery had pulled over all kinds.

His stretch of Interstate 95 got them all. It was close enough to New York City to suck up all the crazies coming north, and since as many crazies were hot to visit the Big Apple as escape from it, he got them coming in both directions.

It was worse in the summer. In winter, snow kept the chronic speeders within reasonable excess. Sometimes the snow kept them off the roads entirely. Even crazies had flashes of common sense.

But in midsummer everyone was on the road, sane or otherwise.

Yes, Slattery had pulled over all kinds. Topless blondes at the wheels of cherry-red convertibles. People humping in the back seat while doing ninety. Once, he pulled over a lime green Volkswagen Jetta to find an Irish setter at the wheel and the other occupants swearing up and down the dog had been exceeding the speed limit, stone deaf to their protestations.

But this was something new.

It wasn't that he'd never seen an armored personnel carrier barrel by. A lot of military traffic convoyed up and down 95. Usually they were spattered green and brown. Sandy colored during the Gulf War.

This particular APC was a smoldering red in the predawn light. And it was going like a bat out of Hades down the high-speed-breakdown lane.

Slattery pulled out from behind the Burger Triumph billboard and fell in behind it.

The license plate reflected his headlight glow. Not a military plate. Massachusetts. That was interesting. Some of the most certifiable drivers ever to blow through Slattery's life were from the Bay State. It was said there was a lot of inbreeding up there.

Punching up his on-board LEAPS computer, Slattery ran wants and warrants. The plate came back redhot. Seemed the very same vehicle had rolled over a Rhode Island State cruiser earlier in the evening. Literally rolled over, mashing it as flat as Ohio.

Slattery called it in. "Dispatch. Fifty-five pursuing fire-engine red armored personnel carrier south on 95. Mass plate 334-E. Vehicle comes back wanted in Rhode Island."

"Proceed with caution, fifty-five."

"You bet your sweet life," Slattery muttered, replacing the dash mike. He lit up his light bar and made the siren keen.

The APC probably would have accelerated, but it appeared to be pushing the envelope. It was too heavy to have much pickup, Slattery figured. And it was already doing seventy-five.

Hanging on its tail, Slattery let the strobing light bar and wailing sirens work on the suspect's nerves.

Trouble was the suspect appeared not to have any. He held the road at a rock-steady rate of speed.

Tiring of this, Slattery roared into the opposite lane and began pacing the other machine.

He got his second big shock of the night.

The driver of the fire-engine red APC was tricked out like a full-dress samurai.

Now, Slattery had seen a lot of weird stuff on I-95. Not once, not twice but on three distinct occasions, he arrested Batman in full leather flying down the road. Each time he arrested him, there was a different guy under the cowl.

None of this was on Halloween, mind you.

But this guy looked serious. His black armor looked serious. In fact, it looked like real armor. And with the light bar slashing crazy shards of multicolored illumination into the APC interior, the samurai glanced over briefly like a bored robot, then turned his attention back to the road as if a pacing state cruiser were no more of concern than a buzzing yellow jacket.

"Have it your way," Slattery muttered. Flooring it, he roared ahead of the APC and cut in front. He wasn't fool enough to stop dead. Visions of being the meat in a crushed-car sandwich came vividly to mind.

Instead, he eased up on the gas just enough to make the APC slow. It tried to scoot into the next lane. But the big red machine wasn't built for scooting. Slattery stayed ahead of him every mile of the way.

"Gotcha," he muttered.

After a while the APC engine began to sputter and miss. Slattery began thinking it was his lucky day.

The APC rolled to a gradual stop, engine sputtering.

When it was hung up on the soft shoulder on the road, Slattery brought the cruiser circling back. He parked it nose to nose with the APC, his high beams blazing into the APC interior.

The samurai sat rigidly behind the wheel, as if he had no eyes to be blinded with.

In the brief seconds as he apprised dispatch of the situation, Slattery got a good look at the samurai's face.

He hadn't any.

A flat black shield reflected his beams. That was all. It was creepy. But Francis X. Slattery had a job to do.

"Assistance en route," dispatch advised.

"Affirm," he said, hanging up the dash mike. Unholstering his SIG-Sauer, Slattery stepped out of his vehicle. He was on the wrong side of the road, but when dealing with samurai, it might pay to resort to the unexpected.

Slowly, to show he wasn't afraid, Slattery walked up to the passenger side of the APC. He saw that that side was marred by meaningless graffiti. Unless it was Japanese graffiti. Who could tell?

With one big hand, he rapped on the passenger-side window. "Roll it down, sir," he said with just the right amount of steel in his voice.

The samurai stayed put. His head rotated on his neck until he was looking at Slattery—if that black, featureless regard could be called looking.

"Right now," Slattery ordered. "License and registration."

A lot of years on the job told Slattery never to show fear or concern. He had his side arm in hand, but kept it below the samurai's line of sight. That way, he was within policy.

But the samurai showed no inclination to play by the rules. He stayed put.

So much for by-the-book. Now it was time to get serious.

Slattery snapped the weapon up. "Out of the vehicle! Now!"

Without any bullshit, the samurai obeyed him. He stepped out of the APC. It happened so fast Slattery had trouble taking it in.

The driver's-side door didn't open. The samurai just stepped out. He was suddenly just...there. Standing. Then he was coming around to Slattery's position, the loose, ebony plates of his armor jumping with every assured step.

"Hold it."

The samurai advanced. He was walking toward him as if the pistol Slattery held in a firm Weaver's grip was meaningless.

"Stand or I will shoot. I *mean* it."

The samurai kept coming. He strode into the high beams, his gleaming body resembling an upright black beetle balanced on its hind legs. He had a very confident walk.

Slattery discharged his weapon.

He squeezed off two quick shots, held fire and saw to his consternation the samurai was still coming. Shooting for the head this time, he snapped out three rounds. The weapon bucked and convulsed in Slattery's hands as he emptied the clip.

The damn samurai walked on, calm, cool and collected like the monster in an old horror flick. Impersonal. Unconcerned. Unstoppable.

Slattery retreated to the guardrail, dropped his clip and shot a fresh one home. Bringing the weapon up, he resumed fire.

The SIG roared and danced, casting angry gun flashes on everything. Including the short black sword that was suddenly in the samurai's hands and swinging back to take a swipe at him.

The blade swung up and over, weaving in midair as if the samurai was toying with him.

Slattery's SIG fell silent. He thumbed the clip out.

And the hovering blade came down with a sudden sharp chop—to bite into his shoulder at a diagonal and remove Francis X. Slattery's entire right shoulder from his torso.

It jumped off his body like a side of ham.

Slattery's horror-filled eyes followed it down.

It lay in the ground like a giant chicken leg, dressed in red-spattered Connecticut State trooper khaki.

The disconnected hand clutched the SIG, and his finger kept squeezing the trigger in some feeble nervous reflex. But it had no strength left. It was dead but didn't know it yet.

Then, legs buckling, Slattery fell atop it.

Francis X. Slattery had seen many weird sights on the job. Now he watched helplessly a black armored samurai climb behind the wheel of his cruiser and go roaring away.

Then he saw no more. He was dead.

That was how the backup cruiser found him.

AN APB WENT OUT and within the hour, Slattery's cruiser was found abandoned. Beside the vehicle lay the body of a local teenager. Bifurcated as if a guillotine had missed his neck and chopped him clean in two across the waistline.

They found his missing Camry in Pennsylvania, not far from the Amtrak station at Reading. No one connected the samurai with the Reading train station. Local authorities assumed he had stolen another car. But without a dead body to connect to another missing vehicle, they had no clue what car he'd be driving, if any.

All anyone found was a pay phone beside the abandoned vehicle, the receiver dangling.

No one connected it with the missing samurai, either.

There the trail ended.

10

When they returned home, Chiun insisted that Remo circle Castle Sinanju three times before parking.

"I think the coast looks clear," Remo said dryly as he completed the third pass.

"You can never tell with *ronin,* who are more sneaky than *ninja,*" Chiun said bitterly.

Remo shot the rental car into one of the parking slots. Chiun got out first. He examined the windows of the house. A few upper ones were open for ventilation.

He examined both doors before allowing Remo to use his key.

Even then he insisted they hang back, with both doors open.

Their ears searched the interior. Hearing no heartbeat or other telltale signs, Chiun entered first.

Splitting up, they combed the building.

When every room had been checked, they rendezvoused as agreed in the bell-tower meditation room.

"Look, Remo."

Chiun was pointing to the telephone on a low taboret. It was hooked up to a message machine. The red light was blinking.

"Must be Smith," Remo said, starting across the room.

Chiun intercepted him with his tiny body. "Are you mad? Smith is dead."

"Oh, right. I forgot. Who could it be? We don't know anyone else."

"It is the *ronin,* checking to see if we are home. Do not fall into his cunning snare, Remo."

"A ghost using the telephone?"

"He absconded with your dragon. If he can drive one infernal white device, he can dial another."

"How would he know our number?"

"How would he know to find us where he found us in the first place?" Chiun retorted. "Ghosts know all manner of dark secrets. That is one privilege of being a ghost. They lurk invisible. They spy unsuspected. There is no defense against their vaporous wiles."

"Seems to me a ghost smart enough to use telephones and cars wouldn't take a zillion years to walk across the Atlantic."

"*Ronin* are inconsistent. No doubt he is crazed from harboring centuries of grief and shame."

Remo's eyes were on the monotonously blinking light.

"Maybe Smith called us before the wreck."

"From a train? Do not be ridiculous, Remo."

"They have rail phones now. Just like on airplanes."

"It is the *ronin,*" Chiun hissed. "He is very clever."

"For a guy who walked the wrong way to America," Remo said dryly.

Chiun eyed Remo thoughtfully. "You cannot let go of your emperor. That is your problem."

"I still can't believe Smitty's dead."

"He will never die in our hearts. Even if his noble bones have been consigned to the cold clay, we will remember him always. Now, cast him out of your mind. We must pack."

And because he knew the Master of Sinanju was right, Remo allowed Chiun to chase him from the room.

THE SUN WAS COMING UP as Chiun was going through his steamer trunks some twenty minutes later.

Upstairs the telephone rang and rang.

Standing up, Chiun raised his voice. "Do not dare climb the tower stairs, Remo. I know what you are thinking."

Remo's voice came from down the hall. "I'm in the bathroom, Chiun."

"Stay there. I am still about my packing. Answer no telephones."

"Who would be calling us at this hour?" Remo called back.

"A houseless ghost knows no rest. We will ignore the fingerless fiend."

But the phone rang and rang and rang. It stopped after nearly fifty rings. Almost at once it rang again. And kept ringing.

Remo came out of the bathroom dripping from a cold shower. He wore a towel around his waist. Except for his freakishly thick wrists, he looked as ordinary as soap.

He poked his head into the room where Chiun was busy packing.

"Are you thinking what I'm thinking?" he asked.

Chiun did not look up from folding kimonos. "You are thinking wrong."

"Harold Smith is the only guy I know who would flog a telephone line like that. Then hang up and go round all over again."

"It is the *ronin*. In the days of Kang, they would knock on any door for hours until given food."

Remo cocked an ear ceilingward. "Sound's like Smith's ring to me."

"You are imagining things."

"Maybe the *ronin*'s leaving a message. Think I'll mosey upstairs and eavesdrop."

Chiun leaped to his feet. "You will do nothing of the sort!" he said, pointing with a threatening finger. Realizing it was his blunted index finger, Chiun hastily made a fist and shook it at Remo.

Remo said, "I won't pick up the phone, I promise."

"The *ronin* will hear you eavesdropping. They are like that."

"Oh, get off it, Chiun."

"Remo!"

But Remo had floated up the stairs.

In the bell tower the phone kept ringing. And ringing. Oddly the message machine wasn't picking up.

Remo saw why when he looked more closely. The tape was used up.

Rewinding, Remo set it at the beginning and hit Playback.

A weak voice croaked, "Remo. Smith. Call me. Urgent."

Beep.

"Remo. This is Harold Smith. As soon as you are back, contact me the usual way."

The voice was stronger now.

Six messages later the voice of Harold Smith was quite strong. And very annoyed.

The Master of Sinanju had entered by this point.

"Sounds like Smith to me," Remo told him.

"Yes , it does sound like Smith," Chiun admitted.

"Sounds like he's still with us."

"The *ronin,*" said Chiun, shaking his head. "It only sounds like Smith. He has disguised his voice."

Beep.

"Call me at Folcroft. Please."

"How many *l*'s in that message?" Remo asked Chiun.

"Four."

"Japanese have trouble with their *l*'s. Don't tell me different. That's Harold Smith."

Chiun's face puckered up. His eyes narrowed. His fingers clenched and unclenched. All except the right index finger, which he kept curled.

"Go outside," he spit. "Call Fortress Folcroft from a pay telephone. If he lives, say nothing of the *ronin* to him. If it is a trick, you will know it because the answering voice will say *'moshi moshi.'*"

"What is a *moshi moshi?*" Remo asked.

"A Japanese hello."

"I'll be back," said Remo, popping down the stairs.

Chiun called after him, "If you are ambushed, at least you have no fingernails to lose. But mind that you retain your fingers. If you lose one, I will never speak to you again."

"What if he throws a finger in my face?"

"Better you lose a finger than allow the House to be doubly shamed. If you lose a finger, throw it back in his face, Remo."

"Do thumbs count?" Remo wondered aloud.

"Mine, yes. Yours, not at all. Now go."

Remo went out the rear entrance and crossed the street to the Oriental market at the intersection of three streets. There was a pay phone bolted to the brick building. Slipping a dime into the slot—Massachusetts had to be the last state in the Union where the pay phones took dimes—Remo leaned on the 1 button.

He waited for the automatic connection.

The phone never rang. Instead, Smith's lemony voice said, "Remo?"

"I didn't hear it ring," Remo said suspiciously.

"That sometimes happens."

"How can you pick up a phone before it rings?" Remo asked, all the time matching the lemony voice against his memories of Harold Smith's distinctive voice.

"It did ring. On this end. The phone company has instituted a policy of dissynchronous rings. The ring you hear on your end of the line is not the ringing on this end."

"Why would they do that?" Remo asked, thinking it sure sounded like Harold Smith. Right down to the constipated consonants.

"It is to foil persons calling relatives long-distance and hanging up after one or two rings as a signal they have arrived safely. The phone company's lines were being used without charge."

"They sound as cheap as you," Remo said.

Harold Smith cleared his throat. "Actually it is very thrifty of them."

"It is you, Smitty!" Remo exploded.

"Who else would it be?" Smith asked querulously.

"We heard about the train wreck and went bombing down. Three different people said you died."

"A man named Howard Smith was killed. Coincidence."

"Well that coincidence cost me my Dragoon. Someone stole it while we were combing the wreckage."

Smith groaned. Then he said, "I must ask you to return to the wreck."

"Why?"

"My briefcase was, er, left behind."

"I know. I salvaged it."

"You have it!" Smith's voice skittered on the dangerous edge of sounding pleased, and Remo's suspicions flared up again.

"Yep. Figured I couldn't let it fall into innocent hands."

"Its secrets are invaluable."

"Actually it's as wet as a drowned cat. I was thinking of the rescue workers who would've been maimed if they tried to pick the lock."

"It would have served them right," Smith said flatly.

"Spoken like a man with a new lease on life. You know, Smitty, I hear about people having close shaves who see the world differently afterward. I guess we can't add you to that happy list."

"I had a near-miss. Near-misses do not count. The world has not changed in my absence."

"Well, Chiun and I thought you were dead."

"I am not dead. And I have an assignment for you."

"What's that?"

"These train derailments. It is time we looked into them."

"Just because you nearly died in one? Aren't we a little behind the curve?"

"I have been following them for over a year. I suspect sabotage."

"I suspect mismanagement. Didn't the government get involved in Amtrak years ago?"

"It is a quasi-governmental agency."

"Isn't that kinda like bring semipregnant?"

"Freight lines are suffering, as well. There was a derailment in Texarkana the night before last. I want you and Chiun to go there."

"What are we looking for?"

"According to the preliminary NTSB report, they cite human failure on the part of the engineer. The report hadn't been released to the public, but I would like you two to look into it. You will be Department of Transportation agents. Liaise with the NTSB chief investigator. He was very quick to cite drugs. *Too* quick. I would like to know more."

"Want us to hold him upside down and shake the truth out of him?"

"Be discreet."

"Chiun will be wearing a flaming red kimono trimmed with silver-and-gold salamanders. That discreet enough for you?"

"Why are you being so testy, Remo?"

Remo leaned against the brick. "Oh, I don't know. I guess thinking you were dead and finding out I kinda missed your sour old puss put me in a mournful mood. Now I wish you'd you go back to being dead. I liked you better dead."

"I am not dead. Go to Texarkana. Report as needed."

"And happy rebirth day to you, too," said Remo, hanging up.

BACK AT THE BELL TOWER, Remo broke the news to the Master of Sinanju.

"Bad news. Smith is alive."

"He gave you the secret password, naturally?"

"What secret password?"

"Arrgh! You failed to verify it was Smith! Must I do everything myself?"

"Believe me, it's Smith. Two minutes into the conversation, I started hating the sound of his voice and he gave us a dippy assignment."

"What assignment?"

"We're looking into the train derailments, starting in Texarkana."

"I do not know that place."

"Oh, believe me, Chiun. You'll love Texas. And Texas will love you."

"Is that one of the flat, square provinces far to the west where the buffalo roam and the roughnecks play?"

"The phrase is *rednecks* and I'm sure we'll bump into a few of those."

"We will go because we are obliged to go. And Texas will be the last place the faceless *ronin* will seek us."

"Let's go," said Remo as Chiun turned to pick over his steamer trunks. They were half-packed. The open ones spilled elaborate brocaded kimonos, tatami mats and many of the papyrus scrolls Chiun had brought from Sinanju, on which were inscribed the inked histories of his village.

"You will take the silver trunk with the lapis lazuli phoenixes."

Remo groaned. "Not that one again."

"Do not drop it, and above all do not open it under any circumstances."

"Didn't I lug this thing across half of Mexico last time out?"

"Now you will lug it to exotic Texarkana, where men's necks are red and never a discouraging word is heard."

"I think I'm going to rewrite that last part of the song," grumbled Remo, lifting the trunk onto his shoulders.

11

Melvis O. Cupper didn't like what he was hearing.

"No drugs," the Texarkana medical examiner was saying.

They were in the county morgue. The body of Southern Pacific engineer Ty Hurley lay on the porcelain autopsy table, his head and a few disconnected parts piled at the top of the table, above the main portion of his torso.

Hurley looked as if he was about to be sewn back together. But Melvis knew nothing would ever put the poor bastard together again. Out of respect for the dead, in his big red hands he held his white Stetson with the black letters NTSB stenciled on the crown.

"Mind closin' his eyes for me?" Melvis said.

"They bother you?"

"I'm fixin' to talk about the poor fella behind his back and all, I don't care to have him starin' at me like that."

The ME shrugged and dropped a sheet over the head and loose parts. Somehow that made it creepier. Melvis could have sworn the shrouded eyes were peering through the thin cloth. He thought he could see the outline of the pupils against the whites.

"You sayin' absolutely no dope?"

"No drugs, no liquor. Not even aspirin traces."

"What about amphetamines? Surely you found some of those. After all, he was a dang engineer. They live on the stuff."

The ME shook his head in the negative. "No illicit substances in the system."

"Check the stomach?"

The ME lifted a clear plastic bag that sagged with a blackish substance.

"What's that?" Melvis grunted.

"His last meal. Moo Shi pork."

"Looks like regurgitated saw grass to me. How can you tell?"

"Same way I can vouch that the blood is clean. Analysis."

"Dang, I was countin' on dope."

"The dead man struck a stalled car. You know just as I do that wasn't his fault."

"I know that. But why didn't he brake?"

"He was decapitated."

"That's the part that bothers the fool out of me, I don't mind sayin'," said Melvis Cupper in the cool fluorescent atmosphere of the county morgue. "There wasn't enough glass in the cab to chop him up like that."

"Impact forces can sometimes wrench a man's head clean off."

"I got a good look at the neck stump. Looks like a clean cut. And a wrenched-off head would pull out all manner of plumbin', wouldn't it?"

The ME frowned. "I must admit you're right about that. Well, there are some factors we haven't accounted for yet."

"That's what I been sayin', Doc. What happened is plumb inexplicable. That's why I was hopin' it was dope."

"Drugs wouldn't explain what happened here."

"Not to you and me. But I gotta tell you, when I run into somethin' I can't otherwise explain away, dope fills the bill. Covers up a wealth of sins and omissions. In fact, I highly recommend it to you."

"You have a different way of looking at your responsibilities than I do," the ME said firmly as he sheeted the headless nude body.

"Appreciate you not takin' that tone with me, Doc. I got more of these fandangled derailments these last two, three years than I care to count. There's a big one back East right this minute I'm supposed to look into once I get done here."

"You'll have to find your answers elsewhere," the ME said formally. "My report will say no drugs in the system. And death by traumatic decapitation."

"Dang."

A voice from the suddenly open door asked, "Melvis Cupper in here?"

"That's me," Melvis said, turning.

The first one through the door didn't make Melvis's eyebrows quirk up much. He was six footish. On the lean side. Short dark hair and deep-set eyes that sank back into his head so he seemed to have hollows instead of eyes, like on a skull. His wrists were mighty big, though. Reminded Melvis of Popeye the Sailor Man.

He wasn't Texan. Not in a white T-shirt, tan chinos, fancy leather loafers and no self-respecting hat on his head.

"Who might you be?" Melvis demanded.

The man flashed an ID card, identifying him as Remo Renwick from DOT—the Department of Transportation.

Melvis was handing it back when the second man popped through the swinging door.

Now, here was an entirely different article. He swam in silvery silk skirts like a lady. But he was a man. Old as sin, too.

"And this 'un?"

"Chiun. Derailment specialist on loan from Washington."

"Him!"

"Yes," said the little old Asian. "I am very familiar with trains."

"That so? You don't look much like a railroad man from the cut of your skirts."

The face of the tiny Asian stiffened. "I am old enough to have ridden steam locomotives."

"That so? What kind?"

"My first engine was a Mikado 2-8-2."

Melvis's eyes popped like white grapes. "You don't say! And where might that have been?"

"The Kyong-Ji Rail Line."

"Never heard of it. Must be east of Texas."

"West. For this train wended its way through my native Korea many years before you were born."

"Do tell."

"Can we get on with this?" Remo asked.

"What's the rush?" Melvis countered.

"The Department of Transportation is very interested in this derailment."

"NTSB has it covered. You gents can wait for the official report like everyone else."

"The preliminary one says drugs."

Melvis cleared his throat noisily. They had him there. "We just been discussin' that little detail, the doc and me. Ain't that right, Doc?"

"Drugs are not present in his system," the ME said flatly.

"So much for the preliminary report," Remo Renwick said pointedly.

"Now, don't get all carried away. We're still compilin' data."

Remo Renwick drifted over to the dead engineer on the dissection table. "This the engineer?" he asked.

"Yep. I wouldn't lift that sheet if I was you. It's kinda raw under there."

Ignoring him, Renwick lifted the sheet, picked up the head and examined it as if it were a basketball he was checking for leaks, then tossed it to the old Korean. The little guy caught it as if catching heads was something he did all the time.

"See now!" the ME protested.

"Let 'em have their fun," Melvis said. "They look like right ready boys."

The old one had the head upside down and was looking at the stump. The younger man was poking about the other stump.

"Check this out, Chiun," he said.

The little guy drifted up to the neck stump, which was red but bloodless. It had been thoroughly washed and disinfected.

"Decapitated, plain as day," Melvis said.

The little guy shook his head. "No."

"If that isn't decapitation, what is?" Remo asked.

"I will explain later." His eyes went to Melvis and the ME. "Away from these prying ears."

"Those are right unfriendly words to use around a fellow public servant."

"His head came off. That's decapitation," Remo was telling the old Korean.

"Later," Chiun argued.

Remo looked Melvis in the eye. "Give me a rundown."

"You read the preliminary report?"

"I did. He didn't. Let's hear it."

"Engineer hit a sport vehicle at the crossing at Big Sandy. Tore the thing apart, dragged it a few miles down the line, then plowed smack into the freight yard at Texarkana. Engineer ended up discombobulated. A lot of rail fouled and boxcars on their side. Not much else to tell."

"Where did the man lose his head?" asked the little Korean, going right to the jackpot.

"That answer we ain't exactly shook loose. Some think it was at the crossing." Melvis eyed the ME. "There's others who hold that it came loose in the big freight-yard wreck."

"What's your opinion?" asked Remo.

Melvis rocked back on his ostrich-skin boot heels, squeezing his white Stetson in both hands. "I'm reservin' judgment on that particular point."

"I would like to see the place where this tragedy took place," said Chiun.

"Which? The first wreck or the big one?"

"The beginning."

"Suit yourself. I got a car outside."

As they started out of the autopsy room, Melvis remembered something. "Doc, you keep that sorry fella on ice. I got me a feelin' we ain't done with his sorry ass just yet."

On the way out Melvis's hard-bitten attitude softened as he asked Chiun, "You really ride steam locomotives in your youth?"

"From Kaesong to the railhead at Sinuiju. And back. Many times."

"Man, I was born eighty years too late. I hanker for the clean smell of steam and coal smoke."

"Steam is heavenly, I agree."

Remo looked at them both as if they were crazy.

WHEN THEY RETURNED to the rental car, Remo took the wheel and waited for Chiun to close the passenger door.

"What's this about steam?"

"It is my cover," Chiun said airily. "I am conversant with trains."

"Just let me do the conversing, okay?"

"We will speak of this later."

"For crying out loud, we have a fifty-mile drive ahead of us."

"You drive. I will think."

"Suit yourself," said Remo, waiting until Melvis pulled out of his parking slot. Then he fell in behind him.

On the way out of town they drove past the freight yards. A derailment team was putting a boxcar back on the rails with a pair of Caterpillar tractors.

Chiun craned his neck to see the operation.

"What are you watching?"

"It is very interesting to see how they do it in this day and age."

"Huh?"

"When I was a youth, oxen were employed."

"They really had trains in Korea way back then?"

"Yes. In Pyongyang they were called *ki-cha,* which means 'steam cars.' We called them *cheol-ma.*"

Remo blinked as he searched his mind for the English translation.

"Iron horse?"

"Yes. We called them iron horses."

"Funny. That's what the Indians used to call them in the days of the transcontinental railroad."

"Why should that surprise you, Remo? My ancestors settled this land."

"Let's not get carried away. Just because one of your ancestors came across the Bering Strait and pitched a tent doesn't mean every Hakawi and Poohawk is Korean."

"I have been reading of late. Your historians claim that America was settled by Koreans."

"Tell that to Leif Eriksson. Or Columbus, for that matter."

"It is true. This was a barren land until Koreans came. We conquered the wilderness to live in harmony with the land. Until the evil white man came, despoiling all."

"You been watching that Kevin Costner series again?"

"He actually wept when describing the horrors whites inflicted upon my ancestors' noble Cheyenne cousins."

"He could use an egoectomy," Remo grumbled.

"I am thinking of petitioning Emperor Smith for the return of my ancestors' stolen lands."

"Never happen."

"Oh, I do not want it all, Remo. Just all the land west of the Kutscn River."

"Where?" asked Remo, recalling *kutsen* was Korean for "muddy."

"You occupiers call it the Mississippi," Chiun sniffed.

"Save us all a world of grief. Don't even bring it up."

"Only the land closest to Korea is of interest to me, Remo. I do not think my ancestors traveled very far west, I do not recognize the eyes of the Powatans or the Mohawks. I suspect them of being Mongol vagabonds."

"Pocahontas was a Mongol? Is that what you're saying?"

"I defy you to find a trace of Koreanness in that tart's face," sniffed Chiun.

They followed Melvis's car through piney scrub hills. Oil-derrick farms bristled here and there. Finally they turned off onto a dirt road that ran alongside a rail bed. A freight train barreled by, and the Master of Sinanju's eyes went to it. A faint smile came to his thin lips.

"What are you looking at?" Remo asked.

Chiun sighed. "There is something about a train."

"You weren't kidding him back there?"

"I admit it. I am a buff."

"I admit it. I couldn't care less about trains. They're slow, noisy and they take too long. And I'm surprised you don't share that opinion."

"Barbarian. You have never known the sublime joys of steam."

"Cross my heart and hope to avoid it, too. I thought the only steam you cared about fluffed your rice."

"Have I never told you of my first train ride, Remo?"

"Yeah. No need to plow old ground. We have a busy day ahead of us."

"No, I insist."

"Look, you told it to me. I know it by heart. Give it a rest."

"Excellent," said Chiun, beaming. "Now, you tell it to me."

"Why do you want to hear your own story back?"

"Because I would like to savor the memory without the distraction of having to recount the details."

Remo said, "Tell me why that engineer wasn't decapitated and I'll tell you your story back."

"I will think about it," Chiun said vaguely.

And Remo smiled thinly. He had gotten out of a tough one. He couldn't remember Chiun's railroad story to save his life.

THE CROSSING at Big Sandy bore few signs that an accident had occurred. Fresh gravel lay in the rail bed, mixed in with older, rain-discolored ballast. The rails gleamed unbroken.

Melvis Cupper stood at trackside as he explained things. "SP hauler hit the sport vehicle along this stretch. Broke it apart and carried it three miles east, throwin' off sparks and hot steel."

"What happened to the driver?" Remo wondered aloud.

"No one knows."

"Anybody run the plate?"

"Never found a dang plate."

"Isn't that kinda strange?"

"Like I said, metal was flang off for three miles. It's probably in the bluebonnets somewhere."

Remo looked at the tracks. They were sunk flush with the ground. Wooden sections lay on both sides of the track for the convenience of crossing vehicles.

"Rail's not very high."

"Yeah. That's so the cars can mosey across."

"Looks to me like you'd have to have four flats to stall out on this spot."

"Maybe he run out of gas."

Remo looked at Melvis Cupper. "You're full of easy answers."

"After this I gotta head east to look into that Amtrak spillover. I got my hands full. This was a common freight derailment. One dead hogger. No front-page headlines. Gotta file it, forget it and move on. Way things are pickin' up, there's more comin'."

Remo noticed the Master of Sinanju lying down beside the rails. He placed one fragile ear to the rail, closing his eyes.

"Is he doing what I think he's doing?" Remo asked Melvis.

"Does my heart proud to see a foreigner who comprehends high iron. Way the Asiatics are floodin' in, you'd think the old ways are not long for this sorry world."

Remo said nothing.

Having satisfied himself that no train was coming, Chiun stood up and began walking the track.

"I guess we walk," said Remo.

They walked. The hot Texas sun beat down, and Melvis Cupper adjusted his Stetson, saying, "You boys really ought to get yourselves hatted up Texas style. Do you a world of good."

"Pass," said Remo.

"What about you, old fella?"

"I have known many summers. I do not fear the sun." His eyes were fixed on the ties.

"Suit yourself. But sunstroke ain't nothin' to wish away."

When they came to the section of track where the wood ties were scorched from the sport-vehicle gas tank going up, Chiun abruptly left the rail bed.

"Where we goin' now?" Melvis asked Remo.

"Where *he* goes."

"That don't answer my interrogative, as we say in east Texas."

"Learn to go with the flow," suggested Remo.

Chiun came to a flurry of footprints. He stooped, examining these. Remo watched him.

Melvis spoke up. "Those tracks won't tell you a damn thing. That's where we all stood the other day, pokin' about."

Chiun stood up.

"Where are the tracks of the escaping driver?" he asked.

"Search me. Figure he hightailed it for Mexico by now."

"Has it rained of late?" asked Chiun.

"Naw. Dry as a bleached cow skull."

"There should be tracks of the fleeing one."

"Well, if you can find 'em, you're more than welcome to 'em."

Abruptly Chiun walked into the underbrush.

Remo soon saw why. A crushed sprig of mimosa showed that a man had walked here in the recent past.

Carefully Chiun placed his feet on the bare spot. His gait became deliberate, cautious.

Remo watched the ground as he followed.

"Who we followin'?" Melvis asked.

"Search me," Remo admitted.

"Hush!" said Chiun. His tone was very serious.

They walked into trackside woods. This was east Texas. Pine and sweet gum predominated. Without warning, Chiun stopped.

"What's wrong?" Remo asked.

"They stop," he said.

"What stops?"

"The tracks."

"Whose tracks? I see only yours."

"Come around. Carefully."

Remo did. Melvis hovered close.

The Master of Sinanju was pointing at the sandy yellow soil. Ahead of him stretched a short set of footprints. They looked like Chiun's. But Chiun hadn't walked this far yet. And Chiun left prints only when he wanted to. Remo followed them back and saw that Chiun was standing in a lone set. Only then did Remo realize that the tracks he'd thought were Chiun's were really older tracks Chiun's feet perfectly fit into.

"Wait a minute..." Remo said.

"Hush."

"What's goin' on?" Melvis muttered.

Chiun's eyes squeezed into slits of deep thought. "These tracks are two days old. Perhaps older. But no more recent."

"Yeah. You're right," said Remo.

Their eyes met. Chiun's chin lifted. A dusty breeze toyed with his wispy beard. He took it between two fingers, the short-nailed index finger and the second one.

"Two days," he repeated. "No sooner."

"No argument there . . ." said Remo.

Chiun turned on Melvis. "What manner of vehicle was destroyed here?"

"Lemme think now. It was a funny one. Oh, yeah. A Nishitsu Ninja."

"Hah!" crowed Chiun.

"Hah what?" asked Melvis.

"Weren't they recalled a few years back?" Remo said.

"Yeah. They kept tippin' over on tight turns. But a few folks spent the money to have 'em fixed up so they were stable. That's why I said it was funny. You don't see too many Ninjas on the road these days. Worst durn rice-burner ever built."

Suddenly Chiun turned, hurrying back to the rail line. He walked them carefully, striding, his fists tight, hazel eyes scouring the rails, the ties and the surrounding brush.

"What's he lookin' for now?" Melvis asked Remo.

"You'll know when I do."

"You're not bein' very cooperative."

"Sometimes the dog wags the tail. Other times it's the other way around. I learned a long time ago to follow along and let the pieces reveal themselves."

Melvis spit. "You would last two days with NTSB."

Chiun stopped so abruptly that Melvis nearly bumped into him. They gathered around. Chiun was looking straight down.

In the center of a tie was a fresh gouge.

"I'm lookin' at a gouge, am I right?" said Melvis.

Chiun nodded.

"Looks like a hunk of metal hit it pretty hard. It's sound, though. No urgency about replacin' it. Am I right?"

"A *katana* did this," Chiun intoned.

"Oh-oh," said Remo.

"What's a *tanaka?*" asked Melvis.

"*Katana.* Sword."

"Sword, huh? I'd put it down as a flyin' hunk of axle or something."

"It's a sword cut," said Remo.

"What sword?"

"The blade that beheaded the engineer," said Chiun.

"You funnin' me? He was decapitated."

"Beheaded."

"What makes you say that?"

"Experience," said Chiun, abruptly leaving the rail.

"Where we goin' now?" Melvis wanted to know.

When Chiun stepped into the rental car, the immediate question was answered.

Remo leaned into the car. "Where to next, Little Father?"

"We must speak with Smith."

"Who's Smith?" asked Melvis.

"Our supervisor."

"I got a cell phone in my rig."

"We need more privacy than that."

"Well, there's gotta be a pay phone somewhere's around. After all, this is Texas."

"Not if he gets his way."

"Say again?" asked Melvis in a dubious voice.

"It goes back to the original settlers."

"The Mexicans? Never."

"No, before them," said Chiun.

"You mean the Injuns?" Melvis exploded. "I'd sooner see the dang Asiatics have it."

"You're getting warmer," said Remo.

12

Harold Smith was at his desk when the blue contact phone rang. He had been cleared to work by the Folcroft doctors who had pulled him from the taxi and administered stimulants.

The first thing Smith had said upon regaining consciousness was, "I must get to my desk."

"It's the middle of the night, Dr. Smith," the head doctor said. "I prescribe rest."

"And I pay your salary," Smith snapped.

The Folcroft staff knew their director. They eased him into a stainless-steel wheelchair and rolled him to his Spartan office, where he peremptorily dismissed them.

Reaching under his desk, whose top was a slab of black glass, Smith pressed the button that activated the buried video terminal. It lurked under the tinted glass. When the screen came on, the amber phosphorescent sign-on cycle was visible only to Smith.

None of the Folcroft staff suspected the concealed terminal any more than they knew of the existence of the four mainframes that hummed quietly in the basement behind blank concrete walls.

This was the nerve center of CURE.

As soon as he had the system up and running, Smith called up incoming reports on the derailment he had just survived, downloading them into his ongoing Amtrak file.

Twenty-odd minutes into this he remembered to call his wife.

"I am fine," Smith said without bothering with a greeting.

"Why wouldn't you be, Harold?" Maude Smith asked sleepily.

"I was on the train that derailed but I am fine."

"Oh, Harold."

"I am fine," he repeated.

"Where are you now?"

"At work."

"You should come home, Harold. You sound tired."

"I will see you tomorrow," said Harold, hanging up and thinking that there was no reason to let Maude know he had been on that wreck. There was no sense worrying her needlessly.

That was hours ago. Smith had toiled through the night, pausing only when he experienced an uncontrollable fit of coughing. His tongue tasted brackish. His stomach was sour. He loaded it up with antacid pills and Maalox, all to no avail.

When his secretary showed up for work, he asked her for black coffee but said nothing about the accident.

The wire feeds on the Mystic derailment were still coming in. The death toll was mounting in slow increments. It looked as if the final fatality total would exceed forty. Smith read that information, making absolutely no connection with his own brush with death.

In his mind a person either survived an accident or did not. One is dead or living; there is no in-between. Harold Smith still breathed. *Almost* didn't count.

The first bulletins were fragmentary and under constant revision. The earliest reports simply attributed the derailment to excessive speed. This was revised to human factors, a euphemism for crew fatigue or drug-induced engineer impairment.

When he read that the train had struck a bulldozer, Smith frowned like a puckering lemon.

"What would a bulldozer be doing on the tracks?" he muttered.

A follow-up report referred to cable being laid in the vicinity of the derailment, and suggested the bulldozer had attempted to cross the tracks and become stuck. There were no witnesses and no missing workmen.

"Ridiculous," Smith said. "There is no crossing on trackage so close to the water and no place on the shore side for the bulldozer to go."

But there the reports stood. A bulldozer had blocked the tracks. That was the end of it as far as the media was concerned. All they cared about were facts—whether true or not.

Smith moved on, looking into the Big Sandy incident.

It was similar. Only it fell within acceptable accident parameters. A driver tried to beat a train at a crossing. It happened with numbing regularity, like squirrels leaping into the paths of cars.

The decapitation of the engineer and subsequent behavior of the runaway Southern Pacific freight train was a different matter. It warranted investigation. Yet the preliminary NTSB report mysteriously cited drug use. It was a conclusion completely un-supported by available facts.

So when Remo had called, Smith sent him to the site, knowing that the Mystic investigation could wait. They were in the salvage stage now. There was nothing for them to do there. NTSB was still en route.

SMITH HAD MADE no progress by the time Remo checked in from Texas.

"Go ahead," Smith said, upon picking up the blue contact phone.

"Smitty, we found something."

"Yes?"

"The engineer was beheaded."

"I know that."

"No, you're thinking of decapitated. This guy was definitely beheaded according to Chiun."

"What is the difference?"

"The difference is a sword."

"I beg your pardon, Remo."

"According to Chiun, the engineer was deliberately beheaded."

"By whom?"

"Well, that's where it gets sticky."

"I am listening."

Remo's voice moved away from the receiver. "Here, Little Father, you tell him. It'll sound better coming from you."

The Master of Sinanju's squeaky voice came on the line. "Emperor, I bring difficult tidings."

"Yes?"

"Your servants have determined that foreign elements have been at work."

Smith said nothing. Chiun would tell it in his own way.

"These crimes have been perpetrated by Japanese agents, possibly only one."

"Why do you say that?"

"In both places Japanese vehicles were employed to block the right-of-way."

"How do you know this, Master Chiun?"

"In the place truly called Mystic, I myself beheld the name of the yellow machine. It was Hideo."

"Yes. That is a brand name."

"Here in this land of roughnecks, a Ninja was employed to work the same end."

"Excuse me—did you say *ninja?*"

"He means a Nishitsu Ninja," said Remo.

"Japanese-made vehicles are very common these days," said Smith. "I doubt this is anything more than coincidence."

"There is more, Emperor. In both places the unmistakable bite of a *katana* blade marked the site of this fiend's depredations."

"Did you say *katana?*"

"You know it?"

"I believe it is a sword used by the ancient Japanese."

Chiun's voice shifted away. "Remo, Smith recognized *katana*. Why did you not?"

"I'm having a slow week," Remo said sourly.

"Since 1971?"

"Get off my back!"

Smith interrupted the impending argument. "Master Chiun, I can think of no reason why—"

"There is more. Last night I encountered a foe the like of which I have never encountered."

"Yes?"

"A *ronin*. Do you know this word?"

"No."

"See?" said Remo. "Even Smith never heard of it."

"Hush. A *ronin* is a masterless samurai," explained Chiun.

"The samurai clans died out long ago," Smith said.

"Would that it were truly so," Chiun said, sad voiced. "I myself beheld one with my own eyes. He escaped. Stealing our dragon."

"It's Dragoon," Remo inserted.

"With which the fiend made his escape. Otherwise, we would have vanquished him utterly, just as you would wish."

"Er, did Remo see this samurai?"

"This *ronin*—no. He emerged from the sea while Remo was busy elsewhere. I alone saw him. He moved with great stealth. Fierce was his mien. Great was his skill."

"From the sea, did you say?" asked Harold Smith.

"Yes. Why?"

Smith frowned. A hazy memory tickled his brain. What was it he had seen?

"Nothing," he said, unable to shake the cobwebs from his brain. "It is nothing. Go on."

"Now that we have solved this mystery, we crave a boon, O Emperor."

"What is it?"

"My pupil and I are in dire need of a vacation. We are thinking of sojourning in sweeter climes. Just for a month or two. No more. We will return if needed."

"This assignment is not over."

"I told you he wouldn't fall for it," said Remo.

"Hush, unwise one. O Emperor, will you not reconsider?"

"This assignment is not over. And I do not accept your findings."

"What is wrong with them?"

"If a—er—samurai blocked the right-of-way with a Nishitsu Ninja, how did he get into the cab to behead the engineer?"

"Perhaps he flung his blade into the man's face."

"In that case the blade will be in the wreckage of the cab."

"Not if the samurai recovered it."

"How? The engine traveled over fifty miles before crashing."

"A mere detail."

"You might look into the engine. If a *katana* turns up, I may reconsider my evaluation."

"It will be done, O Smith."

The line went dead.

"I TOLD YOU he wouldn't fall for it," said Remo after Chiun hung up. The receiver shattered like so much black glass from the force of Chiun's angry gesture.

"That man is impossible."

"You didn't tell him the whole story."

"It is family business and none of his concern."

"Now what?" asked Remo.

"You overheard all. We will examine the engine."

"Even though you know we won't find any *katana*. The *ronin* was carrying it last night. A whole night after this mess."

"We have our instructions," Chiun said thinly.

"You just want to hang around where the ghost samurai don't roam."

They rejoined Melvis Cupper, who was working a pay phone in a local saloon. He clutched a sweating can of Coors in one hammy fist. After a minute he hung up.

"Just got my marchin' orders. I'm Mystic bound."

"We want a look at the engine," said Remo.

"Well, it's in the direction I'm headed, so I guess I can take a little detour."

THE ENGINE LAY on its side in the shattered remains of the Texarkana freight yard. It was a long gray monster, its formerly blazing red nose now scorched black by the exploding utility vehicle.

"Man, it about busts my heart to see one lyin' on her side like that," Melvis said unhappily.

"It's only an engine," said Remo.

"Shows what you know. That's an MK5000C. Sweetest thing this side of steam. Another generation or two, and diesel will finally match the tracktive effort of the old Challenger steamers. Never thought I'd live to say it, either."

Remo was looking at the forward windscreens. They had shattered into crazy spiderweb patterns, but the glass had held. Only a small piece was missing.

"No sign of an entry puncture," he said.

"Entry?"

"Never mind."

There was a gangplank platform hovering over the side access door. They climbed the steps and lowered themselves down.

The interior cab walls were crusted reddish black with dried blood. A few flies buzzed about.

Remo and Chiun looked around. The cabin hadn't sustained much damage.

In the rear of the cab was a long rip in the bulkhead that separated the cabin from the power plant.

"What's this?" Remo wondered aloud.

"A hole," said Melvis.

"Made by what?"

Melvis shrugged. "Flyin' something or other."

"You find the something?"

"They ain't got to the engine yet."

Remo said to Chiun, "What do you think, Little Father?"

Chiun looked the rip over carefully. *"Katana."*

"You sure?" asked Remo.

Chiun nodded. "The blade passed through this hole."

"Okay. How'd it enter the cab?"

"Sorcery."

Remo looked dubious.

"You fellas care to share your opinions with a jug-eared good ol' boy?"

"Let's see that engine," Remo said.

"Probably birds-nested all to hell."

They opened the engine covers, exposing the monster diesel engine. It was still new, a factory-fresh coat of primary yellow paint making it gleam.

"Man, is that a mess," Melvis said.

It was. Wires and metal components lay everywhere. In places the yellow was scorched and blackened. It looked like a bird's nest after it had been picked at by squirrels.

Melvis shook his head. "Never seen one birds-nested so bad."

Remo asked Chiun, "Think it's inside the engine block?"

Chiun shook his head. "It passed through, impaling itself on the tie. You saw it."

Remo shook his head, "Couldn't. If it struck the tie, the trailing cars would have mangled it. And someone would have noticed it among the car parts. Therefore, it's in the engine block if it's anywhere."

Chiun frowned like a death mask drying. "There is an explanation," he said.

"Sure, always is. Look in the engine block."

"First we will look under the engine," said Chiun.

They looked. There was no exit hole in the bottom of the engine. Nor in the back.

"It is a conundrum," said Chiun, absently stroking his wispy beard.

"That's a rabbity kinda word for what we got here," Melvis Cupper allowed.

"Well, I guess there's only one way to find out," said Remo.

"Yes," said Chiun, raising his arms so his wide kimono sleeves slid back to his elbows, exposing pipe-stem arms resembling plucked chicken wings.

Remo turned to Melvis Cupper. "Think you could find a flashlight?"

"I guess I can rustle one up. You wait here now."

Melvis Cupper was gone only five minutes, long enough to forage a flashlight from the freight yards. He was loping back when he heard the wild straining and shriek of metal.

He broke into a run. "Dad-gum it all to hell!"

Remo and Chiun were climbing out of the cab when he got there. Remo was holding a short black sword of some kind.

"What's that?" Melvis demanded.

"*Katana.*"

"I can see that. I got eyes. Where'd you get it?"

"From the engine block."

"How?"

"Reached into the rip in the back of the cab," said Remo as they fell to examining the blade. Melvis clambered into the cab and examined the rent. It was bigger now. Very big. It looked as though someone had used clevis hooks to open it wide.

He poked his head out again. "What kinda tool you boys use?"

"Handy ones," said Remo, not taking his eyes from the blade.

Melvis rejoined them, looking mad. "You DOT boys ain't got no right to poke your noses into my investigation."

"You'd never have discovered this without us."

"Fine, then. That there frog-sticker is NTSB accident evidence."

Remo moved it out of Melvis's reach. "Sorry. Finders keepers."

"I plan on writin' you uncooperative boys up."

"Feel free," said Remo, turning the sword around in his hands.

Melvis's eyes kept going to the blade. "That's what chopped that poor soul's head clean off, you reckon?"

"Looks that way."

"Lopped it off and buried itself into the bulkhead, is what you're sayin'?"

"That's right."

"If that be the case, why ain't it banged up or broke?"

"Good question," said Remo.

The blade was straight, true and without nicks or scratches.

"And while we're gnawin' at the subject, how'd it get in there in the first place?"

"Through the windscreen."

"No hole in the windscreen. Not one big enough to pass that sucker through. Explain that if you can."

"We cannot," said Chiun.

"Then your theory falls all to hell and gone."

"That's life," said Remo.

"Yes, that is life," echoed Chiun.

Melvis Cupper eyed them skeptically. "For DOT boys you two seem powerful casual about your work."

They started off.

"We'll see you around the old camp fire," said Remo.

"Not if I see you gents first," said Melvis Cupper, slapping on his NTSB Stetson.

13

On the flight back east, Remo had one question for the Master of Sinanju. "What do we tell Smith?"

"The truth," said Chiun.

This wasn't exactly the answer Remo expected, so he asked another question. "All of it?"

"Of course not."

"What part are we leaving out?"

"The important part."

"Which is?"

"Family business. It is not for the emperor's ears."

"So we just tell him a loose samurai—"

"Ronin."

"—is responsible for these derailments and let him take the ball from there?"

"He is emperor. His wisdom will guide us."

Remo settled back into his seat. "I can hardly wait to hear his reaction."

HAROLD SMITH LOOKED at the short sword as it was laid on his tinted-glass-topped desk at Folcroft Sanitarium.

Behind him a picture window let in afternoon light. Long Island Sound danced placidly. There wasn't a cloud in the sky or a shadow on the water.

The sword was ebony of handle and black of blade. Smith extracted a pearl gray handkerchief from the breast pocket of his gray suit.

Lifting the sword, he dropped the handkerchief onto the upraised edge. The gray cloth settled, hanging over each side. Reaching under, Smith grasped the dangling ends and gave a firm but gentle tug.

With a faint popping, the linen handkerchief parted like old cheesecloth.

"This is a genuine *katana*," Smith pronounced.

Remo grunted in surprise. "You know that from the sharpness of the blade?"

"Of course. I spent time in occupied Japan after the war."

Chiun favored Remo with a silent look Remo read as *How does he know of this and you do not?*

Remo shrugged in response.

"You say you found it in the locomotive?" asked Smith of Remo.

"It went through the bulkhead in back of the cab and embedded itself in the engine block. I had a hard time pulling it out."

"Impossible."

"Why do you say that?"

"For this blade to have sliced into the engine block is impossible. If possible by some freak of chance, it would have been hopelessly mangled upon impact, if not melted by engine heat."

"Look, I'm just telling you where I found it."

"*We* found it," corrected the Master of Sinanju.

"Right," said Remo. "There's more."

Laying the blade on the desktop, Smith looked up expectantly.

"You start," Remo told Chiun.

Smith's gray eyes tracked to the Master of Sinanju.

Chiun stood with his hands in the sleeves of his kimono, his favored position when at rest. "What I am about to relate may strain your imagination, O Emperor."

"Just tell it plainly," invited Smith.

"On the previous night, in the place correctly called Mystic, I came upon footprints that came from the sea," said Chiun.

"Yes?"

"I followed these and encountered a *ronin*, a masterless samurai, as I have told you."

"How do you know this was a *ronin*, not a samurai?"

Chiun's wispy eyebrows shot up in surprise.

"Er, I looked the word up after we spoke last," Smith admitted.

Chiun eyed Remo as if to ask, *Why do you not ask such intelligent questions?*

Remo pretended to be checking the shine of his shoes.

"I know him to be a *ronin* because his armor bore no mark of his allegiance upon his shoulder."

"No clan crest, in other words?"

"Yes. No *sode-jirushi*. Thus, a *ronin*, not a samurai."

"Continue, Master Chiun."

"As I stalked this wave-tossed one, so-called because that is the meaning of *ronin*, not because he emerged from the sea, I spied the bite of a *katana* blade in the bole of an alien tree."

Smith's eyes eyes flicked to the *katana* on his desk.

"Coming upon the *ronin* in question, he challenged me and I him. We battled. His blade cleaved the air in mighty thrusts, but to no avail, for I am the Master of Sinanju."

"Of course," said Smith.

"Alas, he got away."

Frowning, Smith steepled his bony fingers. "How?"

Chiun made a dismissive gesture. "He was exceedingly crafty. No craftier foe have I encountered. Ever."

Smith's puzzled expression indicated that he wasn't satisfied with the answer.

"Tell him about the fingernail," said Remo.

"What fingernail?" asked Smith.

Chiun winced. "Another matter entirely," he said flatly.

"Oh, come on, Chiun. You can tell Smith."

"Yes. You can tell me, Master Chiun."

Chiun's features tightened. His fisted right hand dropped so the down-sliding sleeve almost covered it. "I lost a nail to the masterless cur."

Smith's puzzled expression gave way to a startled one. "You?"

"A fluke. I am still the Master of Sinanju. No mere *ronin* could best me. But his blade clipped my avenging nail, and it was lost."

Smith looked incredulous.

"No doubt that in my concern for your loss, I allowed myself to be distracted."

Smith nodded. Chiun relaxed. Remo rolled his eyes.

Chiun then continued. "I would have pursued the wretch to the very ends of the earth had not Remo come along bearing your all-important briefcase."

Smith's eyes went to a chair where the briefcase now lay, noticeably warped from its recent immersion.

"Knowing that this was more important than any other matter," Chiun continued, "I allowed the *ronin* to escape with his worthless life. I would not have done this had I suspected the truth I now reveal to you."

Smith's eyes dropped to the *katana*. Chiun allowed himself a faint smile. He had cleared the first hurdle. Now for the second.

"Had I suspected that this wave man was responsible for the train wreck of the previous night, I would have slain him twice over. For the very footprints I discovered in eerie Mystic were present in the sandy soil of the Big Sandy, also correctly named."

"This cannot be the same *katana* he wielded in Mystic," Smith declared. "Not if you found it in the engine block in Texarkana."

"Obviously the resourceful *ronin* availed himself of another. And thus we have a path to this fiend."

"Yes?"

"Contact all sword makers in your land and see who has recently forged a fine blade such as this. For I judge this particular example to be excellent. Possibly the work of a descendant of Odo of Obi."

"Odo of Obi?" said Remo. "Sounds like *Star Trek Meets Star Wars*."

"Ignore this benighted one's prattle, O Emperor. I am sure that Odo of Obi is known to you."

Smith adjusted his Dartmouth tie uneasily. "Er, I doubt this blade was manufactured outside of Japan."

Chiun gestured toward Smith's desktop. "Your oracles may tell you otherwise."

"That will take time."

"There is another way, O Smith. This *ronin* has taken up a new *katana*. It is required that he bloody it. Usually this is done by beheading a luckless commoner. It is a custom known as the crossroad cutting."

"I hardly think that—"

"Your oracles will tell you of any beheading in the provinces near shunned Mystic."

Smith's hands went to his keyboard. "It is worth looking into, I suppose," he said without conviction.

Almost at once he was lost in thought. His gnarled fingers tapped the illuminated keyboard. He stared into his desktop like a man at a Ouija board.

"My God!" he croaked.

"Ah-hah!" Chiun cried in triumph.

"There was a rash of beheadings in Connecticut and Pennsylvania. The first was of a state trooper who pulled over—" Smith swallowed hard "—your APC, Remo."

Remo threw up his hands. "Great. Now I'm wanted for beheading a Connecticut State trooper."

"I can fix that," said Smith, performing some manipulation on the computer.

Remo came around to Smith's side of the desk. "What are you doing?"

"I am changing the APB on the LEAPS system."

"LEAPS?"

"Law Enforcement Agency Processing System." Smith finished inputting commands. "Now the cover name in which the APC was registered no longer traces back to you."

"Who gets the blame instead?"

"A low-level Mafia soldier who has thus far eluded justice."

"Good luck to him," grunted Remo.

Smith returned to the matter at hand. "The trail ends in Reading, Pennsylvania," he announced, reading off the screen.

"Then it is cold," said Chiun. "For three beheadings are more than enough to test his blade. He will waste no more strokes."

Frowning, Smith logged off.

He picked up the captured *katana* again. He was examining the hilt when his thumb, encountering one of the many ornate studs, suddenly depressed one. The blade went click.

Like a fury Chiun reached in and snatched the blade from Smith's hands. It happened so fast, Smith had only time to blink. His eyes read the sudden absence of the blade, and he blurted out the thing his brain told him had happened.

"It self-destructed!"

Chiun's voice lifted. "No. I hold it in my hands. Remo, quickly, check your emperor's fingers for barbs or punctures."

Remo moved in, turning Smith's hands up and down. "Looks clean," he said.

"Sometimes the crafty Japanese ensure that their own weapon is not turned against them by certain artifices," said Chiun. "Poisoned barbs are very common. But I see none here. This is only a stud, but it does nothing.''

''We need to return to the matter at hand,'' said Smith, taking his hands from Remo's grasp. Remo stepped away.

''Why would a man dressed like a samurai derail two trains in different parts of the country?'' Smith wondered aloud.

''A *ronin,* not a samurai, and who can fathom the mind of a cruel Japanese?'' said Chiun, returning the *katana* to the desktop.

''We don't know this man is Japanese.''

''He is a *ronin.* Of course he is Japanese.''

''Did you see his face?''

''No, it was . . . masked.''

''He could be anyone.''

''Smith's right, Chiun. How many times have the police nabbed some dip dressed like a *ninja* breaking into a house? They aren't really *ninja.*''

''Even *ninja* are not really *ninja,*'' spit Chiun. He paced the floor. ''Smith, accept the word of your loyal assassin. The man is a *ronin.* Seek no one else.''

''If he is Japanese, there is a way we might prove this.''

''How?''

''To reach Texarkana from Connecticut in less than a day requires air travel. I will search the computerized airline-reservation files for Japanese travelers.''

Chiun beamed. ''Excellent thinking.'' His gaze grew sharp as it fell upon his pupil. Remo pretended to be interested in the *katana.*

Harold Smith went to work. He logged on and off several times, but when he was done, his face was glum.

"No Japanese nationals left any of the major Texas airports for Connecticut on the day in question."

"Any land in Connecticut?" asked Remo.

"A few. But from other locations. None trace back to Texas."

"We're back to square one," said Remo. "What do we do now?"

Smith was thinking. They could tell because his pinched nostrils were distending methodically. Otherwise, he looked as if he had fallen into a trance.

"The central question at the moment is not whom, but for how long?"

Remo and Chiun looked at him. Smith took up his rimless glasses and began polishing them.

"By that, I mean is this samurai—"

"*Ronin,*" Chiun corrected testily.

"—responsible for the most-recent derailments, or could the last three years of incidents be laid at his doorstep?"

"No doubt he is newly arrived on these shores. Otherwise, we would have heard of his depredations before this," suggested Chiun.

Smith shook his gray head. "No, we can assume nothing."

Chiun turned on his pupil. "Remo, you witnessed a train derail only a year ago. Tell Emperor Smith that you saw nothing out of the ordinary."

Smith's gaze went to Remo.

Remo blinked. "That's right. Remember last summer, Smitty? Chiun had me running all over creation performing the Rite of Attainment?"

Smith nodded.

"I was in Oklahoma City when a cattle train derailed. I pitched in to help."

"Was there anything usual about the derailment?"

"As derailments go, it was a bloody mess. Dead cows everywhere. Other than that—" Remo's face suddenly went strange.

"What is it?"

"Yes. Remo, speak," urged Chiun.

"When I was walking the tracks, I saw something weird. The engineer's head was up a tree."

"Up a tree?"

"Yeah. I figured he'd been decapitated in the wreck, and his head just bounced upward."

Chiun made a low moan and glared at his pupil. Remo avoided his cold regard.

"Last summer, you said?" Smith murmured.

"Yeah. July."

Smith pulled up his Amtrak file, got the incident on the screen and read in silence.

"It was a Santa Fe train. The NTSB cited traumatic amputation as a result of drug use on the part of the deceased engineer."

"Drugs?" said Remo.

"Yes, it says drugs."

"That wouldn't be a Melvis Cupper report, would it?"

"Yes, how did you know?"

"He was trying to blame the Texas mess on a drugged-out engineer, too."

Smith's bloodless lips thinned noticeably. "Perhaps we might talk with Cupper again."

"Shouldn't be hard. Last we heard he was on his way to Mystic to check out the mess up there."

Chiun spoke up. "O Emperor, is there not a more pressing need your loyal assassins might fulfill?"

"Master Chiun?"

"Is this not a task for the FBI, those stalwarts? We are assassins, not sleuths. I am Chiun, not Fetlock."

"Matlock," growled Remo.

"If this marauder is found, we will be happy to dispatch him, but is it necessary to squander our valuable time chasing this fiend? Is not our place here at your side? You have only just escaped death. Who knows that this is not some Japanese scheme to unseat you? I offer my pupil and myself as bodyguards until this dire crisis has passed."

"It is highly unlikely that I was targeted. I had an unreserved ticket. No one could know I was on that train. And if my life was sought, there was no reason to derail a freight train in Oklahoma City a year ago."

"Logic is a dangerous trap," warned Chiun.

"Is something the matter?" asked Smith of Remo.

"Chiun just doesn't want to lose another fingernail to the phantom samurai," Remo suggested.

Chiun puffed up his cheeks like a Korean version of Old Man Winter, ready to vent a blast of angry air in Remo's direction.

"I am certain you will be able to deal with him when the time comes—if it comes," said Smith.

Subsiding, Chiun bowed as if in agreement. His bobbing posture covered the angry glance he threw in Remo's direction.

Remo mouthed the words *Nice try*.

"Talk to Cupper," said Smith. "I will look into the Oklahoma City parallels, if there are any."

"As you wish, O diligent one," said Chiun, bowing out of the room.

"Later," said Remo, following.

Outside the building Chiun exploded. "Are you mad, dragging an old head into this!"

"Look, it may prove this samurai—"

"Ronin."

"—has been active for a while."

"So?"

"That means he's not your wave-tossed ghost *ronin* just washed up on shore."

"What makes you say that?"

"Because if he were after the House, he'd have found you long before now."

"You were in Oklahoma City when that train of beasts fell over on its side?"

"Yeah..."

"Where in Oklahoma City?"

"Sleeping in a hotel room behind the tracks, hiding from you."

"Ah-hah!"

"Ah-hah what?"

"The toppling of the train was to lure you into an ambush."

"So why wasn't I ambushed?"

Chiun's face froze. His mouth paused in open mode. "Why must you and Smith insist upon heaping white logic on everything?" he sputtered.

"Beats ignoring reality."

"You would not know reality if its brazen talons roosted upon your thick head and looked down into your face with its blazing ruby eyes," said Chiun, getting into the rental car.

"You know," admitted Remo when he got behind the wheel, "it *is* kind of a big coincidence that that train should derail when I was in Oklahoma City and another one when Smith was riding it."

"We will resolve to ride no train for the rest of our days—bitter and galling as the prospect may be."

"Suits me just fine," said Remo, sending the car through the Folcroft gates. After the Dragoon, it felt like driving a Tonka truck.

14

Melvis Cupper was watching the track hands rerail the baggage car at Mystic, Connecticut.

He liked nothing better than watching the rerailers work. They were a special breed. And since part of his investigation involved observing the proceedings but prevented him from actually participating and therefore breaking a sweat, he took his ease at trackside while the Hulcher crew set the clevis hooks at the four corners of the car.

Two side-mounted Caterpillar tractors were hunkered down on either side of the right of way. A supervisor was on his stomach looking up at the work. He wore a white safety hard hat. All eyes were on him. Or rather, on his hands.

It was a hell of a thing to watch.

With only hand gestures, he signaled the boom hands to lift the north end of the car. The twin Cats screeched as they strained to lift the car off the soft, gouged earth. The wheel assemblies dangled uselessly.

In less than a minute they walked the car over the rail bed and dropped her down, true as an arrow, onto the blocks.

The supervisor got off the ground and wiped his

hands, signaling the crew to move to the next car in line.

"Just like pickup sticks," Melvis said happily.

An hour later the last car had been rerailed, the track crew brought up a bucket and began to attack the bent rail.

The dreaded cry, "Watch the rail!" rolled out, and Melvis dropped off his perch and betook himself to a point well back of the festivities.

The bucket dropped down and started bringing up rail section. Most of it came up easy, but there was no way of telling when a stressed or bent length of steel would snap or break with catastrophic results.

Melvis was watching this operation when he felt a hard tap on his shoulder. The tap came just as the bucket dug in again.

"Lordy, I've been hit. God da-yam!" he howled, clutching himself.

"Relax. It's just us," said a voice that sounded vaguely familiar.

Still holding his numb shoulder, Melvis turned. His eyes squinted up. "You fellas again. Next time don't come sneakin' up on a man like that. Was sure a block of rail bit me. What'd you use to get my attention anyway? Crowbar?"

Remo Renwick wriggled his index finger. The old Korean named Chiun stood beside him, face unreadable.

"You must bench-press lead sinkers with that thing, then. Hey, you forget to fetch me that old *tanaka* sword?"

"Sorry. It's still being looked at."

"Had to leave it out of my report, you know."

"You leave a lot of things out of your reports, don't you, Melvis?" Remo said.

"What's that supposed to mean?"

"Oklahoma City. Remember it?"

"Yeah. A damn mess. All those dead folks and twisted-up cars. Sure hope they hang the horse-thievin' dastard what blew up that building."

"I mean the derailment last summer. Cattle train."

"Oh, that one. A Santa Fe. Warbonnet, too. Damn shame. They're threatenin' to get rid of the warbonnet color scheme now that the Santa Fe has merged with Burlington Northern."

"You blamed the engineer."

"Man was on drugs. Why won't these freight hoggers ever learn?"

"They found his head in a tree."

"Hey! How'd you know that? It wasn't in the official report."

Chiun spoke up. "We know many things that we should not. It will go better for you if you tell us all you know."

Melvis hesitated. "What do y'all want to know?"

"What really derailed that train?" asked Remo.

"Impossible to tell for sure. That's why I put down dope. When in doubt, the engineer was high as a kite or strung out. Covers a multitude of sins. Also NTSB expects a nice neat and tidy answer for the final report. Trouble is when a train hits the bumpers it leaves such a dang mess you can't hardly tell a push-pull consist from a cow-and-calf set after the dust is all done settlin'."

The two looked blank.

"Tell us about the engineer," Remo asked just as a section of rail snapped behind them.

They looked back. The track gang was okay. Nobody hurt.

"Man's head was sheared off as sweet as honeysuckle," Melvis replied. "By that, I mean it might have been chopped by a guillotine. 'Cept for the conspicuous lack of a blade."

"Flying glass?"

Melvis nodded. "Plenty of it. But I don't think that's what got him."

"Then what did?"

"I couldn't tell back then. But now that you bring it up, a sword like what you boys pulled outta that big block coulda done it."

The two exchanged hard looks.

"How'd the head get up the tree?"

"That's the part that had me plumb bumfoozled back then. The head couldn't have been ejected by the derailment. But as you boys surely know, toss a basketball out a window and it'll describe a downward arc. This head was stuck way high up that tree. Can't see how traumatic ejection would account for it. Someone had to have hung it up there."

The two looked at each other again.

"But I put down dope because, like I said, it covers a passel of sins. Not to mention inexplicables."

Chiun eyed him coldly. "There is more. I can see it in your beady eyes."

"You're right sharp, you are. I left out one little item."

"What's that?"

"The poor engineer was decapitated—"

"Beheaded," said Chiun.

"—a few miles back of where his head was actually found. In other words, I think someone was in the cab with him, lopped his pumpkin right off, causin' that terrible wreck. She was goin' mighty fast on the turn where she wiped out."

"Someone got in the cabin, cut off his head but managed to jump clear after the derailment?" asked Remo. "That's what you think really happened?"

"And tossed the head into the tree for reasons known only to the Almighty and the lunatic what done it. Now maybe you can see why I wasn't about to write that whopper up. It ain't natural, not to mention sensible. The NTSB abhors such things."

"What's your read on this mess?" Remo asked, indicating the rerailed train, whose cars stood dented and muddy on a good section of rail.

"This? Now, this one is textbook. Piece of heavy equipment on the rail. Engineer couldn't have seen it in time to stop. Smashup with cars in the water. Happens all the time."

"That so?"

"You can't say different."

"Come with me," said Chiun, beckoning.

Reluctantly Melvis followed them past the track gang.

"I sure hope you boys aren't about to upset my little red wagon. I've been pullin' her a long old time and I hope to pull her a lot longer before I go for my gold watch and that last lonesome terminal."

The pair said nothing. They walked off the rail bed on the landward side of the line. In a section of forest they showed him a patch of dirt where footprints had disturbed the earth.

"These look familiar to you?" asked Remo.

"Sure. Looks like your friend here was walkin' about."

"What about these?" Remo said, pointing to another scatter of imprints.

Melvis rubbed his blunt jaw thoughtfully. "Hmm."

"Big Sandy, remember?"

"That's your friend's footprints. You can't fool me."

"They are the same size, true, but not the same," said Chiun. And placing one sandaled foot beside a print, he pressed down. When his foot came away, it was obvious they were not the same. Just similar.

"You sayin' the fella what jumped the track at Big Sandy was here, too?"

"Definitely," said Remo.

Melvis Cupper contorted his face in thought. He chewed his lower lip. He squinted one eye shut, then the other. "If that don't beat all," he muttered.

"He was at Oklahoma City too."

"That's conjecture. Pure, unabashed conjecture. I don't hold with conjecture. No, sir. Don't hold with it a-tall."

"Tough," said Remo. "You're stuck with it."

"Yes," says Chiun. "Put that in your report and smoke it."

They walked away.

Melvis hurried after them. "Now, wait a goldang minute."

They kept walking.

Puffing, Melvis drew abreast. He walked in front of them, stepping backward and trying not to trip over ground roots.

"You fellas came along the other way, am I right?"

"Right," said Remo.

"So how y'all know those tracks where there?"

"That is for us to know and you to find out," said Chiun.

Melvis eyed them pointedly. "You were here before."

"Possibly," said Chiun.

"You were here before NTSB! How is that possible? There wasn't time for you to get on-site before me."

"You ask too many questions," said Remo.

"Yes. Of the wrong person. Better you learn to ask the correct questions at the proper times," Chiun warned.

Melvis was trying to think of a good comeback for that when his beeper went off. "Oh, hell. I hope this ain't another one."

It was. Melvis ran to his rental car and dialed a number on his cell phone.

"Da-yam."

"What is it?" asked Remo.

"You boys might want to check in with your supervisors, too. There's big doin's out Nebraska way."

"Derailment?"

"Worse. Looks like they got what they used to call in the old-timey days a cornfield meet."

Remo said, "A what?"

Chiun gasped. "No!"

Remo did a double take. "You know what that is?" he asked Chiun.

"Of course he does," spit Melvis. "Any man who rode steam locomotives before they turned antique knows what a cornfield meet is."

"Well, I don't."

"I rest my case," Melvis Cupper said. Turning his attention back to the cell phone, he barked, "I'm on my way. This one was only a crossing derailment anyway. Happens every dang day.''

When he hung up, Remo and Chiun were looking at him like a pair of unhappy Sunday-school teachers.

''Nobody has yet proved different,'' Melvis retorted defensively.

15

Over Nebraska, Remo began to suspect why a corn-field meet might be called that. Rows of waving corn marched in all directions like a green-clad army on parade drill.

The waiting NTSB helicopter had taken off from Lincoln, Nebraska, and picking up a double ribbon of tracks running due west through flatland country, followed them. After a while a parallel set of tracks appeared.

Over the rotor whine, Melvis Cupper was peppering the Master of Sinanju with questions. "Tell me more about that steam loco you used to ride when you were a young 'un. Narrow gauge or standard?"

"Narrow," said Chiun.

"No foolin'. Elephant ears?"

"Elephant ears are African."

"Bumpers instead of a cowcatcher, am I correct?"

Chiun made a yellow prune face. "Cowcatchers are a white innovation. Even the Japanese do not use them."

"You ride coach or first-class in them days?"

"My family was given its own coach by the oppressors in Pyongyang."

Melvis slapped his knee with his hat. "No foolin'! You had your own private coach? Goldang!"

"It still resides in Pyongyang, awaiting the call to serve," Chiun said blandly.

Melvis turned to Remo. "You hear that? He has his own railroad coach. Man, that is the way to fly."

"Yes." Chiun allowed a trace of pride in his eyes. "There is something sublime about steam travel."

Remo interrupted. "How come I never heard about this?"

"The next time we are in Pyongyang, I will treat you to a ride. If you do not displease me before then."

"No, thanks. I'm not big on trains."

"What's a matter?" Melvis grunted. "Never own a Lionel set when you were a shaver?"

"No," said Remo.

"You missed out big, then. I feel sorry for a man what never owned a train set growin' up."

"Save it," said Remo, scanning the horizon.

There were over the flat heartland of Nebraska now. Cornfields as far as the eye could see. Below, the corn was tassling, showing golden gleams here and there.

"Avert your eyes, Remo," Chiun warned.

"I'm looking for whatever it is we're looking for," Remo complained. "I am not thinking of corn."

Chiun confided in Melvis. "Recently he has become a corn addict."

"White lightning?"

"Worse. Yellow kernels."

"Never heard of that brand of moonshine."

"He has Indian blood, and you know how they are about corn," whispered Chiun.

"Say no more. We had piles of Injuns down in the Big Empty—before we chased their savage asses off."

"I see something ahead," said Remo.

Melvis leaned past the pilot. "What? Where? I don't see nothin'." Melvis gave the pilot's right earphone a snap. "Do you?"

The pilot shook his annoyed head.

"Train wreck," said Remo.

"It over on its side?"

"No."

"Well, you're lookin' at the rear end. It's the head end I'm frettin'," Melvis said, leaning back and licking his lips. "Brace yourselves. A cornfield meet is one hellacious sight if you've never taken one in."

"I see the cornfield," said Remo, "but not the meet part. Is that *meet* with two *e*'s or *meat* like in beef?"

Melvis shuddered visibly. "If it's as bad as I fear, it could be a bloody blend of both."

It was, Remo saw as the helicopter buzzed the train.

There was an Amtrak passenger train down below. Twelve cars long. The last car sat perfectly on the rails as if waiting at a crossing. The rest were all over the place. Two trailing Amtrak coaches, still coupled, formed a big silver V across the right-of-way. Another lay on its side. One was split open like a foil-wrapped package that had exploded.

The train resembled a long silver snake with a broken and dislocated spine.

The head end was where it was really messy. And as they overflew it, Remo understood exactly what a cornfield meet was.

Both engines were still on the rails. The silvery Amtrak engine was mashed into the nose of another engine, a black one. It looked old and spidery somehow, even though it had telescoped in a third of its length. The Amtrak engine had come through the impact no better. It had taken hits in both directions. The following car had slammed into its rear. Consequently the Amtrak engine body had folded up like an accordion.

"Oh, man," Melvis moaned. "Headlight to headlight. They're the worst kind of head-ons."

As they dropped down, they could see the fatigue pup tents where the injured were being treated. Stretchers lay in rows, empty but spattered with red. A few were completely red like flags. Ambulances sat about the cornfield, but it was obvious the worst of the triage was over.

All at once Melvis Cupper began moaning, "Oh, Christ. O sweet Jesus. Tell me it ain't so."

"What do you see?"

"Oh, the horror. I can't look at it no more." And he tore his eyes from the engine. A second later they gravitated back. It was as if he were seeing it for the first time all over again.

"Oh, my momma. I just wanna bust out cryin'. Oh, to die so young like that."

"What're you talking about?" asked Remo, not seeing any bodies.

"The damn engine! Look at it. Oh, will you look at that sweet monocoque body all banged up to hell and gone."

"Which engine?" asked Remo.

"The Amtrak, you idjit. That there's a brand-spankin'-new Genesis Series 1. GE built. Unibody monocoque design. Bolsterless trucks. They even got a Holster cab at the rear of the unit so one crewman can move it forward and back. Jesus, there ain't hardly five or six in operation yet and now one's dead."

Remo looked at Melvis.

Melvis looked back. "Hell, I'm about fixin' to cry. Excuse me."

And he grabbed a handkerchief and busied it about his eyes.

Remo looked to the Master of Sinanju. "Who knows how many people are dead, and he's weeping over the engine."

"He is a fool. Only steam is worthy of his tears."

Remo said nothing. His eyes were on the wreck, which was growing larger every second.

The chopper settled, flattening the prairie grass like hair under a blow dryer. They got out.

Melvis walked up to the engine, saying, "Oh man, I just hope she ain't derail prone. Cause if she is, then you can kiss Amtrak goodbye. This was supposed to be the locomotive of the future. One of 'em, anyways."

"What's this other thing?" Remo asked, pointing to the black engine.

"That? Why, it's a . . ."

They looked at him.

"Give me a second now. It'll come to me."

Melvis scratched his head on both sides and scrutinized the scrunched engine from front, back and sides.

"Don't rightly know," he admitted. "Looks like it might be some kind of switcher or work train."

"What is it doing on the same track as Amtrak?"

"Fair question. Over yonder lies the Union Pacific lines. They haul freight. Uncle Pete livery is what they call Armor yellow, so this ain't one of theirs.

Don't know what else runs on this line. This ain't exactly my neck of the woods."

Melvis led them around to the other side of the joined-at-the-nose Siamese engines. The stink of diesel fuel was high in their nostrils.

When they rounded on the other side, they walked into a camera. It went click in their faces.

Reacting to the sound, Remo and Chiun suddenly broke in opposite directions. They came to a dead stop, a safe distance away.

Feeling the breeze, Melvis turned. "Thought you boys was right behind me."

"Who are you talking to?" a musical, twangy voice asked.

Melvis took one look at the willowy girl in fringed buckskin jacket and bright blue bib jeans and asked, "Who in heck are you?"

The woman let her camera hang down in one hand as she dug a business card out of her jeans. "K. C. Crockett. *Rail Fan* magazine."

Melvis's face lit up. "*Rail Fan!* Why, I subscribe to that." He yanked out a card. "Melvis O. Cupper, NTSB. And if I gotta tell you what the initials stand for, you ain't who you say you are."

"Thank you kindly," said K.C., taking the card. She had a corn-fed smile and hair only slightly less red than copper. Her eyes were electric blue.

Remo and Chiun came up.

Melvis jerked a thumb at them. "These here are two boys from DOT."

"Can I have your cards too?" K.C. asked brightly.

"I do not have a card," said Chiun.

Remo offered his. "Can I keep it? I collect them," K.C. asked.

"Sorry," said Remo, taking it back. "Only one."

"They're from back East," Melvis told K.C. Eyeing Chiun, he added, "*Way* back East."

"Pleased to meet you all. I was riding the *California Zephyr* when it hit. Sure was an experience, let me tell you. But I got some nifty shots of the wreck. Maybe I can make the cover this time."

"You were on the train?" Remo asked.

"Last car. We were going along right smooth when smash! Lights out, *boom-boom-bang-ba-boom* and we were in the ditch faster than pooh through a possum."

"You're a right lucky lady," said Melvis.

"All except for being defiled in the middle of the Nebraska flatlands," K.C. said ruefully.

"That's means left behind," Melvis told Remo and Chiun.

"We have an investigation to conduct. Remember?" Remo said.

"Right. Right. We're gettin' to that." Addressing K.C., Melvis said, "Me and the DOT boys here were just tryin' to make out what this other engine was. Maybe you know, bein' with *Rail Fan* and all."

K.C. squinted one eye and then the other at the black engine. She wore a green-striped white engineer's cap on her head, and she adjusted the bill several times.

"It ain't a switcher."

"That's for sure," Melvis agreed.

"Not an Alco, either."

"Don't have any livery to speak of. Which in itself is plumb peculiar. K.C. gal, you happen to know whose track this is?"

"Burlington Northern."

"Sure ain't a Burlington Northern diesel. Their color scheme is Cascade green."

K.C. nodded. "Whatever it is, it sure don't belong on this line."

"Sure is a shame about this Genesis."

K.C.'s face fell. "And it was my first Genesis, too!"

"Hate to break it to you so rough, but it may be your last if Amtrak loses the good fight. This wreck sure won't persuade Congress to keep her goin'."

K.C. broke down at that point.

"Now, don't you get me started," Melvis blubbered. "I'm a sentimental cuss when it comes to high iron."

While they shared a handkerchief, Remo and Chiun started looking through the scattered debris.

"Maybe one of these pieces will tell us something," Remo said.

Melvis called over, "Man, if true rail fans like me and K.C. here can't tell by lookin' at the back end, no fragments will help."

"It's gotta be something."

"Perhaps it is Japanese," suggested Chiun.

Melvis perked up. "Think you'd recognize her if she were?" To K.C., he said, "That little fella used to ride steam trains back in Korea all the time. Family had their own private car."

"Golleee," K.C. said, eyes drying. "Doubly pleased to meet you, sir. Would you kindly consent to an interview for my magazine? I don't think we've ever run an article on Korean steam."

"Can we save this for the next convention?" Remo demanded.

"Allow me to examine this beast for clues to its ancestry," Chiun said loftily.

The Master of Sinanju began to walk around to the black engine, Remo and Melvis following, while K.C. peppered him with questions.

"What kinda engine was it?" K.C. asked.

"A Mikado 2-8-2," Melvis said proudly.

"Never heard of it. Was it a narrow gauger?"

"Yep," Melvis said.

"Elephant ears?"

"No ears. No cowcatcher. Just bumpers," said Melvis.

"Whose tale is this?" Chiun demanded.

"Sorry," said Melvis, grinning sheepishly.

To Remo, Chiun said, "Why do you not hang on my every word as these two do?"

"My brain hasn't been steamed," Remo grumbled.

"Aw, you're just sore on account of you were born too late to catch the steam bug."

"You could run every train on earth off Niagara Falls, and I wouldn't care," said Remo.

Melvis and K.C. gasped like two old maids.

"Such language!" K.C. said. "Shame on you. This great nation was built on rails. Trains don't pollute, fall out of the sky like planes or lose a body's luggage, either."

Chiun came to a dead stop. Throwing his head back, he struck a heroic pose, hands fisted, tight to his hips. "It is not Japanese," he pronounced.

"How do you know?" asked Melvis.

One long-nailed finger—on the undamaged, left hand, Remo noticed—pointed to a sooty string of seemingly meaningless letters and numbers low on the side of the black engine.

"Japanese do not use the English letter *l*."

"You got a point there."

"So what is it?" asked Remo.

"Look," K.C. said, whirling.

Remo and Chiun whirled in unison, eyes going in the direction of her excitedly pointing fingers.

On the parallel UP track, a train was coming. The engine, Remo saw, was painted in mottled desert-camouflage livery.

"Do I see what my eyes are tellin' me I'm seein'?" Melvis asked breathlessly.

"If you're not dreaming, neither am I," K.C. breathed.

"What is it?" Remo asked, concern in his voice.

"I do not know," Chin said grimly, "but it is painted a warlike color."

"That there must be one of the last units on the Union Pacific still tricked out in Desert Storm camouflage colors," Melvis said, awe coloring his tone.

"What?"

"It's true. Back durin' Desert Storm, the Union Pacific painted a number of their SD40-2's just like that one yonder to show support for our troops in the Gulf."

"Kinda takes your breath away, don't it?" K.C. said.

"Amen. Diesel always makes my heart go hippity-hop."

As the engine rattled by, both Melvis and K.C. took off their hats and laid them over their hearts. The rest of the train consisted of old boxcars painted in assorted colors, their sides dusty and peeling.

"Makes your heart pound like an old kettledrum to see such a rare sight, don't it?" Melvis said. "And look at them Hy-Cube boxcars. They're runnin' on eight-wheeled trucks. I never saw the like of it."

"Down Sonora way I once saw an Alco RSD12, highballing like a bat out of hell." K.C. blushed. "Excuse me—Hades."

"High nose or low?" Melvis asked as the railcars flitted by.

"High. Painted burned orange."

Melvis sighed. "Life can be sweet sometimes."

"I got pictures of it. Wanna see 'em?"

"Swap you an Alco RSD12 for a FPA4, with Napa Valley wine-train livery"

"Deal!"

As Remo watched with increasing incredulity, they pulled out their wallets and began exchanging snapshots of diesels they had known and loved.

While they were lost in reminiscences, Remo found a thin piece of twisted black metal. "This look like a piece of a fan blade to you, Little Father?"

Chiun examined it with narrowing eyes. "Yes."

"Awful big fan."

Remo called over to Melvis. "How big of a fan on the Genesis?"

He had to repeat the question and go spin Melvis around in place before he got his attention refocused.

"Hey, none of that now!" Melvis roared.

"What's this look like to you?" Remo demanded, holding the metal in front of his face.

"Looks like a whopper fan blade."

"Off what?"

"Ain't off the Genesis," K.C. said.

"That's a fact. Looks too old."

"So it's off the other engine?" suggested Remo.

"Gotta be."

"The fan blades are mounted on top for cooling the engine, right?"

"Yeah, but that looks too big to be off an engine-fan blade."

"So that leaves what?" Remo asked impatiently.

"You know," K.C. said, "I once heard about a critter called a rail zeppelin."

"Ain't no such animal," Melvis insisted hotly.

"Is, too."

"Let her tell it," Remo said, giving Melvis an eye-popping neck squeeze.

"Back in the thirties, when they were experimenting with high-speed rail, someone built a streamlined railcar with a great big old airplane engine attached."

"Do tell," said Melvis, fingering his collar.

"It's true. The propeller was in back, pusher style. When she started to spin, the rail zep took off like nothing natural."

"How fast she go?" asked Melvis.

"Don't rightly recollect. But they broke a few land-speed records for that time."

"This doesn't look like an airplane blade," Remo said.

"He's right, at that," K.C. said.

"So that means what?" said Remo tiredly.

"Hell, only thing I can think of is a rotary-plow train," said Melvis.

"What's that?" asked Remo.

"You seen snowplows?"

"Sure," said Remo.

"Imagine a big old engine with a big old rotary-plow blade framed in the front, like a big old lamprey's mouth with whirlin' fan blades instead of teeth."

K.C. looked back at the squashed black engine. It had round portholes on its sides instead of windows.

"Could be a rotary-plow engine, at that."

"Except for one dang thing," Melvis inserted.

"What's that?" Remo asked.

"It's the middle of summer. What would a plow engine be doin' out on the middle of corn country goin' the wrong way on a passenger line?"

"Causing a derailment," said Remo.

"You sayin' this is calculated sabotage?"

"Look at it. Wrong-way engine. Head-on collision. What else could it be?"

Melvis scratched his head. "Maybe the engineer was on dope."

"Which one?" asked K.C.

"Why, the plow engineer, of course. Otherwise, why would he take her out six months after the last snowfall and be goin' the wrong way on occupied track?"

"Sounds sensible to me, much as I shrink from the notion of an engineer on drugs," said K.C.

"They don't raise engineers like they used to," Melvis said sincerely.

"Or engines," said K.C., looking at the demolished Genesis.

Melvis rocked back on his boot heels. "Yes, siree, this could be the end of Amtrak."

"You keep saying that," said Remo. "Why?"

"Yes. Why?" asked Chiun.

"Don't you two know? The Amtrak contract with the freight lines runs out this year. Congress is fixin' to defund it. Amtrak can't pull her weight financially, except on the Northeast Corridor and a few other places. The freight boys are all het up because they gotta give passenger traffic the priority, sidelinin' their consists when they got goods to haul, while Amtrak just blasts on by."

"So the freight lines would like to see Amtrak out of business?" said Remo.

"Sure as shootin' they would."

"Perhaps they are behind this outrage," said Chiun.

"That's a good theory. Except for one teensy little fact."

"What's that?" asked Remo.

"The freight boys are experiencin' more derailments than Amtrak. They're gettin' it worse by a ratio of three to one."

Chiun piped up, "Perhaps they seek to throw suspicion from themselves. It is often that way on 'Fetlock.'"

"Which?" asked K.C.

"Never mind," said Remo.

"Look," Melvis said hotly. "It can't be the freight lines. See those tangled-up rails? Somebody has to clean them up. And that same somebody has to pay for the cleanin' up. It sure ain't Amtrak. They don't hardly own a solitary stretch of high iron in the nation. The freight lines control it all. They're the ones eatin' the cleanup bill." Melvis suddenly looked around. "That reminds me. Shouldn't the Hulcher boys be here by now? What's keepin' them?"

Remo asked, "Who are they?"

"Hulcher. They're only the kings of rerailin' train sets. You saw them workin' back at Mystic."

"You were at Mystic?" K.C. said excitedly. "Jiminy, that was a wreck. Wish I'd seen it."

Remo squeezed her neck, and she subsided, too.

Of Melvis, he asked, "Hulcher the only people in that business?"

"No, just the biggest and best."

"Every time a train goes off the tracks, they make money, right?"

"Oh, don't you blaspheme," K.C. cried, her buckskin fringes shivering in anger. "Don't you speak against Hulcher."

"Hell, don't even think what you're thinkin'," said Melvis. "They're railroad men. They wouldn't cause wrecks. Besides, they don't have to. These rail lines are over a hundred years old. They're bound to throw a train or two just from age and orneriness. No, Hulcher ain't back of this. No way, no how."

"Well, someone is."

"I say it's dope. Dope is a scourge upon the land. Show me a derailed GE Dash-8 or a flipped-over Geep, and I'll bet my momma's Stetson there's cannabis in the air."

"Either that, or the evil antirail Congress is at work," said K.C. with a perfectly straight face.

"Let's at least find out where this plow engine came from before we go blowing up Congress, shall we?" suggested Remo.

16

The rotary-plow engine was out of Hastings, the next stop for the *California Zephyr.*

It was normally kept in a shed by a siding. The shed was still there, but there was no engine inside. No yardman, either.

"Maybe the yardman took her out and went the wrong way, accidental-like," Melvis said.

"If it isn't snowing, is there a right way?" asked Remo.

"Now that you mention it, no."

"They're too slow to run on the same track as a fast train, even going the right way," K.C. interjected.

"What's fast about the *California Zephyr?*" Melvis grunted.

"The old *California Zephyr* was fast."

"This ain't the old *California Zephyr,* I hate to tell you."

K.C. grinned. "It suits me. I'm only heading to the big Rail Expo."

"The one in Denver?" Melvis said, face brightening.

"That's the one."

"Man, do I *yearn* to go to that shindig! They're gonna have every brand-new kind of spankin' engine there is from every nation on earth. And a few old ones too.''

''And I aim to bag 'em all,'' said K.C., lifting her camera.

Melvis cleared his throat and asked, ''Anybody ever tell you you got the prettiest Conrail blue eyes?''

K.C. blushed like a beet. ''Aw, shucks.''

''Can we get back to the investigation?'' asked Remo.

Melvis grew serious. ''Allow me to kindly remind you this is an NTSB investigation. That there's an NTSB chopper what brung us here. And if you don't like it, you can lump it and walk.''

''If we leave,'' Chiun said haughtily, ''we will take our stories of the famed Kyong-Ji line with us.''

''Now, hold on a cotton-pickin' moment here! I wasn't meanin' you, old-timer. Just your skinny-ass friend here. He can hightail it back to whatever he's from. You and I, on the other hand, are gonna do some serious confabulatin' about Korean steam. I ain't hardly asked all the questions I got stored up in my poor brain.''

Chiun's eyed thinned. ''I will consider this offer if the investigation goes well.''

''Well, let's get a move on.'' Melvis looked around. ''I guess that dang plow engineer is the meat in a cornfield-meet sandwich for sure.''

A changing breeze brought a metallic scent to Remo's and Chiun's sensitive nostrils. They began sniffing the wind carefully.

Melvis eyed them dubiously. ''You boys turn pussycat all of a sudden?''

''I smell blood,'' said Chiun.

''Ditto,'' said Remo.

Melvis joined in tasting the breeze. "I ain't smellin' nothin' but diesel and ripenin' corn."

"Blood," said Chiun, walking north.

Remo followed him. The others fell in line.

THEY FOUND the man's head before they found the man. The head was in two parts. He had been split down the center of his face, the line of separation falling between his eyes, dividing the bridge of his nose perfectly. He must have had a gap between his two front teeth, because on either side of the two halves the teeth had survived the sudden cleaving intact and unchipped.

The blade had come down that perfectly.

The Master of Sinanju picked up the two head halves and clapped them together like a husked coconut. It was evident from the horrified expression on the dead man's face that the swordsman had been facing his victim.

"One stroke down, separating the two portions, and one across the neck," said Chiun grimly. "The Pear Splitter Stroke, followed by the Scarf Sweep."

K.C. said, "I ain't never seen such a thing."

Melvis piped up, "Honey, I seen a lot worse. Why, once down Oklahoma way I saw a man's head up in a tree like a pineapple just a-waitin' to be picked. The look on his face was about as hornswoggled as this poor soul's, come to think of it."

"The rest of him must be around here," Remo said, looking around.

They found the body a short distance away. He lay on his stomach in the high prairie grass, with his hands tucked under him, as if he'd fallen in the act of unzipping his fly.

"Musta spliced the poor feller as he was takin' his last leak," Melvis muttered. "A right unkind thing to do, you ask me."

Remo turned the body over on its back. It rolled over as easily as a log. And just as stiff. Rigor mortis had set in.

The hands were frozen at his belt line, as if they had held something before he died. His fly was closed.

"My mistake," Melvis said.

Kneeling, Remo examined one thumb. It was rash red, and a slight indentation was visible in the fingerprint area.

"What's this?" Remo wondered aloud.

"His dead thumb," said Melvis, winking in K.C.'s direction.

"I mean this indentation."

Melvis got down and took a hard look. "Search me."

"Let me see," said K.C. She got down with them and looked the thumb over. "You know, way up in Big Sky country I did a photo feature on those new RC units."

"RC?"

"Radio Controlled. They got transmitters now that can move a locomotive around the switching yards without an engineer in the cab. The transmit-power switch has a little silver ball at the end of it. Makes a deep dent just like this one has."

Melvis scratched his own thumb absently. "You don't say."

"Sure. It's got the Brotherhood of Locomotive Engineers union all in a lather. The freight bosses can cut the crews down to two, sometimes one, by giving a yardman one of those contraptions and have him move rolling stock around without need of engineers.''

Melvis set his Stetson over his heart and looked mournful. "A way of life is surely evaporatin' when even an engineer is prone to layoff."

"Ever heard of a rotary-plow engine run by RC?" Remo asked K.C.

"No, but that don't mean it couldn't be."

Remo stood up. The others followed suit.

"Whoever killed this guy took his RC unit and ran the plow down the track," he said.

"It's possible," Melvis admitted.

"Except for one thing," said K.C.

"What's that?"

"I think that thing glinting in the sun over yonder is the RC unit in question."

They went over to the glint. It was the RC unit. It had a stainless-steel case and shoulder straps so that it could carried, leaving the hands free to work the controls.

"So much for that theory," Remo said.

"Looks like it's been busted open," Melvis muttered.

"Why would anyone do that?"

"Got me," said K.C. "Maybe he wanted to get the radio frequency."

"So where's the desperado what skragged this poor feller?" Melvis wanted to know.

"Perhaps he was in the plow engine," said Chiun.

"Suicide," Melvis said, smacking one fist into a meaty palm. "Suicide! That's it! Suicide. Drug-induced suicide. Man cut up his fellow worker and in remorse lit off with the plow engine and run smack-dab into the *California Zephyr,* going out in a blaze of diesel glory.''

"Sounds thin,'' said Remo.

"Maybe he had diabetes to boot.''

Everyone looked at Melvis with expectant expressions.

"There was a Brit who had diabetes,'' Melvis explained. "Couldn't get his leg amputated for love or coal, so he lay down on a track and let a highball do it for him. Bad leg came off clean as bamboo. Maybe this feller had a terminal illness, and this was his way of goin' out.''

"What manner of imbecile would commit suicide by crashing into an approaching locomotive?'' Chiun demanded.

Melvis and K.C. looked at one another. Out of their mouths came the same answer.

"A rail fan!'' they exclaimed.

THEY TOOK the transmitter back to the crash site. K.C. got it working and threw the train into reverse.

No one expected a reaction, but a beacon light atop the train began flashing yellow and the train lurched backward, dragging the Genesis with it. It crawled painfully for all of two feet, then stopped dead.

K.C. shut down the transmitter. "They're rigged to control only one train at a time. You got to reset it for another.''

"How much of a range?'' asked Remo.

"Maybe twenty miles. With repeaters, more.''

"So the murderer could have stood way back at the shed and sent the rotary plow this way without having to see what was happening?''

"It's possible. All you gotta do is set the cab controls and start her up by RC. If you're looking to run it smack into the *California Zephyr,* all you need is the right track and the correct direction. It's not like you gotta steer anything."

"The question is, who?" said Remo.

"All we gotta do is pry them two sad-sack engines apart and maybe we'll get our answer," Melvis offered.

"An excellent suggestion," said Chiun, throwing back his silvery sleeves with a flourish.

He marched up to the mashed locomotive pile.

"What's he up to?" Melvis asked Remo.

"He's going to separate the locomotives," Remo said casually.

"You mean he *thinks* he's gonna separate the locomotives."

"He thinks it, too."

Reaching the wreck, the Master of Sinanju examined it carefully. He turned. "I may need assistance."

"Hah," said Melvis.

"Back up the ugly engine."

"Won't do nothin'. You saw that with your own eyes."

"Do it anyway," said Remo.

"I got it," said K.C. Raising her voice, she said, "Just call out when you're ready. Hear?"

"I am ready," returned Chiun.

Melvis turned to Remo. "Ain't you gonna stop him? He could hurt hisself."

Remo shrugged. "I learned to let him have his way a long time ago."

K.C. threw the plow locomotive into reverse.

The engine grunted, clashed backward. Tangled steel and aluminum groaned like a tortured beast.

And the Master of Sinanju inserted a hand into the tangle. He did something very quick with his hands. Abruptly, with the sound of a giant spring letting go, the plow engine backed off from the mangled Genesis, trailing thin struts and pieces of flat black blade.

"Did you see that!" Melvis exploded. His eyes were popping from their sockets.

"No," said Remo.

"See what?" said K.C., her head coming up. "I was looking at the controls."

"Nothin'," said Melvis. "But I sure heard a sprungin'."

"I heard it, too," said K.C. She grinned. "Guess we got lucky."

Melvis gave Remo a sharp eye. "A lotta that around these two. Hope it's catchin'."

They ran up to the separated engines. The exposed noses were mashed flat. The housing containing the snow-eating fan blades now looked like a grille. The Genesis snout resembled a kicked-in loaf of bread. Crushed air hoses and power conduits drooped from the bottom, as if a hand grenade had gone off in a snake pit.

"Well," Melvis commented, "they say the Genesis is the homeliest loco since the old Union Pacific M-10000, but a head-on sure didn't improve her profile any."

Blood was streaking down the one side. It was enough to tell the Genesis engineer had taken the brunt of the impact.

Remo climbed the access ladder of the Genesis, looked in the broken window and climbed back down.

"Dead," he said.

"Too bad."

"But he still has his head."

"Why wouldn't he?" Melvis demanded.

"Never mind," said Remo, jumping down.

They circled around the other engine. The entire front end had been pushed back into the firewall, cab and all.

"If he's in here," Melvis said, "he's mashed flatter than an elephant's pillow."

"Only one way to find out," said Remo. He started up the twisted access ladder.

"Now what do you think you're doin'?"

Remo said nothing as he reached the engine roof. Kneeling there, he examined the steel roof plates under him.

"Find me a crowbar," he called down.

"Take more than a crowbar to open that sardine can. You need a can opener the size of a canoe paddle."

"Humor me," said Remo.

"Come on, little lady. We can swap lies while we look."

And when they started off for the emergency crew farther down the line, Remo got to work.

He used his fist. Bringing it down, he popped a line of rivets. Moving his fist, he popped another. He worked quickly, striking key stress points until the rivets began hopping in place like tiny animated toadstools.

When he had the roof plates nice and loose, Remo lifted them free and looked down.

There was still a little space left in the cab. About three inches. It was a tangle of metal. But there were no body parts or any smell of blood, brain or bowels.

Standing up, Remo called after Melvis and K.C. "Never mind the crowbar. I got it open."

Remo had to repeat it three times before the pair stopped talking with their hands and looked back.

They came charging back whooping and hollering.

Melvis climbed up as Remo jumped down. He gawked at the open roof, looked down inside and asked, "How'd you do that?"

"I popped the rivets."

"I can see that. With what?"

"Pocket rivet popper," said Remo. "Forgot I had it on me."

"Fingernails of the correct length would have been more seemly," Chiun undertoned.

Melvis climbed down again and said, "I wouldn't mind havin' me a handy gadget like that. Let me take a gander."

"Sorry. Get your own."

"You know what you just done up there ain't within the purview of the DOT."

"Sue me," suggested Remo.

"NTSB might just do that little thing."

"There's no engineer," Remo argued.

"He coulda jumped clear."

"Not if he were suicidal," K.C. remarked.

"You keep your pretty little cowcatcher out of this. Pardon the expression."

K.C. offered a frown and yanked her engineer's cap low over her eyes.

"No engineer means you can throw drugs, diabetes and accidental derailments out the window," said Remo.

"Let's not be rushin' events. Maybe that guy back there set the engine to runnin' and had an accomplice lop his head off."

"Couldn't happen that way," K.C. said.

Melvis squinted up his homely face. "How's that?"

"See this here tilt reset switch?" she said, indicating the RC control panel. "If the engineer falls over or drops dead, the tilt function comes on, signaling the air brakes to clamp down."

"A fail-safe?" asked Remo.

"Yep. Once the RC is dropped, you have to reset everything. And that poor guy back there is too long dead to have been the one to wreck the train. It was the one who killed him that did the deed, sure as the corn grows high in July."

"You don't say," Melvis blurted.

K.C. stuck out her tongue at him. Melvis grinned back.

"Enough," said Chiun. "This deed is the work of a *ronin*."

"A what?" Melvis and K.C. asked in unison.

"A *ronin*."

"Never heard of a *ronin*. You, K.C. gal?"

Reaching into the bib of her farmer's jeans, K.C. extracted a dog-eared paperback book. Remo saw the title: *Kovac's Engine Handbook*.

"*Ronin, ronin,*" she murmured. "How you spell it?"

Chiun said, *"R-o-n-i-n."*

"Nope. No Ronin locomotive in here."

"He's not talking about an engine," Remo said.

"Then what is he talking about?"

"A *ronin* is Japanese."

Melvis grunted. "No wonder. *Kovac's* covers only U.S. of A. motive-power units."

"Diesel or electric?" K.C. asked.

"Neither. Samurai."

They blinked.

Just then Melvis Cupper's pager started beeping.

"Sure hope that ain't what I think it is," he complained, charging off in the direction of the emergency crew.

They took their time following him. When they caught up, Melvis was handing a cellular phone to an Amtrak worker in a white plastic hard hat and orange safety vest.

"We got a haz-mat situation down the line a piece," Melvis bellowed. "Not twenty miles from here."

"How's the engine?" K.C. asked in a stricken voice.

"Dunno. Look, I can't take you boys with me on account of it's a hazardous-materials situation, and you're general pains in the butt anyway. Adios and happy trails."

Melvis tried to push past the Master of Sinanju, whose right sandal suddenly darted between Melvis's ostrich-skin boots.

Melvis fell flat on his face, and the Master of Sinanju stepped onto his back.

"I will not allow you to stand again until you have agreed to take us with you," Chiun said with measured vehemence.

"You're a nice old geezer, I do admit it," Melvis grunted. "But if you don't get offa my back in five seconds, I'm gonna rear up and wash over you like the Galveston flood."

Face bland, Chiun shifted his sandals apart.

"Better tell your friend to do what Mel said," K.C. said anxiously. "He can't weigh much more than ninety pounds."

Remo shook his head. "He's on his own."

"How can you say that about such a sweet old man?"

"I meant Melvis," said Remo.

"Last chance," bellowed Melvis. "I'm countin' backward from three."

Chiun tucked his hands into his kimono sleeves.

"Ready? Three!"

Chiun closed his eyes. He seemed to be concentrating.

"Two." Melvis arched his back.

Chiun showed no sign of moving.

"One!"

Chiun tapped one toe softly.

Melvis suddenly collapsed like a deflated tire. He went "Oof!" as his face jammed into the soft soil. He began making strenuous noises like a rooting hog. His blunt fingers gouged the earth as he strained to lift the incredible weight of the old Korean from his broad back.

The Master of Sinanju simply stood there, eyes closed, serene, a vagrant breeze snatching at his wispy beard.

Puffing, Melvis twisted his face around so he could breathe through his gulping mouth.

"What'd you do—set a boulder on my back? That ain't fair."

"There ain't nothing on your back except that little old man," K.C. pointed out.

"Don't you prevaricate at a fellow rail fan. I know a dad-gum boulder when one lights on my poor spine."

"I will step off if you agree to take us with you," said Chiun.

"Dang it, you got me flummoxed. Okay, doggonit, I agree."

And Chiun stepped off. He alighted gently as if he weighed no more than a small child.

Melvis got himself turned around, stared up at the Nebraska sky and concentrated on getting air in and out of his wheezing lungs.

"What the hell happened?" he gasped at last.

Chiun smiled thinly. "I thought like a boulder."

"That's some powerful imaginin'. You near to squashed me flat."

"To squash you flat would have required thinking like an elephant. I did not wish to do that to you, a fellow appreciator of steam."

"Appreciate that," wheezed Melvis. "I surely do."

THEY FLEW approximately thirty miles due east, over the Union Pacific track. Corn and prairie predominated.

"What's in the big trunk?" K.C. asked Remo after they had lifted off. Melvis had insisted three freeloaders were as inconvenient as two, so what the hell.

"I don't know," Remo said truthfully.

"Then why are you guarding it like it contains the family jewels—pardon the indelicate expression."

Remo cocked a weary thumb in Chiun's direction. "Ask him."

"What's in the trunk?" Melvis repeated.

"Sloth."

"You got a sloth in there?"

"That is not the sloth I speak of." Chiun eyed Remo, who watched the flat green ground surging beneath them.

"The only sloth I know of climbs trees and eats grubs."

"There is another species of sloth. It is a cousin to shame."

"That is definitely a different critter."

"Why is she coming along?" Remo asked Melvis.

Melvis leaned over and lowered his voice. "I kinda like the shimmy of her caboose—if you know what I mean."

Remo was about to point out the undeniable fact of the ten-year age difference between them when they came upon the wreck.

"It's the Desert Storm consist!" K.C. said.

"Yeah, and if it ain't in a pickle, I'm an unhung rapscallion."

Chiun's eyes flashed. "Why are soldiers guarding that train?"

"Take her down lower, pilot," Melvis said, jerking the pilot's right earlobe like a sash cord.

The chopper pilot sent the helicopter angling down.

That caught the attention of the soldiers. As if hooked up to the same nervous system, they turned in unison and pointed their weapons at them.

"Dang if they don't look like they're hijackin' that train!"

The tiny figures lit up their tiny weapons. Tiny flashes of stuttering light showed here and there.

The arriving rounds were tiny, too. But they stung.

"Up! Pull her up," Melvis howled as the Plexiglas bubble began to spiderweb and frost up before their eyes.

17

Before the helicopter dropped out of the Nebraska sky, Major Claiborne Grimm figured it couldn't get any worse.

He was wrong. And it was already as bad as he could imagine it ever getting.

Short of all-out thermonuclear exchange, that is.

The desert camouflage Peacekeeper train had been rolling on high iron en route to the Strategic Air Command airbase in Omaha, making good time. It was a routine train movement. Norton Air Force Base in San Bernadino, California, to Omaha. A month later it would retrace the trip.

No one would know it wasn't an ordinary freight consist of the Union Pacific line. It looked ordinary. The production-model SD40-2 diesel engine was right off the line. The modifications enabling her to operate in wartime were indistinguishable even to the most ardent rail fan. Her armor, bulletproof glass, silvery flash curtains and hidden surveillance cameras wouldn't show up if the unit were photographed at a dead stop with a telephoto lens and made into a *Rail Fan* magazine gatefold.

The desert camo livery was getting old, but the beauty of it was that it was functional.

Back in the early days of the MX missile program, the brass would never have dreamed of slapping military-style camouflage coloration on a Peacekeeper train. The whole idea was to disperse the nation's MX arsenal along its rail system, staying mobile so the Russkie spy satellites couldn't pinpoint them. If they couldn't pinpoint them, they couldn't target the U.S. nuclear force for a surprise first strike.

It was a gigantic shell game, and it had cost the American taxpayers untold billions of dollars in research-and-development costs until Congress slashed defense funding and the Air Force voluntarily abandoned the MX program.

Congress thought that was the end of it. The American public thought that was the end of it. But it was not the end of it.

The Air Force had possession of the only multibillion-dollar train consist in human history and it wasn't about to mothball it. Not in the uncertain post–Cold War world, where the once-mighty Soviets had reverted to being the plain old Russkies—and who knew which way they would jump?

So Major Claiborne Grimm found himself riding the rails every month or so in the launch-control car overseeing train operations.

It was a routine run until he got the nervous call from the first car in line, the security-command car.

"Major. Airman Frisch here."

"Go ahead, Airman."

"Engineer reports we have a man on the track."

"Jesus."

"He wants to know if we should brake."

"Of course he should brake. Tell him to brake."

"But, Major, security—"

"Brake the damn train. If we run a civilian over, we'll have local authorities crawling all over our Hy-Cubes. All we need is for it to get out that we're running an unauthorized nuclear program and all our asses will be decommissioned."

"Yes, sir."

The sudden screaming of the air brakes warned Grimm to grab for something solid. Still, he was thrown off his feet when the train began decelerating.

His eyes went to the launch-control officers sitting at their dual consoles, one at end each of the launch-control car.

They signaled they were okay. Grimm wished he could say the same. His heart was up in his throat, and his stomach was butterflying something fierce.

"Man, just please don't have hit anyone," Grimm moaned.

With a clashing of tight-box couplers, the consist finally knocked tc a dead stop.

Only then did Grimm lever himself off the stainless-steel floor and hit the intercar intercom.

"Engineer, say status!"

The engineer's voice was tight and strangled.

"Too late," he said. "He went under my engine."

"Damn civilians," he said, not sure which man he was thinking of—the careless fool under the trucks or the engineer, who was himself a civilian sworn to secrecy.

Grimm hit the button connecting him to the security car. "Security team. Detrain. On the double."

Turning to his second-in-command, Grimm said, "I'm turning operational control over to you. Do not under any circumstances open this car to anyone except myself. Do you understand?''

"Yes, sir."

"And the password of the day shall be—'Hotbox.'"

"Hotbox. Yes, sir."

"If this is a hijacking and I give 'Redball' as the password, you have my permission to take off with all due speed leaving me defiled. Do you understand?"

"No, sir. What is defiled?"

"To be defiled," Major Grimm said, unlocking and sliding open the single escape door, "means to be left in the dust."

Stepping down, Major Grimm saw that the security team was all over the consist.

Running over to the security officer, he said, "Report."

"We hit a man on the tracks. We're looking for him now."

"Man on foot?"

"Yes, sir."

Grimm looked to the train. His eyes automatically went to the second boxcar, where the MX Peacekeeper missile crouched like a cougar awaiting the launch command. For as long as he had been in charge of ferrying the beast through cornfields and prairie, he wondered if he was carrying a live one. His superior officers refused to confirm or deny that the aluminum-tipped titanium warhead packed live Mark 21 reentry vehicles or inert dummies. The possibility that they might be dummies offered absolutely no comfort at all.

His empty side-arm holster slapping his thigh, Grimm joined the search.

"Any sign?" he asked, bending down to join an airman peering past the unique eight-wheel trucks, cocked .45 in hand.

"No, sir."

Grimm could see plainly that no body or any detached parts thereof lay under the consist.

Getting up, he walked the length of the train.

At each checkpoint he received "No, sir" and puzzled faces.

Someone handed Grimm a pair of field glasses, and he trained them down the length of track. It ran straight as a ruler, and if there was a body mashed into the ties, it was bound to show.

But it didn't. Grimm climbed to the roof of the last car.

Kneeling, he scanned the line. No body. No splash of red to show that a civilian had been struck. The surrounding prairie was likewise clean.

Clambering back down, Grimm said, "Anybody see anything? Anything at all?"

"Just the engine," the security officer reported.

"I think we should talk to the engineer," Grimm said, loping back to the engine. "Have your men stand ready."

"Yes, sir."

THE ENGINEER REFUSED to open his cab until Grimm gave him the password of the day.

"Hotbox."

"Wasn't that yesterday's password?"

"Yesterday's was 'Reefer.'"

"That's right, it was." The door banged open. "C'mon in."

Grimm climbed the ladder. He shut it behind him. "We can't find a body," he said tightly.

"We ran right over the poor dumb SOB."

"What'd he look like?"

"Dressed all in black, like one of them whatcha-macallits." The engineer was snapping his fingers as if that would help his memory.

Grimm pitched in. "Bikers?"

"No."

"Protesters?"

"No. No. One of those Jap skulkers."

"Ninja?"

"Yeah! That's it. He was dressed like a dirty low-down, egg-sucking *ninja*. Face all muffled sneaky-like and everything."

"Oh, shoot," said Claiborne Grimm, jumping from the cab. "We got a *ninja* on board! We got a *ninja* on board!" he called out.

The security officer looked blank as a blackboard. "Sir?"

"A *ninja!* You know what a *ninja* is?"

"No, sir, I do not."

"Japanese spy. Dressed all in black. They say they can get close enough to spit in your eye before you notice 'em. Masters of stealth, camouflage, infiltration—the whole nine yards."

"Oh, shoot."

"That's what I said. We gotta do a car-to-car search. I want security teams stationed at each end of the train. The minute he shows his *ninja* face, blow his head clean off. We can't take any chances."

The security teams were deployed.

Grimm led the search team. The security officer took another contingent to the rear-end car.

They worked from car to car, going over every square inch.

The rail-garrison consist was set up to be self-sufficient. There were bunks, a shower and even a kitchenette. In theory, they could remain mobile for weeks at a time. The downside was the consist was as cramped as a nuclear submarine.

Grimm's team checked the engine cab, the crapper and the security car, even though the security team had been stationed there all during the contact.

He skipped the second Hy-Cube car, which housed the missile. The only way in and out was through a locked access hatch or if the roof doors split open on command. Even though it made no sense to do so, he returned to the launch-control car.

"Hotbox," he said. The door fell open.

Back inside, he asked the second-in-command, "Everything okay here?"

"Yes, sir. Did—did we hit him?"

"I wish we had. We may have a *ninja* aboard."

"Oh, God."

There was an immediate search of all available hiding places. They even emptied the wall waste receptacle.

"No *ninja* in here, Major."

"Let's keep it that way. Don't open the door for anyone except me."

Grimm passed through to the next car just as the rear-end security team was entering from the other end.

"Any sign of that fool *ninja?*"

"No sir, Major sir."

"Damn. Could we have messed up?"

"Not possible, sir. All hiding places checked out clean."

Grimm went to the intercom and got the security car. "Security cameras. Anything?"

"No, Major. Nothing visible on the outside of the car. Sensors indicate nothing crouching along the right-of-way."

"Damn. He must be on the train. He's not on board. So where the hell is he?"

"Did you check the missile-launch car?"

"Now, how would he get in there? It's locked up tighter than my mother-in-law's constipated ass."

"Well, he is a *ninja*, Major. You know how they are."

"I'm beginning to get a nasty inkling," Grimm said bitterly.

Exiting the car, they locked it up and surrounded the Hy-Cube car.

Grimm faced his security team. "I need a volunteer to enter the MLC car."

Several airmen raised their hands. One stepped forward. Grimm decided he liked the man's initiative. "You game for this, Airman?"

"Yes, sir. I've seen a lot of *ninja* movies. I know what the little buggers are likely to do."

"Okay. Just don't get yourself strangled."

Two airmen ducked under the Hy-Cube car and undogged the underside hatch with a special tool. The volunteer airman crawled under next and, flashlight in one hand and side arm in the other, started to squeeze in.

"See anything?" Grimm hissed.

The airman's "No" was hollow.

His belt disappeared, and then his legs pulled up and out of sight.

They waited for word. Five minutes by Major Grimm's watch. When it was ten, Grimm hissed, "What's keeping that airman?"

The security officer shrugged helplessly.

Taking a flashlight, Grimm crawled under and used the light. He washed light all over the access tunnel and saw nothing.

"Airman. Call out."

Silence came back.

"Airman!"

"Maybe he can't hear way in there," someone suggested.

"Damn. Somebody rap on the side of the car."

Flashlights banged the side of the modern Hy-Cube boxcar.

"Airman!" Grimm shouted.

The airman failed to respond or reappear.

Ducking out from under the car, Major Grimm said, "I need another volunteer. One with *ninja-*movie-watching experience preferably."

This time Grimm got sheepish expressions instead of waving hands.

"The national security of the U.S. of A. may be at stake here. If I don't get a volunteer, I'm going to have to pick one."

Two men stepped forward, faces stiff.

"Fine. You both go in. One first and the other right behind him. Make a human chain. That way, we don't lose voice contact."

It was an excellent plan. It fell apart when the first airman thrust his upper torso into the access hatch and fell back down on his butt—minus his head.

The head tumbled down to fall into his lap. It looked very surprised. The mouth opened and it seemed to be trying to say something when the eyes rolled up to show whites, and a tiny sigh escaped from both ends of the severed windpipe.

"Get that body out of the way!" Grimm snapped.

The security team started dragging and vomiting.

"Okay. We have the *ninja* cornered. All we got to do is flush him out. Suggestions?"

"Can we open the roof doors?"

"Not without activating the launch sequence."

No one seemed to cotton to that idea.

"Where's that other volunteer?" wondered Grimm, looking around.

The second volunteer was standing in the back of a knot of airman like a shy gym student trying to escape the coach's gaze.

"You! Yes, you. Your turn."

"Yes, sir," the airman said in a thick voice.

"Here is what you do. We're going to hoist you in feetfirst."

"Yes, sir."

"You go in that way so he can't get at your neck."

"Yes, sir," said the airman, blood draining from his face.

"You know he's in there. He knows you know he's in there. Maybe he's crawled back a ways. You go in with your combat knife and you hunt him down. Blade to blade. You stick him good. A dead *ninja*'s just as good as a live one, if not better. Got that?"

The airmen felt his side arm being pried from his stubborn fingers.

"Can't have you shooting in there," Grimm said. "Not with all that propellant."

"Yes, sir," gulped the airman.

They got him into position and, on the count of three, they hoisted him feetfirst.

The lower body went in fine, but the heavier upper body was where they got stuck.

"Push harder," Grimm hissed. "Get him the hell up in there."

The poor airman was standing on his hands, and his hands were being supported by the strong blue backs of several security airman. They were arching and grunting in their effort to get him all the way up there.

For his part, the airman looked as though he wanted to cry. Then he did. "Help!"

"What is it?" Grimm hissed.

The airman's eyes were frightened china saucers. "I'm going in!"

"That's what we want."

"No! Something's got my legs. Pull me back! Pull me back!"

And the airman's voice was filled so full of horror that Major Grimm hastily countermanded his order. "Out! Pull him back! Now!"

But it was too late. The airman went up slicker than a fox into a rabbit hole, torn right out of the hands of the security team.

A single drop of clear liquid fell back. They never figured out if it was drool or a tear.

They heard the *swish,* a meaty *thunk,* and then the airman's loose head dropped down.

It didn't die all at once. The mouth was distinctly working.

Reaching in, Major Grimm grabbed it. "Speak to me, Airman. What did you see?"

A puff of foul air came from the mouth. Then it dropped slack.

The light in the eyes looking into Grimm's went out.

Distaste on his own face, Grimm passed the head to his security chief, who looked sick and angry at the same time.

From the open hatch a leakage of blood came. It stained the ties a bright red.

"Enough of this damn pussyfooting. We gas the little cockroach out."

Gas masks were donned. Two grenades of CS gas were thrown in and the hatch hastily shut and locked. Not a tendril leaked out of the missile-launch car. It was airtight.

They gave the gas ten minutes to work, then a nervous airman was ordered into the smoking hatch.

Shortly his gas masked head tumbled down.

"There' s only one thing left to do," Major Claiborne Grimm said tightly.

"Sir?"

"We gotta initiate a cold-launch sequence."

"We can't do that without authorization," his security chief sputtered.

"Well, then, we're damn well going to have to *get* authorization, aren't we?"

THE CALL to SAC headquarters in Omaha was booted up the line to the desk of General Shelby "Lightning" Bolton.

"You have a *what*, Major?" Lightning thundered.

"A *ninja*."

"In your missile-launch car, you say?"

"That's an affirmative, General. We send men in, and he sickles their heads clean off."

"How many casualties so far?"

"Four so far."

"Try gas."

"We did. Evidently the *ninja* has his own gas mask."

"Damn. There's gotta be a way to smoke that rascal out."

"There is, sir."

"I'm listening, major."

"A cold-launch sequence would open the roof doors. We can get the drop on him from above, then halt the sequence before the missile flies."

The silence on the line was thick as grease.

"Do it," said Lightning Bolton.

"I'll need the launch codes," Grimm said, throat clogging.

A rustle of papers came over the line. "Got 'em right here. Somewheres."

"General, I thought—"

"Hold on."

When the general came back, Grimm finished his thought. "I thought the President was the only man supposed to have those codes."

"For the silo-based stuff, sure. But the Commander in Chief doesn't know the MX program is still hanging on. And it's critical he doesn't. Savvy?"

"Understood, General."

"Good. Now, fire up your on-board fax."

THE LAUNCH CODES IN HAND, Major Grimm explained the situation to his launch-control officers.

"We're going to start her up. You men know the drill. We take each step one at a time. When I say abort, you both abort."

"Yes, sir," they said in unison, eyes glassy.

Going to the on-board wall safe, Major Grimm spun the dial and got it open. He took out the matched launch-control keys and with quiet ceremony surrendered them.

The launch-control officers resumed their seats and inserted the keys on command.

"Turn," said Grimm, who was standing in a film of his own cold sweat. He used to have nightmares about this very scenario.

The keys turned.

Grimm jumped out of the car.

The roof doors were already lifting. Side-mounted stabilizers began deploying. Like great feet they dropped to the roadbed and dug in, stabilizing the MLC car against blast and launch recoil.

Simultaneously the gleaming white MX missile lifted into view, driven by gas actuators.

When fully erect, it was pointing toward the great brazen dome of the noonday Nebraska sky.

At a signal from Grimm, the security team began climbing the Hy-Cube access ladders.

It was the most nerve-racking moment of Major Claiborne Grimm's entire life.

Then the angry rattle of the approaching helicopter filled the air, and the nightmare went into overdrive.

"Shoot that damn thing down!" he roared.

18

Remo watched the helicopter bubble turn to frost under the storm of bullets, heard the overhead turbines clutch up and knew they were about to crashland.

Every instinct said to bail out. They were low enough. He had a fighting chance to jump clear and maybe come out of it alive.

There were only two problems.

Chiun.

And the precious lapis lazuli steamer trunk balanced on his lap.

Remo's eyes went to the Master of Sinanju.

"Let no harm befall my precious trunk if you value your life," Chiun said.

"Look, we're going to crash."

"Protect my trunk with your dead body if necessary," said Chiun.

"I can't believe you said that."

"And I can't believe you two are jawin' while we're droppin' like helpless stones," Melvis Cupper wailed, clutching his seat.

The rotor cut out completely. It still turned, but not under power.

"Hang on!" yelled the pilot.

"To what—the damn chopper?" said Melvis. "I'm holding on to it. What's *it* gonna hold on to?"

Air, as it turned out.

The spinning rotor blades went into autorotation mode, acting as a parachute and brake at the same time.

The storm of bullets abated when the soldiers on the ground realized they had bagged the helicopter.

The aircraft landed hard on its runners. Everyone bounced in their seats. In a minute the grounded bird was surrounded by hard-faced soldiers in camo fatigues.

"Out! Out of there now!" a red-faced major was shouting.

No one moved at first. They were still getting used to being alive.

"Are these guys on our side or the other?" Melvis undertoned, keeping his hands in plain sight.

"What other?" asked K.C.

"You got me."

Remo spotted the arm patch on the major's shoulder. It showed a freight train superimposed over a vertical missile. Two United Nations-style stalks of wheat framed the image.

Around the circular edge of the patch were the words Rail Garrison Peacekeeper.

"I think they're on our side," said Remo.

"Yeah? Someone should point that useful little fact out to them," muttered Melvis.

The pilot stepped out carefully, hands held high.

Two soldiers fell on him and forced him to his knees at the point of M-16s. Flexible plastic handcuffs pinned his wrists behind him.

The rest stuck their M-16 muzzles in through the cockpit door he had left hanging open.

"What's in that box?" a soldier demanded of Remo.

Remo indicated Chiun with a toss of his head. "Ask him. I'm just minding it."

The soldier looked at Chiun and said, "You Japanese?"

"Watch your tongue!" Chiun squeaked.

"What's in the box, sir? I need an answer."

"None of your business," sniffed Chiun.

"Major, we appear to have a Japanese national and a box of unknown origin here."

The major came up to see. He took one look at the steamer trunk with the lapis lazuli phoenixes and two looks at Chiun and stepped back hastily. "These people are obviously accomplices. If they move, shoot them."

"You can't shoot me," said K.C. "I'm a U.S. citizen and photojournalist." As proof, she snapped their pictures.

A soldier spoke up. "Sir, her camera appears to be of Japanese origin."

K.C. subsided.

"Nobody talk." The major turned, calling back toward the train. "Find him?"

A handful of soldiers balanced on top of a huge boxcar with an open roof signaled back.

"No."

"What the hell is that stickin' up outta that there Hy-Cube?" Melvis asked.

"Nothing," the major said.

"It's a powerful big length of nothin' to be nothin'."

"Avert your eyes."

"I'll have you boys know I'm with the NTSB," Melvis said. "And I don't appreciate your form of hospitality."

"Just stand easy."

"I am getting out," said Chiun in a loud voice.

"Here we go," groaned Remo.

The major snapped. "No. Don't get out. You—in the T-shirt. Hand over that box."

"Remo, if you surrender that box, I will never speak to you again," Chiun promised.

"I'm not handing over the box," said Remo.

"If you don't surrender that box, I will have you shot where you stand," the major said in his steeliest voice.

"I'm sitting," Remo pointed out.

"For God's sake, hand him the dang box!" Melvis yelped. "It ain't worth gettin' skragged over. Especially if you ain't got a notion what's in it."

"If I hand over the box, there'll be trouble," Remo said.

"If you *don't* hand over the box," the major snapped, "I will assume you are in league with the enemy."

"What enemy?" asked Remo.

"Forget I said that. Now relinquish the box."

"I am getting out now," Chiun repeated in a loud voice. "Please do not shoot me with your fearsome weapons."

"Not until we have secured the box."

"That will never happen."

As it turned out, the Master of Sinanju was absolutely correct. It never happened. Something more dramatic occurred, distracting everyone from the box in question.

An airman called over from the big boxcar with the missile sticking up from it like a gigantic tube of white lipstick.

"We found him!"

The major whirled. "The *ninja?*"

"What *ninja?*" asked Remo.

"I didn't say that word."

"No, sir. Airman Dumphey!" came the reply.

"What about the you-know-what?" the major shouted.

"The *ninja*'s not in here."

"If he's not in there, where can he be?"

That question was answered indirectly but in the most dramatic fashion possible.

MAJOR CLAIBORNE GRIMM had one eye on the Hy-Cube and the other on the captured helicopter when it happened. His side arm was trained on the chopper.

As far as he knew, everything was under control. They had the *ninja* cornered, the missile in prefiring position and the helicopter crew under control. It was just a matter of getting everyone locked down for interrogating.

The very last thing Major Grimm expected to hear was the gigantic sound like a massive shotgun blast, the overwhelming *whoosh* that preceded by mere seconds the mushroom cloud of boiling white steam generated when the detonating explosive charge in the missile canister turned thirty gallons of stored water to instant steam, scalding the airmen atop the boxcar and sending the MX Peacekeeper missile vaulting into the sky like a piston ejected from a mortar tube.

The tip of the missile popped up from the expanding steam cloud.

It was the last thing Grimm expected to see.

"Oh, dear God," Major Grimm said in a small, horrified voice. "We have launch."

The next thing was no surprise. Given the changed circumstances.

Vaulting two hundred feet above the train, the missile paused, seeming to hang in the air like a long white balloon. A heartbeat elapsed. Grimm's stricken eyes went to the cold exhaust bell of the stage-one engine.

Once it ignited, there was no calling the MX back.

Grimm waited for the eruption of flame that would send the missile streaking downrange toward its unknown destination. They had not input any targeting coordinates. It could come down anywhere. Russia. China. Hawaii. Even Ohio.

For a heartbeat the future of humanity hung in the balance, and Major Claiborne Grimm saw himself going down in history as the man who triggered nuclear Armageddon—if there was anyone to record anything past this fateful day.

"Please drop into the Atlantic," he beseeched the God he suddenly believed in with all of his pounding heart. "Or the Pacific. Or anywhere harmless."

The MX obliged him. It came down in Nebraska some two thousand yards south of the train. The stage one engine nozzle never fired. The force of its steam-driven expulsion expired, and gravity took hold, pulling the long tube back to earth. It struck lengthwise, exploding into a fireball that looked for all the world like a raging mushroom cloud.

The blast of heat withered prairie grass and wilted the standing ears of corn, while everyone with sense dropped to the ground.

EXCEPT REMO WILLIAMS.

He threw himself over the streamer trunk and waited for the shock wave to roll over the helicopter.

It wasn't much of a wave. More heat than force. The chopper wobbled like a big bubble. That was all.

By the time everyone realized they were not going to be incinerated, the Master of Sinanju had calmly collected all Air Force side arms and rifles in the vicinity from the fear-stunned hands of various airmen and was methodically dismantling them.

Remo figured it was safe to leave the trunk on the seat, and joined the Master of Sinanju.

He found Chiun standing on the back of the major.

"Get off me!" the major demanded.

"Not until you apologize," Chiun said.

"For what?"

"For referring to me by that unspeakable word."

The major grunted and strained. He cursed such a blue streak that K. C. Crockett covered her ears as her face turned the color of beets.

Finally Grimm gave up. "What word?" he asked.

"The *J* word."

"He means 'Japanese,'" Remo said helpfully.

"I apologize for calling you Japanese," the major said with no enthusiasm whatsoever.

"And you will never do this again," Chiun prompted.

"And I will never do this again."

"So help me Jesus," added Melvis.

Remo looked at Melvis.

"Just keepin' things honest," he said.

"I will allow use of the other *J* word," said Chiun.

"So help me Jesus," the major gasped.

"It pays to make certain," said Melvis in a satisfied voice.

The major got to his feet, saying, "They're going to bust me down to airman once this gets out."

Remo asked, "What's this about a *ninja?*"

The major stiffened. "Claiborne Grimm. Major. United States Air Force. Serial number available upon request."

Remo handed him a business card. Grimm took it. "FBI?"

"Let me see that!" Melvis said, taking the card from the major. He read it once, and his eyes jumped to Remo's composed face. "You told me you were with DOT. And your last name was Renwick."

"Cover," said Remo.

"Remo Llewell?" Melvis said, reading the name aloud.

Remo retrieved the card. To the major, he said, "We're interested in your *ninja.*"

"If you can find him, you can keep him," Grimm said in a bitter voice.

Major Grimm led them to the train. He explained the problem in a surprisingly small number of words, considering how many were cusswords.

Chiun drifted up to Remo's side. "See, Remo? Did I not assure you Japanese were behind these horrible crimes?"

"Not now," Remo muttered.

"What I don't understand is how that durn MX launched without orders," said Major Grimm.

"MX? Didn't they scrap that program?" Remo asked.

"They canceled the program. We didn't throw away the prototype train."

"Are we talkin' new-clear here?" Melvis demanded.

"If we were," Major Grimm said, "we wouldn't be standing here exercising our jaws right now. We were carrying a dummy-warhead array. Thank God."

"Amen," said K.C.

"You the guy that called in the haz-mat situation?" Melvis wanted to know.

"My superior must have," Grimm admitted.

Remo blinked. "You have a top secret, unauthorized nuclear program and you reported a hazardous-material problem to the NTSB?" he blurted.

Grimm shrugged lifelessly. "State environmental regulation."

"Well, you got a pretty hazardous situation goin' on over on that cornfield," Melvis drawled. "I can still hear that sucker a-poppin' away."

"Popcorn," said K.C. She smiled. "Smells good, too."

Chiun eyed Remo. "Remo, do not think what you are thinking. You have risen above your corn-eating redskin ancestors."

"I'm thinking about the *ninja*," Remo said sourly. "Let's see where he is."

THEY DIDN'T FIND the *ninja*. But they discovered where he had been.

The two launch-control officers were at their consoles, hands on keys, keys in their slots and turned all the way over to the final launch-firing position.

Their heads were on the floor looking astonished.

"Da-yam," said Melvis, pushing K.C. back. "You better not see this, gal. It's a mess."

A camera was pushed in. "Take pictures?" K.C. asked. "For my magazine."

Stepping into the command car, Major Grimm looked at his dead launch-control officers and said, "It's impossible."

"What's impossible?" Remo asked.

"We had that slippery *ninja* cornered in the missile car. The car was surrounded. There is no access from that car to this one. How did he get in?"

Chiun was looking at the raw neck stumps, which oozed blood in the last, slow gulps of the dying hearts below them.

"A *katana* did this," he intoned.

"You sure, Little Father?"

"No *ninja* did this deed."

"My engineer reported a *ninja* on the tracks," Grimm insisted.

"Let's talk to your engineer," suggested Remo.

THE ENGINEER WAS ADAMANT. He spit a string of tobacco juice, dug in his heels and made his voice boom so it could be heard over the snap, crackle and pop of the burning MX missile.

"It was a *ninja*. Short as a tree stump, all muffled in black and as mean looking as an oncoming barrel-assing Baldwin diesel."

"You sure?" said Remo.

"Abso-positively. He even had on one of them funny-looking *ninja* hats."

"Hats?"

"You know—the kind that sorta look like a fireman's helmet from the back."

"*Ninja* don't wear helmets," said Remo.

"I know a *ninja* when I see one."

The Master of Sinanju used his sandaled toe to draw an outline in the dirt.

"Like this?" he asked, indicating an ornate flanged helmet.

"Yeah. You got it. Exactly like that."

"That," said Remo, "is a samurai helmet."

"Samurai—*ninja*—what's the blasted difference? The little bastard was chock-full of mischief any way you spell it."

"Why would a samurai attack my train?" Major Grimm demanded.

"He is not a samurai, but a *ronin,*" sniffed Chiun.

"What's that?"

"A masterless samurai."

"You mean he was free-lance?"

"Yes."

"My question stands. What would he want with my train?"

"To derail it," sniffed Chiun. "Obviously."

Major Grimm looked over the mess that was his Peacekeeper train. Dead, scalded airmen were being lowered down from the missile car. Other bodies were being laid out and covered with Air Force blue blankets, while the surviving security team attempted to sort out which unanchored head went with which truncated corpse.

And out in the field, corn was popping and hissing as the MX missile slowly melted into incandescent aluminum slag.

"When this gets out, they're going to bust me down to toddler," Grimm moaned.

"We still have a samurai to catch," reminded Remo.

"Ronin," corrected Chiun. "Why can you not get it right?"

19

"There's only one thing to do," Remo said as he surveyed the stopped Peacekeeper train.

"What's that?" asked Major Grimm, whose expression now matched his family name.

"Take the train apart, car by car."

"This consist costs upward of sixty billion dollars. That's *billion* with a *b*. And I'm responsible for it."

"How low can they bust you down to?" Remo asked.

"I said toddler before, but now I'm thinking sperm."

"Maybe you'll meet a nice egg and get to start fresh," said Remo, starting down the tracks.

Grimm followed, feeling helpless, and the old Korean took to the other side. They walked from car to car, setting their ears to each car as they came to it.

Hearing nothing, they moved on.

At the equipment car, the second-last of the train, Remo stopped. Dropping to one knee, he signaled the Master of Sinanju on the other side.

Remo went to one end and Chiun the other.

The sound that came next was hard to describe. It might have been a coupler knuckle fracturing under pressure. That, of course, was impossible, Grimm told himself. It would take a collision to snap a tight-box coupler. Or a shaped charge.

No one saw what happened, but when Grimm saw Remo and the old Korean rejoin each other on the other side, they gave the last two boxcars a hard push.

The cars started rattling down the tracks, in reverse.

The sheared-off coupling came into view at that point. The broken face gleamed the color of new steel. The cars slowed to a natural stop.

Major Grimm waved a contingent of security airmen to surround the detached boxcars.

"We got him isolated from the rest of the train," Remo told him.

"What happened to that coupler?"

"Gave way," said Remo.

"It's a tight-box coupler. They don't break easy."

"This one did."

"Can't argue there," Grimm admitted.

"Watch this end," said Remo. "Come on, Little Father."

They went around to the other end of the boxcar, and this time the noise was like metallic thunder.

Then the end car was rolling free. The prairie was flat, so it didn't roll far. Just enough to isolate the equipment car.

Remo hovered beside the equipment car. "He's definitely inside."

"How do you know?"

"We can hear his heartbeat."

Grimm experimented with listening. "I don't hear anything."

"Rock and roll will do that to your eardrums."

Remo addressed the old Korean. "Okay, Chiun. Do we go in or just take the car apart?"

Chiun's face frowned into a tight mask of determination. "We must be careful. There is no telling what deceits this *ronin* has at his disposal."

"Why don't we just shoot the fool out of that thing?" Melvis suggested.

"We do things our way," said Remo.

"This man has an excellent idea," snapped Chiun. Spinning, the Master of Sinanju raised his voice in the direction of the Air Force security team. "Shoot the Japanese fool out of this car!"

Remo shrugged.

At Major Grimm's direction, a firing squad was assembled. They lifted their M-16s into line.

"Ready...aim...*fire!*"

The M-16s blazed away. Smoking cartridges hopped into the Nebraska sunlight, falling to earth like spent brass grasshoppers.

The boxcar side shivered under the drumming storm of rounds. Paint peeled. Indentations like silver washers cratered the peeling boxcar paint.

When they had expended their clips, Major Grimm ordered the firing squad at ease.

Remo walked up to the boxcar. He put his ear to it. "I don't hear anything."

"He is dead," intoned Chiun.

"I thought he was dead to start with," muttered Remo.

"Now he is doubly dead, if not triply dead."

"What say we crack her open, then?" Melvis suggested.

Remo started for the door. "I got it."

That was as far as he got.

The samurai jumped from the boxcar. He came out through the closed door without bothering to open it.

Everyone was caught off guard. Including Remo.

Remo's entire body was one gigantic sensing organ. That was why he usually left his arms bare. So his sensitive body hairs and skin were receptive to shifts in air currents and other atmospheric vibrations.

Remo hadn't been aware the samurai was coming at him until he emerged from the door.

He popped from the blank door like a black soap bubble, landed in a crouch and came clumsily to his feet.

His *katana* was sheathed. Over his shoulder was slung a black leather bag, which hung heavy under the weight of its contents.

It was broad daylight, so everyone got a good look. The sun gleamed on his black plates, made the ornate helmet smoulder and most unnervingly of all, showed very clearly that the samurai had no face.

"Mercy!" said K.C., who started backing away. A dozen steps later, she turned and ran.

Remo moved in on the samurai. Out of the corner of his eye, he saw Chiun flitting in from another angle.

They intercepted the apparition at the same time.

The *ronin* had no chance to draw his blade. Remo and Chiun were on him.

They each threw a blow, Remo directing the heel of his hand at the flat, blank face, intending to turn it to jelly. The Master of Sinanju came around spinning, one sandaled toe seeking a fragile kneecap.

Both connected. Remo struck the featureless face dead center. Chiun's foot bisected the knee joints. And passed through.

Encountering no resistance, Remo found himself plunging through the black, solid-looking form.

The Master of Sinanju spun past him, his flashing toe nearly catching Remo on the fly.

Recovering, Remo reversed. He brought an elbow back. It sank into the back of the samurai's flanged helmet.

The *ronin* strode on unconcerned.

Hissing like an angry cat, the Master of Sinanju recovered from his wild spin and stamped his feet hard. "*Ronin!* Hear me!"

The *ronin* may have heard, but he walked on, arrogant, purposeful, sword flashing from its sheath. He waved it from side to side to warn any other challenger he meant business. He looked like a batter warming up.

Major Grimm thought he was seeing things. But it had happened so fast he couldn't be sure. Appropriating an M-16 from a stupefied airman, he lined up the muzzle on the samurai's advancing chest. "Halt or I will shoot."

The samurai declined to halt. Or so his body language indicated.

So Major Grimm opened up.

The bullet track was noisy but abbreviated. There was no way he could have missed.

In fact, the boxcar directly behind the menacing figure began collecting more bullet indentations.

The samurai kept coming, unfazed by the noise and the hammering lead.

"Hand me another," Grimm called.

Another rifle was clapped into his hands. He raised the weapon, planted his feet wide apart and laid the sight on the precise center of the shielded face.

Grimm waited until they stood nearly toe-to-toe, then opened fire. The clip was only half-full. Still, sufficient rounds snarled out to obliterate the head, helmet and all.

The samurai walked into the still-chattering muzzle. Major Claiborne Grimm saw the last muzzle-flashes disappear into the black face. The muzzle sank all the way in as the samurai came on. It looked as if he was deliberately and contemptuously swallowing the weapon.

Major Grimm was brave. Not to mention stubborn. He held his ground. Right to the point when the samurai walked into his body.

Then he fainted on the spot.

Grimm missed the rest of it.

Remo and Chiun got in front of the *ronin*, once more blocking its way.

They rained blows, punches, snap-kicks and, in the case of the Master of Sinanju, assorted invective on his unperturbable head.

The *ronin* didn't so much as flinch from any of it. He just walked on, swinging his blade with slow menace.

Chiun followed him, kicking at the back of his knees with strenuous fierceness, while Remo settled for taking the occasional swipe.

"You know what this reminds me of?" Remo complained.

"I do not care," said Chiun, kicking out again and again.

"Wonder what's in that sack?" said Remo.

"It is a *kubi-bukuro*. It is for carrying captured heads."

"Looks full to me."

"Just take care that your head does not join his collection," spit Chiun, shaking his fists in the *ronin*'s glassy face.

The *ronin* trudged on, head lowered like a striding bull.

Eventually they had to give up trying to arrest him.

WALKING BEHIND the ronin, Remo and Chiun lowered their voices.

"You see, Remo?"

"Okay. It's just like you said."

"The House is haunted."

"If the House is haunted, why is he walking away from us?"

"That is not the question. The question is where is the *Nihonjinwa* walking to?"

The answer developed before very long. The *ronin*, ignoring them with a pointedness bordering on insult, swinging his blade from side to side, looked east, then west. He was looking for something.

But all that lay ahead was the still-smoldering MX missile and the unending cornfields of Nebraska.

"This is starting to look like *Field of Dreams* in reverse," said Remo.

"What do you mean?" demanded Chiun.

"Once he gets into the corn, he's going to be tough to stay with."

Chiun hitched up his kimono skirts resolutely. "We cannot let him get into the corn."

"Any idea how to stop him?"

"We must draw him into battle."

"Feel free."

Suddenly the Master of Sinanju hurried up. He got in front of the *ronin*. Blocking the way, he set his hands against the waist of his kimono and made his face fierce.

"*Jokebare!*" he thundered.

The *ronin* slowed.

"*Jokebare!*" Chiun repeated, then launched into a bitter stream of invective Remo had trouble following. Some of the words sounded vaguely Korean, but most did not. Probably Japanese, he decided. The two languages shared a lot of words in common.

To Remo's surprise, the *ronin* stopped dead in his tracks.

He stamped one foot into the ground. The ground didn't respond. Not with sound or a trembling of dirt.

Lifting his *katana* high, he laid it across one shoulder, then the other.

"What's he doing?" called Remo.

"I do not know," Chiun said, low-voiced. "I am not familiar with this stance."

"Well, he's gotta be doing something."

The *ronin* was. On his third draw back, he suddenly swung his blade all the way around. His squat upper body turned with it. When he let go, the *katana* unexpectedly flew toward Remo.

Remo's eyes saw it coming. His other senses detected nothing. It flew fast, going into a methodical spin like a helicopter blade winding up.

"Remo! Take care!" Chiun called.

Normally Remo could dodge bullets blindfolded by sensing the advancing shock waves. There was no wave here. According to his senses, the sword didn't exist. But his eyes read it coming. His Sinanju training, receiving conflicting signals, told him to dodge and not dodge at the same time.

Since to his heightened senses, it was all happening in slow motion anyway, Remo studied the phenomenon.

The blade was coming on a horizontal spin, exactly at the level of his neck. It meant to behead. But a blade that could not slice air had no hope of cleaving flesh.

Remo folded his arms.

The blade spun closer.

Chiun voice was a high, batlike squeak. "Remo! Remember the finger!"

So Remo flipped the *ronin* the bird.

The spinning blade was only inches away now.

At the last possible moment, something changed. The air roiled not an inch from his face. A swishing sound reached his ears. Strangely it started in mid-swish.

And as the first warning signals reached his brain, Remo started to duck. It was pure instinct. He was going down before his brain started processing the incoming information.

A meaty smack sounded just above his head.

That was Remo's first indication that the blade had struck something.

But what?

Fading back and to the side, Remo straightened.

There stood the Master of Sinanju. He was holding the *katana* by its ebony hilt. His other hand joined the first, and he lowered the blade resolutely.

Remo blinked. "What happened?"

"I saved your worthless life."

"No way. I had already ducked."

"I arrested the blade before it could separate your dull melon of a head from the magnificent body I have trained."

"Not a chance," Remo said, returning Chiun's side.

The Master of Sinanju held the blade firmly in both hands, the blade tip touching the ground, making a dent. It was real. It had weight.

Then they remembered the *ronin*. Remo and Chiun turned their heads in unison.

A vile greenish black smoke was boiling out of the downed missile. The flames were dying down, but the smoke was thickening. It rose into the sky like a black dragon in the throes of its death torment.

The surrounding flatlands were hazy with chemical smoke. The wind was blowing away from them, but the haze in the air started to sting their eyes anyway.

There was no sign of the *ronin* anywhere in the haze.

"He's in the corn," said Remo.

"No, he walked into the fire," insisted Chiun.

"Why would he do that?"

"Because he can with impunity," said Chiun.

They ran to the burning MX missile.

"No tracks that I can see," said Remo as they approached.

"Of course not. Ghosts do not make tracks. Except when they wish for devious purposes."

"If he's a ghost, shouldn't his blade be a ghost, too?"

"Do not split hairs with me, Remo. We must find him."

They didn't.

The poisonous smoke from the destroyed MX missile prevented them from getting too close. Moving upwind, they examined it from every angle with searching eyes.

If the *ronin* had walked into the smoking missile, there was no way to tell.

"I say we try the corn," said Remo.

"One of us must stay to see that he does not emerge from the smoke."

"I'll go."

"No, you will only gorge yourself on corn."

"Okay, *you* go."

"Yes, I will go. See that he does not not escape under your very nose."

And Chiun flashed into the corn.

Remo watched the smoking missile, one eye on the corn.

The tall ears waved in a soft breeze but otherwise didn't move or rustle. Chiun was slipping through the rows with such stealth the *ronin* would never see or hear him coming.

THE MASTER OF SINANJU plunged into the lurid forest of corn. Its scent called to him. Its golden allure whispered of forbidden pleasures. He ignored them all. He had one goal, one purpose.

Unfortunately he also faced many paths. North or south? Perhaps west. His hazel eyes raking the ground discovered no tracks. His ears heard nothing of his foe. And the only scent on the wind was the maddening reek of uncooked corn, which swayed like brazen harlots with long yellow hair.

In the end it was the overwhelming numbers, not his illusive foe, that defeated him. Holding his nose,

he raced through the cornrows back in the direction
he had come.

AFTER FIFTEEN MINUTES, the Master of Sinanju
emerged, looking unhappy.

"No luck?" Remo asked.

"Luck has nothing to do with what has happened
in this riceless land," Chiun spit. "He is not in the
corn."

"In other words, you lost him."

"Pah! My senses were dazzled by the malevolent
miasma of raw corn."

By this time Melvis Cupper trotted up. "I seen it all
and I deny it ever happened," were his first words.

Remo looked at him. "You're a big help."

"It ain't my idea. That major woke up and said
that was the way it was going to play. I see no reason
not to oblige him."

"You know as well as we do that a samurai caused
both train wrecks."

"I don't know what you're talkin' about. I got only
one wreck. This here's a haz-mat situation No derailment. No striking train. No cars in a ditch."

"What about the missile?"

"I don't do missiles. I'm strictly a high-iron-and-
steel-wheel man." Melvis lowered his voice. "Somebody should drop a dime in the general direction of
the EPA, though."

"So what are you going to report caused the Amtrak collision?"

"That? That was suicide. Yessir, naked suicide."

"Homicide is more like it," said Remo.

Melvis puckered up his weather-beaten face. "Tell
you what. We'll split the difference. Let's say for the

sake of sayin' there was these two sexually confused persons. One gave the other AIDS. The infected party takes the head off the party of the second part and then goes out in a blaze of diesel and glory. End result—homo-suicide.''

"That's bull and you know it," said Remo.

Melvis put on a crooked grin. "You knew I was weak from the first time you laid eyes on me."

20

They waited until the MX Peacekeeper missile burned itself out.

A cursory examination of the white-hot slag heap that remained led to one inescapable conclusion.

"Looks like he went into the corn after all," said Remo.

"Pah," said Chiun.

The Master of Sinanju paced back and forth before the slag, face tight, eyes squeezed to slits that reminded Remo of the seams of uncracked walnuts. He shook his fists at the ascending smoke.

"We're going to have to report this to Smitty," he reminded.

"I do not care."

"We're going to have to get our stories straight."

Chiun frowned like a thundercloud getting ready to rain. "I no longer care. I have been twice bested by a mere *ronin*. My ancestors are surely weeping tears of blood over my shame."

K. C. CROCKETT WAS waiting for them at the helicopter. She gave them a nervous corn-fed smile as they approached.

"Thought I'd guard your box for you," she said sheepishly.

Chiun bowed in her direction without saying anything.

"You didn't catch your spook, did you?" she asked.

"No," said Melvis. "It was the durnest, dangest, most spiflicated thing you ever did see. And I take my hat off to the Almighty that I don't have to write it into any report."

"Just as well. It ain't good to catch spooks."

"We're going to need a lift back to Lincoln," Remo told Melvis.

"Suits me fine." Melvis showed K.C. his Sunday smile. "Don't suppose I could interest you in a ride goin' my way?"

"Thank you kindly, but I'm bound in the opposite direction. The Denver Rail Expo awaits."

"I might be persuaded to fly thataway. Eventually."

"Mighty neighborly of you. If I don't get a passel of pictures for my magazine, it's back to the farm for me."

"Gonna shoot a lot of steam, are you?"

"That, too. But my assignment's to get all I can on the new flock of maglev trains."

Without warning, Melvis staggered back as if hit on the head by a falling steer. "Maglev!" he barked. "Why you have to go fool with that heathen crap?"

"Maglev's not crap!" K.C. flared. "It's the future."

"In a pig's ass!" Melvis roared. "How can you be for steam and maglev both? It's like prayin' to Satan *and* St. Peter."

"You are a close-minded old reprobate, you know that?"

The two glared at one another. There was blood in Melvis's eyes and disappointment in K.C.'s.

"Guess I can forget about that lift, huh?" K.C. finally said in a soft, dejected voice.

Melvis looked as though he wanted to bawl. He squared his shoulders manfully. He yanked down the brim of his Stetson to shadow the pain in his eyes.

"I'm a steel-wheel man. I don't hold with maglev. It's against the laws of God, man and nature. I'm sorry, but you and I have got to go our separate and distinct ways."

"Guess it wasn't meant to be. I'll just hafta hitch a ride on that there Desert Storm train."

"Adios, then," muttered Melvis, turning away.

"See y'all," K.C. said to Remo and Chiun. Pulling the bill of her engineer's cap low, she loped off, shoulders slumping.

Walking back to the helicopter, Remo asked Melvis, "What was *that* all about?"

"That," spit Melvis, "is the chief reason Hank Williams sung so lonesome and died so young. And if you don't mind, I can't talk about it no more. I'm plumb heartbroke."

Glancing back at the Master of Sinanju for understanding, Remo saw Chiun brush a vagrant tear from the corner of one eye before averting his unhappy face.

HAROLD SMITH was feeling better. He no longer smelled mulch when he exhaled. His coughing had almost abated. He had traded the hospital wheelchair for his comfortable executive chair. And his secretary had brought him two containers of his favorite lunch—prune-whip yogurt.

He was deep into the second cup when his computer beeped, and up popped a report of a head-on collision between the *California Zephyr* and an unidentified engine in the Nebraska flatlands.

Smith read the report, instantly categorizing it. It looked like a serious accident. He captured the report and added it to his lengthening Amtrak file.

The file was quite extensive now. He had been analyzing it all morning. The train crashes and derailments over the past three years were almost evenly divided between the Amtrak passenger system and the various long-haul and short-line freight railroads. A few tourist and excursion lines had been affected, as well. Even a Philadelphia streetcar line reported an accident.

There was no pattern. No line had been targeted over any other. No one kind of engine bubbled up over any other. It was not equipment failure of the rolling stock. Crew fatigue or negligence was cited with the most regularity, but Smith knew train crews were a convenient NTSB scapegoat. His computers had already crunched the numbers and discounted some twenty percent of those attributions as NTSB laziness and scapegoating. The Oklahoma City cattle-car wreck of last summer and the more recent Southern Pacific disaster at Texarkana proved that.

The yogurt was a fond memory when the blue contact telephone rang, and Smith scooped it up.

"Smitty. Remo."

"What have you learned in Connecticut?"

"Not much. We're in Nebraska. We hitched a ride with our good buddy Melvis, who by the way is full of beans, beer and bull."

"I suspected as much. You are on top of the Nebraska collision, I take it?"

"That was last hour's wreck," Remo said dryly. "We're at the MX railcar disaster now."

Smith frowned. "Do you mean CSX?"

"No. MX—as in rail-launched Intercontinental Ballistic Missile."

"Remo," Smith said patiently, "the MX program was voluntarily abandoned by the Air Force more than three years ago for budgetary reasons."

"Surprise. The Air Force has been playing a little shell game with Congress. They've been running an MX train through corn country all this time."

"I will put a stop to that," Smith said, his voice turning steely.

"Save your dime. The program was just scrubbed. They lost their missile, and the train is kinda banged up."

Smith's voice became urgent. "Remo, begin at the beginning."

Remo explained what he'd discovered at the *California Zephyr* crash site, up to and including the beheaded rotary-plow engineer.

"The *ronin* again!" Smith gasped.

"Yep. We didn't see him at the crash, but he was all over the MX train. There are a lot of U.S. airmen without heads, and one MX missile in the corn. Good thing it was a dummy."

Smith swallowed his horror. "You saw this *ronin?*"

"Saw him, chased him, lost him in the corn. Sorry."

"Why would a *ronin* attack the U.S. rail system?"

"Maybe he knew about the MX train and was trying to nail every train he could until he found it."

"That theory is farfetched."

"Maybe you'd like Chiun's theory better."

"Put him on."

"I'd better tell it," said Remo. "Chiun thinks this guy is the same one who had a run-in with an old Master centuries ago and is only now catching up with the House."

"Preposterous!" Smith exploded.

"Chiun, Smitty says your idea is preposterous. Unquote."

Harold Smith heard the Master of Sinanju say something pungent in the Korean language.

"What did he say?"

"You don't want to know, Smitty. Look, he may not be a ghost but he sure as hell acted like one. He popped out of a boxcar like an amok hologram. We couldn't lay hands on him. He was there but wasn't, if you know what I mean."

"How did he get away?"

"We followed him. He got tired of that and threw his *katana* at me. That was the weirdest part, Smitty. On the way it suddenly turned solid. I kept my head only because I ducked."

"You kept your fool head because I arrested the deadly blade!" snapped Chiun.

"Take your pick, Smitty," Remo said wearily.

"You have the *katana* still?"

"Yeah. Want it for your collection?"

"Yes. And I want you both here."

"Gotcha. We're on the next flight."

Hanging up, Remo looked down at Chiun's unhappy face. "You heard?"

"Every word. You explained my side of the story improperly. It is fortunate that Smith has recalled us, so that I may rectify your many errors."

"Don't forget to tell Smitty which assassin lost the *ronin* in the corn."

Chiun made a sound like a steam valve hissing.

FIVE HOURS LATER, Remo and Chiun stood in Harold Smith's Folcroft office once more. The second captured *katana* lay on the desk beside the first. Smith was examining the workmanship of the new blade.

"It is identical to the first," he said.

"Big deal," said Remo. "See one *katana,* you've seen them all."

"You have located no blade-smith, Smith?" asked Chiun.

Smith shook his gray head. "No such blades are being forged in this country."

"For a ghost," Remo said, eycing Chiun, "this guy sure has a ready supply of cutlery."

Chiun frowned. "He is a ghost. You cannot deny that, Remo."

"He was ghostly. That much I'll go along with."

"A ghost is a ghost."

"Ghosts don't go around derailing trains as part of their earthly penances. Especially *ronin*."

"What logic is this?" spit Chiun.

"He's Japanese, right?"

"A *Nihonjinwa,*" spit Chiun. "A stupid Japanese."

"So why is he wrecking U.S. trains? Shouldn't he be wrecking his own?"

"You call that logic?"

"Yeah, I call that logic. If he were after the House, he wouldn't be in the derailing business. He would be in the beheading business."

"He is in both!" Chiun flared.

"He's more interested in derailing than beheading."

A phone started ringing. It wasn't the blue contact phone nor the Rolm phone Smith used for Folcroft business. The ring was muffled.

Reaching down, Smith drew open a desk drawer and took up a fire-engine red telephone receiver.

"Yes, Mr. President?"

Smith listened. So did Remo and Chiun.

"Yes, Mr. President. But you understand as Chief Executive you are not empowered to order CURE into action. You can only suggest missions."

Smith listened to the President of the United States.

"I will consider the matter," said Smith. "Thank you for the call." And he hung up.

"That was the President," Smith said, closing the drawer.

"Do tell," said Remo.

"He wants the organization to look into these derailments."

"So you told him no?"

"No. I told him that I would consider it. There is no point in alarming him with our recent findings at this juncture."

"I'd say all the dead bodies, not to mention the near-nuclear catastrophe over the last day or two, is worth an alarm or two."

"This President would be ordering us into action at the drop of a hat if encouraged to think of CURE as an instrument of executive-branch power," said Smith. His eyes went to the new *katana*.

"Be careful," said Remo. "It's got a button on it like the other one. We avoided touching it."

Smith nodded. Removing a Waterman pen from his vest pocket, he tapped the handle. It sounded solid. Carefully he laid the blunt end of the pen to the button and pressed it.

The button made a distinct click.

And the blade sank into the black glass of his desktop as if slipping into a pool of still black water.

Aghast, Smith recoiled.

"Did you see that!" Remo exploded.

Everyone got down on the floor and tried to see under the desk. They saw nothing at first. Then the blade reappeared.

Like a falling feather, it floated through the kick space, touched the floor and promptly sank into the varnished pine planking.

"What's under this floor?" Remo asked.

Smith croaked, "The laundry room."

"Have it evacuated," Remo said, racing for the door, Chuin, a flapping silvery silk wraith, at his heels.

Smith grabbed the telephone.

BY THE TIME they reached the laundry room, the door was hanging open, and two workers in starched whites were outside, looking rattled.

"You see a floating sword by any chance?" Remo demanded.

"You tell us. Did we?"

"Not if you value your jobs," said Remo, going in.

Inside they looked up at the ceiling. It was unbroken. But that was to be expected. They looked down at the floor. No sign of any blade. There was nothing in the big industrial-size washing machines except hospital laundry.

"The basement!" said Chiun.

Exiting, they warned the laundry-room staff to stay out of the room until told otherwise. They looked more than happy to comply.

They bumped into Harold Smith as he stepped out of the elevator.

"We think it's in the basement," said Remo. Smith nodded.

They took the stairs. At the foot of the creaky wood-plank steps, Smith flicked on the lights.

He didn't get much in the way of illumination.

"You know, you might have sprung for light bulbs brighter than twenty-five watts," Remo said.

"This is not a work area," said Smith.

They searched the basement and found nothing.

"It has dropped into the very earth itself," Chiun intoned. "Never to be seen again."

"What's directly under the laundry room?" Remo asked Smith.

Smith blinked up at the pipework radiating from the big boilers and furnaces that supplied Folcroft with heat and steam. He seemed to be reading them like a map.

"The computers!" Smith gasped. Hastily he took a key ring from his vest and strode to a concrete wall broken by a wooden door.

Unlocking the door, he opened it. A steady industrial humming became audible. Reaching in, Smith tugged at a drop cord, and a dangling naked light bulb came on—another twenty-five-watter.

They entered.

The room was a small space crammed with mainframe computers and short jukeboxlike optical WORM drive slave units. They were the source of the low humming—and the heart of CURE's information-gathering network.

In the center of the floor, looking as solid as the concrete on which it lay, sat the *katana* blade.

Gingerly they surrounded it.

"Looks solid to me," Remo said.

"Looks can be deceiving," Chiun warned.

Smith bent down and touched it. Feeling substance, he picked it up.

"Solid one minute and then the next not," he murmured.

Remo nodded. "Just like in Nebraska."

"Pressing the button caused it to dematerialize," said Smith.

"What caused it to undematerialize?" asked Remo.

"Sorcery," said Chiun.

"There is a logical, scientific explanation for this phenomenon," Smith insisted, "and I intend to discover it."

BACK IN SMITH'S OFFICE, the two *katana* swords lay on the black-glass-topped desk.

"Matter obeys fixed laws," said Smith.

"Sorcery obeys others," suggested Chiun.

He was ignored.

Leaving the second *katana* blade, Smith picked up the first. He pressed the button. Nothing happened.

"A button suggests what, Remo?"

"Turning something on or off, I guess."

"And that suggests..."

"Electricity."

"Exactly." Smith held up the end of the hilt, examining it carefully. He squeezed. He pushed. He pulled. But he obtained no result.

"You're not looking for batteries, are you?" asked Remo.

Chiun said, "The white mind is like a runaway train. It always follows the same track. Emperor, this is beyond your plodding white science. Do not attempt to fathom what you cannot comprehend."

"Let me try," suggested Remo.

Smith handed over the *katana*.

Remo looked over the blade hilt.

"Feels pretty solid to me," said Remo, hefting it.

Chiun bustled up, saying, "Therefore, it is not."

"What's that supposed to mean?"

"That I am correct and you are not."

"Who lost the *ronin* in the cornfield?"

And while they were arguing, Remo squeezed the hilt and the end popped open like a flashlight.

Instinct caused Remo to release the hilt. Both he and Chiun flew to opposite sides of the room before the blade struck the floor. It bounced, and out from the open hilt spilled a train of short yellow cylinders.

Smith was coming around from behind his desk as Remo and Chiun approached the fallen blade with caution.

Smith picked up one of the cylinders. "A battery," he said.

"What make?"

Smith blinked. "I cannot read it."

Chiun took it from Smith hands. "Japanese! I was right! Look, Smith, it is Japanese."

"What is the brand name?"

"Who cares? It is Japanese. That is all that matters."

"I would like to know the brand name, please."

Chiun read the label.

"Gomi."

Returning to his desk, Smith got his computer up and running.

"What are you doing?"

"Researching the Gomi brand name."

"What good will that do?" asked Remo.

"The power required to enable that blade to defy scientific law is not likely to be something one purchases off the shelf. These batteries are specially made."

"For *katanas*?"

Smith nodded. "For *katanas*."

A minute later Smith said, "Gomi is the industrial brand name for Gomi products, and the brands Gomi and Hideo are connected to Nishitsu."

"Hideo was the name of the dozing yellow bull of Mystic," Chiun crowed.

"He means the bulldozer that was parked on the tracks at Mystic," explained Remo.

"Remo," Smith said slowly. "Has it occurred to you that everything we have seen so far can be explained by the technology we know to have been pioneered by the Nishitsu Industrial Electrical Corporation?"

"Yeah, it has. But this guy isn't the Krahseevah."

"Do not speak that hateful name," said Chiun.

"We have twice before dealt with a foreign spy who was sent to this country to pilfer industrial and military secrets."

"Tell me about it. But that was a Russian kleptomaniac, tricked out in an electronic suit that gave him the power to walk through walls. He was a thief, but he never hurt anyone. Besides, he's dead as far as we know."

"What we know is very little. But the electronic garment he wore was designed by Nishitsu Osaka. And if they built one, they could duplicate it."

"The only time the Nishitsu name has come up in this was when the Southern Pacific train hit a Nishitsu Ninja," Remo pointed out.

Chiun smiled broadly. "It all now makes supreme sense."

"It does?" Remo and Smith said together.

"Yes. Emperor, your rails are under attack by the scheming Japanese. It is obviously part of a plot to humble your mighty nation."

Remo looked at Chiun with a vague, incredulous expression. "What happened to the finger-flicking ghost *ronin?*" he blurted.

Chiun composed his face into bland lines. "Do not be absurd, Remo. Whoever heard of a ghost whose sword required batteries?"

"I'll let that pass because I like clinging to my sanity. So answer me this—how does wrecking our railroads bring the U.S. to its knees?" Remo wanted to know.

"That is so obvious I will not deign to answer it," Chiun sniffed, presenting his back to Remo.

Remo and Smith exchanged glances.

"Actually it's as good a theory as we have right now," Remo admitted.

Chiun beamed. They were learning wisdom. It was almost enough to take his mind off his missing fingernail.

Smith was opening the first *katana* when his computer beeped.

He went to it. Remo came around when he saw the color of Smith's face go from light gray to ghost white.

"Another derailment?"

"Yes. A Conrail freight and an Amtrak passenger train. In Maryland."

"Anyone hurt?"

"Unknown at this time. Strange. This is very strange."

"What's strange?"

"This accident has happened before. Exactly this way." Smith swallowed. "And it was one of the worst in Amtrak history."

21

Cora Lee Beall would never forget the sound as long as she lived.

That long scream of metal that preceded the dull *crump* of impact, followed by the booming cannonade of passenger coaches slamming into a suddenly stopped engine. Then an awful silence.

And after the silence, the horrible moans and screams of the injured rose up from the settling dust like fresh-made ghosts discovering their fates.

It had happened at her backyard right here in Essex, Maryland.

Cora Lee had been unloading her washing machine. The sound yanked her out of that household chore like a bluefin tuna pulled out of the Chesapeake Bay.

When she emerged from her house, she saw the coaches lying on their sides, piled and jammed together like foolish toys in her backyard. Big as they were, they reminded her of little toys.

One had skidded on its side, scalping the lawn and crushing her clothesline flat. The same clothesline she would have been standing at in another minute or two. Another coach lay open, as if an old-fashioned claw can opener had been taken to it, spilling its precious cargo.

It was a day and an experience Cora Lee would never forget and hoped never to witness again. The sound was what stayed with her. Not so much the blood and the torn of limb. After things got back to normal, in the first of the nights without sleep, Cora Lee heard those sounds again and again in her mind and ultimately came to the sorrowful conclusion they had cut her life exactly in half. After that first long, piercing scream of steel wheels on steel rail, her life was never again the same.

That was back in January 1987. Almost ten long years ago now. How the time had flown. Gradually the gouged earth softened, and the scars were healed over by the seasonal rains. New grass grew. Cora Lee got herself a brand-new washer-dryer stack, never again to air out her laundry in the backwash of the *Colonial*. She finally got to the point where she could look at the passing trains and not flinch.

True normalcy never did quite come back into her life, but the years took care of the worst of it.

So on a July day when Cora Lee was lounging on a redwood chair as the day's wash tumbled in the dryer, sipping a mint Julep and looking out over the rail bed, the last thing she expected on earth was to hear a long, familiar scream of steel under stress.

Cora Lee dropped her drink and sat frozen. Before, she had only heard the disaster. This time she saw it happen with her own eyes.

The *Colonial* came shrieking by, steel wheels spitting sparks. She knew what a hotbox was. When a moving wheel-set overheated, it would spark and begin to fly apart. This was no hotbox. Every wheel was in agony. The *Colonial* looked more like a ground-skimming comet than a train. The wheels were locked, sliding not rolling. She knew enough about trains to know the air brakes had been applied. Hard and fast.

Her stricken gaze went to the engine, and her heart jumped and froze even as her body sat paralyzed.

Coming down the line on the same northbound track was a lone blue Conrail freight engine.

"This can't be happening," she said. Then she screamed it.

"This can't be happening. Oh, dear Lord!"

But it was. Exactly like 1987, when the *Colonial* slammed into a Conrail engine that shouldn't have been there, and sixteen had died.

The sounds that followed might have been played by the tape recorder of her memory and pumped out through a quadrophonic sound system.

The long scream of steel ended in a dull, ugly *crump*. Then like steel thunder the coaches slammed together and flung themselves about.

"Oh, Lord, this is the end of me," Cora Lee said just before the flying fragment of broken rail smashed her apart like a cotton sack filled with so much loose meat.

MELVIS CUPPER'S BEEPER went off within fifteen minutes of the derailment at Essex.

He was at the Omaha airport bar, knocking back frosty Coors, lamenting the wretched unfairness of life and improvising old railroad choruses as the spirit moved him.

Oh, her eyes were Conrail blue,
She wore a Casey Jones cap.
But she lusted after maglev speed.

Which everyone knows is crap.
So now I'm off my feeeeed.

On that high note, the pager beeped.

"Oh, hell," Melvis said, shutting off his pager and seeking out a pay phone.

His supervisor was direct. "Got another one for you, Cupper."

Melvis groaned. "Where is it *this* time?"

"Essex, Maryland. *Colonial* slammed into a wrong-way Conrail diesel."

"Hell, Sam. You soused?"

"You're the one slurring his *s*'s, Mel."

"I may be drunk as a boiled owl, but even I can remember through the haze that Essex, Maryland, was the site of that hellacious wreck back in '87. *Colonial* plowed into a Conrail humper then, too. Conrail hogger was on drugs."

"You always say that."

"That time it was true. He ran a signal he shouldn't, confessed and got his ass suspended for life."

"Damn. I remember it now. You're right. That's downright weird."

"Weird or not, I'm on my dang way," said Melvis, hanging up. It took him six tries. He kept missing the switch hook.

"Damn Jap phone," he muttered, handing the receiver to a bewildered child.

An NTSB HELICOPTER was waiting for Melvis at the Baltimore-Washington international airport. He was on-site thirty minutes later.

"Don't tell me that's one of them new Genesis II engines," he moaned as the chopper was settling.

"What's that?" the pilot asked.

"Never dang mind," Melvis said, slapping on his Stetson and ducking out of the winding aircraft.

The on-site Amtrak director of operations shook his hand and said, "We're still processing bodies here."

Melvis said, "I aim to stay outta your way. Just want to get a preliminary gander at the point of impact."

The man pointed the way and rushed off.

Melvis walked down, picking his way carefully. He almost tripped over the bottom half of a leg that lay in his path. It was naked except for an argyle sock with a hole big enough to allow one cold toe to poke out.

"That boy shoulda listened to his mama about keeping up his socks," Melvis muttered, clapping his Stetson over his big chest out of respect for the dead and dismembered, which were plentiful.

The train cars had performed every acrobatic stunt from flying sideways to gouging their wheels into trackside ballast, Melvis saw as he passed the mangled mess.

The compacted engines were as bad as in Nebraska. The monocoque body of the Genesis had gotten the worst of the deal. There was a joke in the industry that the Genesis looked like the box the real locomotive had come in. Now it looked like the box thrown out after Christmas Day.

The Conrail freight engine was an SD50 diesel. By some freak it had bounced back from the point of impact.

Melvis decided he should check out the Conrail cab, in case he had another inconvenient headless engineer on his hands.

Climbing up the tangle of blue steel that had been the access ladder, he heard voices, paused and muttered, "Naw. Couldn't be."

A wrinkled ivory face peered out at him through the shattered glass of the gaping nose door. "You are too late," said Chiun.

"Hidy, old-timer," Melvis said with more enthusiasm than he actually felt. "Hell of a way to run a railroad, don't you think?"

Chiun withdrew so Melvis could step in. Remo was there with him, looking unhappy—which seemed to be his natural condition.

"You boys are sure tramplin' up my patch."

"We got here first," Remo remarked.

"You did, at that. What you find—anything?"

"No engineer. No blood."

"So I see," said Melvis. "Well, let me show you how we do things at the NTSB. Follow me down into the necessary."

Melvis led them down into the toilet compartment, where he lifted the scat and sniffed expertly. "Crapper here ain't been used recently," he pronounced. "Not in at least two hours."

Returning to the console, Melvis checked the controls. What he saw bothered the fool out of him.

"Damn controls are set for highballin'. The engineer would have had to jump clear to escape. But if he had, he would surely have splattered his dumb ass all over the trackage. Guess we walk the dang tracks," he said.

"You sniff a toilet and look over some dials and that's your conclusion?" said Remo.

"That," said Melvis, "is why I get the buck buckaroos. C'mon."

They walked the track. A mile, two, then three.

"I see no body," Chiun sniffed.

"This is powerful strange," Melvis admitted.

"Why's that?" asked Remo.

"Why's that, you say? Those freight controls have an interrupter on them. If the engineer doesn't respond to a beep every forty-five seconds by resettin' a switch, the air brakes will clamp down and stop her cold. Fifty seconds at an estimated eighty miles per means if he didn't jump clear by this point, he didn't jump clear. Period."

"Maybe it was radio controlled," Remo said.

"It's possible. Controls were set. But you're single-footin' down a trail I don't care to follow—if you take my meanin'."

"We are doing this incorrectly," said Chiun.

"How's that, old-timer?"

"We are looking for a dead engineer when we should be looking for a live Japanese."

"Lordy, don't say that! Not out loud. I took a vow of silence I wouldn't breathe a word about what happened up there in Nebraska. Don't make me go back on my solemn word."

"So we're just going to put this one down as drugs?" Remo said.

"This? No, not this little shivaree. This is the second time that has happened here. That spells bad track or maybe a chronic switching or signal problem. Now, if you fellers will excuse me, I done all I can until they get all the dead ones cleared away. I'm gonna find me a nice clean motel and grab me some shut-eye. I'm beat down lower than a flapjack.''

WATCHING MELVIS walk away, Remo growled, ''Remind me to tell Smith to have Melvis's ticket punched.''

When Chiun said nothing, Remo looked around. The Master of Sinanju was sniffing the still air.

''What's up?'' Remo asked.

''Use your nose as I do, lazy one.''

Remo tasted the air.

''Do you smell it?'' asked Chiun.

''What?''

''The foul, reeking odor.''

''All I smell is corn,'' Remo said.

''This is not a place where corn grows.''

''You saying our samurai is lurking in the brush?''

''We will follow the scent and see with our own noses,'' said Chiun, taking off.

Sighing, Remo followed. A mile up the line the scent trail drifted inland. Chiun changed direction, eyes switching and sweeping, face determined.

The ground was flat and undisturbed. After a while a pair of footprints suddenly appeared and continued along. They were heelless. Remo recognized them. They were identical to the tracks found near the Mystic and Texarkana wrecks.

''Unless somebody parachuted down and walked off with his chute, I think we have something here,'' Remo muttered.

Farther along, in a copse of spreading hickory trees, the footsteps stopped. The ground was disturbed in a circle, then the tracks continued. But they had changed. They became Western shoes, with deep heels. Where the tracks changed character, the ground was well-scuffed and full of indentations.

"What are these marks?" Remo wondered aloud.

"This is where the *ronin* removed his armor," said Chiun. "Look, the unmistakable imprint of a *do*."

"If you say it's a *do*. I don't know what a *do* is."

"You would call it a cuirass."

"I probably would if I knew what that was."

"The *do* is the breastplate of the *ronin*."

Chiun set his sandaled feet into the new tracks. They were the same size.

Nodding, Chiun continued, saying, "Come, slow one."

"I'm not the one nursing a missing fingernail."

At that, Chiun swirled and blazed his eyes at Remo. "You insult me!"

"No, just pointing out that I'm a full Master, not a spear-carrier. How about a little respect?"

"When we again encounter the *ronin*, it will be your duty to remove your finger and fling it in his face."

"I'll think about it," said Remo.

They walked on. Chiun folded his hands into his kimono sleeves. "A true Master would not hesitate," he sniffed.

"How about I just give him the fickle finger of fate instead?" Remo undertoned.

The track stopped at a busy highway. They looked up, then down. There was a Burger Triumph and a Taco Hell in one direction. The other was deserted except for a sign that said Chesapeake Hotel.

"We will try there," said Chiun.

"What would a ghost *ronin* be doing in a hotel?"

"Awaiting his doom," said Chiun, who picked up his skirts and strode toward the motel.

Remo followed, thinking he had never seen Chiun so determined before.

THE DESK CLERK at the hotel was extremely accommodating when Chiun asked for the room number of his Japanese friend, whose name slipped him at the moment.

"Mr. Batsuka is in his room. Three-C."

"Did he say Batsucker?" asked Remo as they waited for the elevator.

"Batsuka."

"That a first name or a last name?"

"We will wring the answer from the wretch's very lips before we grind his skull to powder," Chiun vowed.

"Don't forget we need to wring some explanations for Smith before the grinding begins."

"If I become carried away in my anger, Remo, I will count on you to restrain me until the all-important answers are ours."

The elevator let them off on the third floor. Room 3-C was to their immediate right, down a red-carpeted hall.

Standing outside the door, they put their ears to it.

"I hear CNN," said Remo.

"And I hear a human heartbeat I have heard before," said Chiun.

"Knock or kick?"

Chiun considered, his facial wrinkles quivering. "We must not alarm him, lest he commit seppuku."

"Knock it is." Remo knocked. *"Maintenance! Gotta look at your john!"*

His ear to the door, Chiun listened. "He is ignoring us," he whispered.

"Bad move on his part," said Remo, knocking again. "Maintenance man!"

Chiun withdrew and his eyes narrowed. "Await me."

Then he disappeared around the corner.

Remo figured Chiun was going to the balcony to cover that escape route. But when the hotel fire alarm started buzzing, he wasn't sure what to do at first.

Chiun flashed around the corner, eyes excited, demanding, "Has he emerged?"

"No. And don't tell me you threw the alarm!"

"It will flush him out."

It didn't. Instead, other doors flew open, including one that disgorged Melvis Cupper, wearing his NTSB Stetson and boxer shorts decorated with longhorn skulls.

"What's doin'?" he asked sleepily.

Chiun shushed him. He placed his ear to the door panel, listening. His face broke apart in shock.

"He has escaped!" he squeaked. "I hear no heartbeat."

Remo slammed the door with his palm, and it jumped off its hinges with such force it rebounded into the hall. Chiun plucked Melvis out of its path just in time. Remo ducked into the room, moving low in case a sword ambush waited him.

He found instead an empty room. The TV was on, showing coverage of the derailment less than a mile away. On the bed sat a heavy stainless-steel box with carrying straps and assorted switches and buttons on top. It was half in and half out of a black leather bag Remo recognized immediately.

It was the *ronin*'s head bag.

On the end table the telephone was off the hook.

A check of the bathroom and closets showed them to be empty. There was no connecting door to adjoining rooms.

"I'm getting a flash of *déjà vu* here," Remo said. He went to the telephone, scooping it up.

"Hello?" he said.

He got a rush of static, indicating an open line.

"Anybody there?"

"Try *moshi moshi,*" hissed Chiun.

"Moshi moshi," said Remo into the receiver.

The static hissed on. Remo hung up.

"I'll be switched," said Melvis, hefting the steel box on the bed. "If this ain't one of them newfangled RC units. See? It's got that little silver ball on the transmit-power switch just like that fickle little filly said."

Chiun floated up, took one look and said, "Behold, Remo. It says Nishitsu."

"Damn Japs will be making our engines before you know it," muttered Melvis.

Going to the telephone, Chiun picked up the receiver and hit Redial.

The phone started ringing.

When the other end lifted, a thin voice said, "Nishitsu."

Remo's and Chiun's eyes met.

Chiun hissed a question in Japanese, and the voice challenged him in the same language. An argument ensued, at the end of which the Master of Sinanju hung up, ripped the telephone from its wall socket and flung it through the glass balcony door and into the pool, where it caused a fat man to roll off his inflatable sea horse.

"Nice going, Little Father," Remo complained. "Now they know we're on to them."

"The better to strike fear into their craven hearts," spit Chiun.

"Let's find out where our *ronin* ended up."

BACK IN THE LOBBY the desk clerk wasn't as cooperative as before.

"We need the phone charges for 3-C," he said.

"Can't you see I have my hands full?" said the distraught clerk, who was explaining to the unhappy hotel guests that the commotion was only a false alarm.

Remo placed one hand on his shoulder and took his tie in the other. "Show you a trick."

The tie became a blur, and when Remo stepped back, the clerk's hands were dangling just beneath his Adam's apple, held together by a tight paisley knot that had been his tie.

The clerk tried to extricate himself. The harder he pulled, the redder his face became. When it shaded toward purple, he realized he was strangling himself and stopped. The purple went away, replaced by a helpless expression.

"Room charges," Remo repeated. "Three-C."

"Uggg," the clerk said, pointing with both hands to an open office door where a freckled redhead chewed gum at a switchboard.

"Much obliged," said Melvis, tipping his hat.

The hotel operator provided the last number dialed and told them Mr. Batsuka had checked in only a few hours before.

"Got a first name?"

"Furio."

"Thanks," said Remo.

From a lobby pay phone Remo called Harold Smith.

"Smitty. Pull up a number for me."

"Go ahead, Remo."

Remo read off the number.

A moment later Smith said, "It is the number of a Nishitsu car dealership in Eerie, Pennsylvania."

"Damn. Our phantom *ronin* was here. Looks like he used a radio-controlled transmitter to run the Conrail engine onto the Amtrak track. The same transmitter he used to wreck the *California Zephyr,* from the looks of things. All he had to do was find the right frequency and he was in business."

Smith said nothing to that.

"He left the transmitter behind, though. It says Nishitsu on it. We had him cornered in a hotel room, but when we broke in, all we found was an off-the-hook phone. But we got a name. Furio Batsuka."

"That is very interesting, Remo. The strands are coming together to form a pattern."

"Not one I recognize. None of this makes sense."

"I have just completed a deep background check. Nishitsu is the parent corporation of the Gomi and Hideo brands."

Remo whistled. "What do you know?"

"Nishitsu technology explains everything we have encountered thus far. We know that the Krahseevah, in his dematerialized atomic state, had the power to transmit himself through telephone lines. That is how he eluded you and Chiun."

"That much I figured out. But what's the point? Why are they attacking our rail system?"

"I know," squeaked Chiun.

Remo looked at him.

"To destroy a nation's roads is the same as sucking the blood from its veins. It was so with Rome. It is so here in the new Rome. We must save our gracious trains from the foreign brigands."

"Railroads aren't that important anymore, Little Father."

"Philistine. Antirailer."

Into the phone Remo said, "You catch that?"

"Never mind. Remo, I have been analyzing my files over the last hour. Recall that there has been a lull in rail accidents over the last three months."

"If you say so."

"Suddenly events have been happening at an accelerated rate, beginning with the Texarkana disaster."

"I'm with you so far," Remo said.

"In almost every recent incident, the engines involved have been new, state-of-the-art vehicles." Smith paused. "Someone is attempting to discredit U.S. motive-power units."

"Couldn't it be just coincidence? I mean, this guy is hitting everything that runs on rails. He's bound to topple a few new engines."

"A pause, and then an accelerated program. The pause was to regroup and restrategize. Recall that these derailments have been commonplace for three years now."

"Yeah."

"Obviously the initial plan was not working. The mind behind this has shifted tactics. The plot is approaching a crescendo."

"So what's the point?"

"I wish I knew," Smith said helplessly. "But we cannot stand by and chase derailments. We must take the initiative."

"None of this would have happened had the foolish white race not abandoned steam," said Chiun loud enough for all to hear.

"I'll drink to that," said Melvis from the other side of the lobby.

"Remo, book a room in that hotel and await instructions," said Smith.

"If you say so," Remo said reluctantly.

Hanging up, Remo faced the Master of Sinanju. "It's a new ball game. We're dealing with a second generation Krahseevah. Smitty says so."

"He is still a *ronin*," Chiun returned. "And he is very dangerous."

"No argument there. But we're dealing with a guy in an electronic samurai suit. The House isn't haunted."

Chiun raised his nailless index finger. "If you fail to avenge this Japanese insult, I will haunt the House forever."

22

Harold Smith was sorting files when his system beeped.

Hitting a key, he got a pop-up window and an AP news-wire report.

There was a derailment in Eerie, Pennsylvania, the town where the enemy *ronin* had presumably teleported himself. A Ringling Brothers, Barnum and Bailey circus train had gone off the tracks approaching Eerie.

Smith's file beeped again as he read the report. A flashing message in one corner of the screen said, "Match found."

Smith hadn't asked for a match, so he was frowning as he instructed the computer to pull it up.

What he read made him gasp.

The wreck in Eerie was identical in every particular to the one that had cost a half-dozen lives in Lakeland, Florida, two years before. It, too, had involved a circus train.

"The pattern is changing again," Smith muttered under his breath.

It was clear that it was. The demolished engine was an ordinary GE Dash-8. Not new. Not new at all.

Thirty minutes later another AP report popped up,

and Smith knew without being told by the system that it would be a match.

It was.

The *Lakeshore Limited* had jumped the track near Batavia, New York. Casualty reports were yet to filter out. But his system matched it to an identical event two summers previously, where 125 people had been injured.

"He is re-creating some of the most catastrophic disasters in recent rail history," Smith blurted. "But why?"

A moment later Smith forgot all about the why. He had a new angle to pursue.

Frantically inputting commands, he commanded his system to list all of the significant rail disasters of the past three years, in order of loss of life and property damage.

The list was not long. But the first entry was headed, "Bayou Canot."

Smith remembered it well. September 22, 1993. The *Sunset Limited* was barreling south to Florida through Alabama bayou country. A towboat had taken a wrong turn and struck a trestle bridge, weakening it. When the *Sunset Limited* went over the bridge, three lead engines and four trailing Heritage cars tumbled into the water. Forty-seven people drowned. That one event doubled the total number of fatalities in Amtrak history overnight. To this day it remained the most deadly Amtrak accident ever.

Suddenly Smith doubted the official NTSB explanation. Odds were Bayou Canot was about to be repeated.

Dialing the Maryland hotel, Smith reached Remo. "Remo. Here are your instructions. Go to Mobile,

Alabama. Find the railroad bridge over Bayou Canot." Smith spelled it. "Then guard that bridge from sabotage. I have reason to believe the *ronin* will attack it."

"On our way," said Remo.

Hanging up, Smith returned to his computer. There was a lot to do, and he had relatively little hard data.

But he did have a name: Furio Batsuka.

Smith began a search of his data base first. It was unlikely to be legitimate, but the possibility had to be factored out first.

Smith was surprised when the global search came up positive. His gray eyes scanned the scrolling blocks of amber text. His expectant expression soon turned sour: "Seattle Mariners slugger Furio Batsuka strikes out at All-Star Game."

Smith didn't bother to read the rest.

"The name is an obvious alias," he said unhappily.

Hunching his shoulders, Harold Smith tried attacking the problem from another angle. Dead ends were to be expected when dealing with industrial-espionage operations, as this assuredly was.

GETTING TO BAYOU CANOT involved a car ride and then renting a motorboat. It was nearly dusk by the time Remo and Chiun got to the boat leg of the trip.

They were puttering down the sluggish river, Chiun standing in the stern like a watchful figurehead while Remo piloted the craft. A mist was rising from the water. The air was moist and humid. And behind them, a lonesome alligator was following lazily in their wake.

When they found the great steel trestle, it was still standing.

"Looks okay to me," Remo said. "Maybe we're in time."

Chiun said nothing. He was waving to the alligator as it followed them to shore with lazy swishes of its tail.

The craft beached on a bank, and Remo hopped out to secure it. Chiun waited patiently in the stern for Remo to pull the boat nearly out of the water. Only then did he deign to step off onto dry land.

The alligator decided to join them.

"Better watch the lizard, Little Father," Remo cautioned.

"Better that the lizard watch me," said Chiun, turning to face the waddling saurian.

The alligator crawled out on his stubby legs and made a determined lunge for Chiun. Chiun watched him approach, his hazel eyes curious.

"This is an inferior specimen."

"Compared to what?" said Remo, eyeing the long, eerie span over their heads.

"The royal crocodiles of Upper Egypt."

"If he gets hold of your ankle, you'll think differently."

That seemed to be the alligator's intent. He kept coming. Chiun let him get within a snout's length. Abruptly the alligator scissored open his jaws and, with a furious forward convulsion, snapped them shut.

If an alligator could show surprise, this one did.

Its lizardy eyes were gawking at the spot where Chiun stood. There was no Chiun. It whipsawed its long head. Right, then left.

And standing serenely on the creature's pebbled back, the Master of Sinanju reached forward to tap the gator on the top of its knobby brown head.

"Yoo-hoo," Chiun taunted. "Here I am."

The gator threshed. Its tail whipped back. Its jaws snapped around like a dog trying to bite its own tail. It bucked. It squirmed. It let out a rare alligator roar.

But the Master of Sinanju rode it as calmly as if it were a lumpy log, not a leathery, muscular eating machine.

"Chiun, will you stop teasing that gator?" Remo warned. "We have work to do."

"I am teasing no one. He is trying to eat me."

"Stop giving him reason to think he can."

And since it was a reasonable request, the Master of Sinanju stepped forward, slamming the gator's fanged jaws shut, simultaneously mushing its head down into the spongy riverbank.

The gator's entire body convulsed, tail slamming in anger, then determination, finally in unmistakable terror as it realized it was utterly powerless to unseat the skirted annoyance on its back.

Chiun waited for the gator to settle down. It lay flat, panting like a flattened, exhausted dog. Calmly, with a sandaled toe, the Master of Sinanju nudged the gator's ribs until it rolled over once, it legs kicking out helpless as broken chicken wings.

"Behold, Remo. A trick you do not know."

Remo ignored the commotion. He was moving through the rank undergrowth, checking the bridge supports.

So Chiun, using only his toe, nudged the helpless alligator over and over like a log, maintaining his balance with nimble steps, until the saurian rolled into the oily bayou waters with a defeated splash.

Chiun stepped off at the last possible moment.

"Good riddance to you, sandworm," squeaked Chiun.

The gator was only too eager to go away. It swam off, tired of tail and discouraged of spirit.

Chiun joined Remo, who was testing the trestle supports with his hands.

"They're solid. Let's go up."

They climbed because it was the easiest way up.

Up on the span, the tracks looked stable. They walked them to make sure. By this time night was upon the bayou. Below, the turbid waters muttered, dark and oily.

"Wonder why Smitty thinks this bridge will be hit?" Remo said.

"It only matters that he does," said Chiun.

"I don't like being way out in the boonies, out of touch, in case something happens somewhere else."

"What could happen? Smith's infallible oracles have whispered secrets to him, and we must all obey."

"Let's just hope we're on ground zero. It could be a long night."

HAROLD SMITH WAS TRYING to follow an audit trail through cyberspace.

The trouble was, trains kept crashing.

He had reasoned that the enemy was moving through the nation's telephone lines in order to attack its rail system. It was a logical deduction. Computerized airline-booking files showed no ticketed Japanese-surnamed passenger moving between the cities in question by air. Rail was too slow. As were cars.

Therefore, the Nishitsu *ronin* was traveling by fiber-optic cable, like a human fax. It had been the mystifying modus operandi of the Krahseevah before he had attempted to fax himself to Nishitsu headquarters in Osaka, Japan, in order to escape Remo and Chiun about three years before.

Nothing more had been heard of him since then. Smith had assumed that the Krahseevah—the name was Russian for "beautiful," which definitely did not fit the faceless white coverall garment he wore—had been unable to transmit himself via orbiting communications satellites as he did through fiber-optic cable. There was no reason to think otherwise. This new opponent's MO was different. He was engaged in acts of sabotage, not theft. And he displayed a callous disregard for human life, while the Krahseevah had never been known to harm anyone.

This was a different foe with a different agenda.

The audit trail assumed a telephone credit card was being used by the *ronin* to travel around. Smith was hunting for such a card.

As all over America new crashes, derailments and rail accidents were being reported, Smith input these new destinations into his exploding data base. Soon, he knew, something would bubble up. With luck only one or two phone cards were involved. The more they were used, the sooner the CURE system would make connections.

The trouble was, the longer it took, the more catastrophes the U.S. rail system suffered.

As he waited, the system beeped again.

This time it was in Boise, Idaho. Another Amtrak crash. The *Pioneer* had derailed in Boise on that exact same spot back in 1993. And Smith had a sudden flash of understanding.

The *ronin* was duplicating past accidents because time was running out, and it was easier to reengineer a successful derailment than create one anew.

Running out for what? Smith wondered.

REMO HEARD the strange sound long after darkness had fallen.

"What's that?"

"I do not know," said Chiun, head lifting.

As they listened, it became a monotonous metallic creaking, like slow gears going through a laborious cycle. An engine muttered.

Reaching in a back pocket, Remo pulled out an Amtrak schedule he had grabbed at the car-rental agency.

"According to this, the *Sunset Limited* isn't due for another hour."

Chiun cocked an ear. "It does not sound like a train, but a devil wagon."

"What's a devil wagon?"

"In the days of the renowned Kyong-Ji Line, a railroad man would ride before the locomotive on a wagon he propelled by pumping a seesaw handle. This was to examine the track to insure the way was secure. Also to lure lurking bandits to their doom."

"You had bandits on the Kyong-Ji?"

"Until the Master of that time, my father, ridded the countryside of these brigands—in return for a private coach."

"No gold?"

"The coach was filled with gold. Shame on you, Remo. It goes without saying."

"Let's see what it is."

BILLY REX DAUGHTERS WAS getting worried. Here it was after dark, and he had another ten miles of cable to lay.

The bulldozer creaked beside the rails at a sedate walking pace, its tracks grumbling as the giant spool paid out fiber-optic cable. It came out of the spool and followed the curve of the specialized front-mounted plow, falling flat into the trench as it was excavated. Later a work crew would tamp it down.

It was the damnedest thing, he thought, not for the first time. Laying the information highway of the twenty-first century on twentieth-century rail with a plow not much different from what men first used to till the soil back in the Stone Age.

But there it was.

And here he was. And if Billy Rex didn't get a move on, the *Sunset Limited* was going to catch him and his dozer on the Bayou Canot bridge and mash man and machine into the trackage like a discarded can of pop.

As he approached the great span, the mists rising from the sluggish waters below made him think of the spirits of the dead who had died in the diesel-soaked, alligator-infested waters below. Billy Rex slowed. There had been a heavy fog the night the *Limited* went into the bayou. It smothered the span so that the hapless engineer thought he was running over solid rail right up until the moment he rode his diesel into oblivion.

Trouble was, slowing down encouraged the damn mosquitoes. They began swarming.

THE TWO FIGURES materialized on either side of the right-of-way like ghosts from the Bayou Canot incident.

"Hold!" one said. He was a strange one, he was. Old as the hills and dressed for a Chinese square dance.

The other was a regular fellow. Lean as bamboo, with wrists like railroad ties. Neither exactly looked like track men. But they looked harmless enough.

Oddly enough, the mosquitoes didn't seem to have an appetite for them. They stayed off a ways, like careful moths shrinking from a flame.

"Can't stop," he called ahead in his friendliest voice as he approached the pair. "Got a schedule to make."

The tall, skinny one spoke up. "Is that a plow?"

"Yep."

"Kinda late in the year for clearing snow."

"Or early," Billy Rex returned sociably.

They were walking alongside him now. Not threatening, just interested. Billy Rex began to relax.

"What is this?" asked the little guy, pointing at the serpentine cable dropping into the fresh-turned earth.

"Fiber-optic cable. We're laying the information highway."

"Along railroad track?" the skinny one blurted.

"Hell, phone lines have been strung along the right-of-way and buried beside it for years and years. This here is just the latest wrinkle."

"I didn't know that."

"Well, a body learns something new every day, doesn't he?"

They were approaching the bridge now. The mosquitoes were really biting now. If the engineers were on the money, the cable would run out about now.

It did. The last plopped into the trench, for later splicing. Billy Rex hit the lever that raised the plow. Then he sent his machine up onto the tracks, jockeyed it true and prepared to cross the bridge as fast as reasonable.

"I wouldn't follow me any farther," he said, slapping at his arms. "Ain't safe."

Suddenly there was a business card in his face. He couldn't read it too well by moonlight, but the skinny guy's voice said, "Remo Bell, FCC," in a voice so self-assured, Billy Rex naturally accepted it. "Pull over."

"This is rail I'm on, not blacktop. I can't pull over."

"Then stop this vehicle or face the consequences," said the squeaky voice of the little old Asian.

"What consequences?" Billy Rex naturally asked.

That's when the bulldozer stopped. Dead. Billy Rex yanked out a flashlight to see what it had hit.

The tracks were clear, except for the leather shoe. It had arrested the plow somehow. Inside the shoe was the foot of the skinny guy from the FCC.

Deciding to be sociable, Billy Rex killed the engine.

"What can I do for you fellas?"

"Spot check."

"Check away."

They looked over his cable, peered under his vehicle as if looking for a bomb, checked his ID and for some reason looked real hard at the bulldozer manufacturer's plate before saying, "Okay, you can go now."

"Much obliged."

"You are very wise to buy American," the Asian squeaked.

Then they watched him start up and negotiate the bridge, ponderous tracks gripping steel rail it wasn't designed for.

The mosquitoes followed, as mosquitoes would. If any malingered to sample the two odd ones Billy Rex left behind, it wasn't noticeable.

AFTER THE BULLDOZER was lost in the darkness, Remo turned to Chiun and said, "I think I know what they're after now."

"And you are wrong," Chiun sniffed.

"I didn't say what I was thinking yet."

"You are wrong, whatever you are thinking."

"We'll see about that." Remo looked up at the moon, whose position in the sky verified what his internal clock was telling him. The *Sunset Limited* was due before long.

They retreated into the undergrowth to watch the bridge for trouble. The night was full of mosquitoes. But all avoided them as if their pores exhaled a natural insecticide, which was closer to the truth than not.

HAROLD SMITH WAS reading the first AP bulletins of the derailment of Amtrak's *City of New Orleans* at Poplarville, Mississippi, when the link-analysis program began reporting results.

There were three active phone cards.

One was issued to an Akira Kurosawa. The second to a Seiji Ozawa. And the third to Furio Batsuka.

A horrible thought crossed his mind. What if there was more than one *ronin?*

Double-checking the times of each accident, Smith decided not. Multiple saboteurs would not explain the short intervals or the lack of simultaneous crashes.

Smith then ran a check on the first name. Akira Kurosawa came up as a famous Japanese director of samurai movies. Seiji Ozawa was the Japanese-American conductor of the Boston Symphony Orchestra. Smith's brow furrowed distastefully at the dual significance of the word *conductor.* He detested opponents with humor.

The news wires were humming now. The multiple accidents were becoming hourly bulletins. And all were Amtrak trains. Another shift in tactics. The reasoning was self-evident. Derailed passenger trains meant significant loss of life compared to freight accidents: Amtrak was not hauling cabbages.

"Someone is deliberately bringing enormous pressure to bear on the U.S. rail system, both materially and politically," Smith said aloud.

The why remained elusive.

While his search programs trolled the net for more incidents, Smith began reviewing the state of the U.S. rail system.

For three years accidents had been an unrelenting plague.

For four, freight traffic was booming. Even the Midwest floods and washouts of '93 had not crimped it.

Amtrak, on the other hand, was in trouble. Service cutbacks had begun to bite. Ridership levels were up, but Smith had begun to suspect some of that could be explained by the opportunists looking for a free ride into lifelong insurance benefits if they survived a rail accident. The so-called Railpax, which allowed Amtrak to utilize existing freight lines on a favored-nation basis, was at an end.

With Congress considering terminating funding, Amtrak's future appeared bleak.

But what possible motive would the Nishitsu Industrial Electrical Corporation have for derailing Amtrak?

There was no clear answer. Smith returned to the matter of the murderous teleporting *ronin*.

Every time one of the phone cards was used, the call was logged by the issuing company's computers. Smith got a readout of the originating call and its destination as they took place. They came up as simple phone charges. In reality they represented the most efficient form of transportation known to man.

And a Japanese company owned it exclusively.

No other Japanese names bubbled up from the ongoing search programs. And every time one of those cards was used, without fail, a rail accident followed within minutes.

Somewhere in the fiber-optic maze of the nation's telephone system, a deadly predator was moving unseen and unsuspected. Soon, Smith knew, the *ronin* would attempt to send the *Sunset Limited* tumbling into Bayou Canot.

It was just a matter of time. If only, he found himself hoping, their nameless enemy would strike at Bayou Canot sooner than later. The carnage piling up was horrendous.

THE *SUNSET LIMITED* first showed itself as a distant gleam of light in the shadowy distance.

"Here it comes," said Remo.

Chiun's head swiveled about, left then right. His sensitive ears were hunting for sounds. "I hear no *ronin*."

"Don't forget. If he's dematerialized, we won't hear his heartbeat. Just like in that boxcar."

"If he skulks amid this eerie backwater, my eagle eye will spy him."

Remo nodded. His eyes were also searching.

Foliage rustled. Herons. Somewhere the muscular splash of a restless alligator disturbed the night.

And down the line the gleam of the twin-beam headlight grew to a white, widening funnel. The trestle began to vibrate.

Remo stepped back. He was looking at the trestle supports. If the *ronin* was going to strike, he would strike here.

A wind picked up. It seemed to be moving ahead of the oncoming train. The light grew, changing the shadows, making them crawl. And lining up on the trestle, the *Sunset Limited* threw the full blaze of her engine headlight along the bridge, making the rails gleam and sparkle.

The *Sunset Limited* hit the bridge at a thunderous seventy miles an hour. The bridge vibrated in response. It rattled for barely two minutes to the thunder of the passing train.

Then the *Limited* was gone. The shadows returned. Night closed in again.

And Remo and Chiun stood at the foot of the bridge and looked at each other.

"Guess Smitty was wrong."

"We must get word to him," said Chiun.

"How? We're in the middle of nowhere."

"Did you not say that trains have telephones now?"

"Yeah. But we're a little late to catch the *Sunset Limited*."

"Not if we hurry," said Chiun.

THEY PUSHED THE BOAT into the water and sent it racing down the waterway.

The tracks wound in a serpentine in and out of the bayou. That made it possible to beach the boat at a point down the line before the *Sunset Limited* reached it.

Taking up positions at trackside, Remo and Chiun waited as the headlights bored toward them.

Gauging its speed, they began to run, ahead of the train and parallel to the track.

The silver train had slowed to fifty miles per hour. Remo and Chiun got up to that speed and held it.

The engine barreled past. They let the forward coaches do the same.

The end car was baggage. Since they were traveling at the same velocity, it was easy enough to hop on at the back, cling a moment, then force the rear door open.

When they worked their way forward to a passenger coach, Remo and Chiun attracted no more attention than normal.

Remo found a rail phone. He activated it with a credit card.

"Smitty. You guessed wrong. The *ronin* didn't hit the bridge."

"I know, Remo," Smith said wearily. "He has been creating carnage in several other places instead. There are many casualties."

Smith filled Remo in on the new pattern of re-created derailments.

"So why'd he skip this one?" Remo asked. "Some of those other crashes are pretty small potatoes."

"He is building toward something. Perhaps he is saving Bayou Canot."

"Saving it for what?"

"That," said Harold Smith with an audible grinding of teeth, "is the question of the hour."

"Well, I may have part of the answer."

"Go ahead, Remo."

"We came across a guy laying fiber-optic cable along the tracks. Did you know they're laying cable along rail bed all over the country?"

"Yes. That is how the SPRINT company has created its telephone system."

"SPRINT?"

"It stands for Southern Pacific Railroad Internal Telephone."

"The railroads are in the telephone business?" Remo blurted out.

"Yes. Some."

"Well, now they're laying cable for the information superhighway, too. Mean anything to you?"

"The Nishitsu Corporation is attempting to sabotage our computer links!" Smith snapped. "This has nothing to do with the rail system at all."

"That's how I read it."

"Excellent work, Remo."

"You are both wrong," sniffed Chiun. "The Japanese are envious of American railroads. Their destruction is the insidious goal."

"Tell Chiun that the Japanese rail system is far more sophisticated than our own," Smith said. "And please return to Folcroft immediately."

Hanging up, Remo said, "You hear that?"

"The man is an inveterate rationalist."

"You're just jealous because I was right and you were wrong."

"You are never right and I am never wrong."

Just then the conductor accosted them and asked if they had tickets.

"I entrusted mine to this lackey," said Chiun, pointing at Remo while breezing haughtily past the conductor.

23

Dawn was breaking over Folcroft Sanitarium when Remo and Chiun finally got back.

"What's the latest?" asked Remo.

Chiun flew to his steamer trunk, checked the lock to make sure it hadn't been tampered with, then relaxed.

Harold Smith was hollow of eye and voice. "There have been a half-dozen derailments and rail accidents overnight. The loss of life is significant. Almost thirty people."

Remo grunted. "You lose more people in one average plane crash."

"That is not how it will play in the morning papers," said Smith. "The National Railroad Passenger Corporation is known for its comparatively good safety record. This will be seen as a symptom of its decline and unworthiness to continue operating."

Remo frowned. "What's the National Railroad Passenger Corporation?"

"Amtrak."

"How do they get 'Amtrak' out of 'National Railroad Passenger Corporation'?"

Smith declined to reply. He was scanning his computer screen. There had been no movement on the part of the *ronin* in more than two hours. None of the three fake phone cards was in play.

"Guess he tucked himself in for the night," said Remo unhappily.

"The last location I have for him is Denver, Colorado."

"Want us to go there?"

"Not yet."

Chiun spoke up. "Emperor, where are the *katana*s of the *ronin?* I would like to examine them."

Smith pointed to one of a row of ancient oaken file cabinets that occupied a corner of the office. "Top drawer."

Chiun went to the one indicated and extracted the matched *katana* blades. Remo drifted up.

"A descendant of Odo of Obi forged these," Chiun said firmly.

"If you say so," said Remo. "What I'd like to know is how they rematerialize."

"A timer," Smith said absently.

"Oh, yeah?"

Smith nodded without looking up from his screen. "I discovered a minitimer in each hilt. Once the button is pressed, the dematerialized state is of short duration but can be regulated. That is how the *ronin* was able to decapitate the Texarkana engineer without entering the cab. He threw the blade through the windscreen, whereupon it rematerialized and decapitated him, then due to the speed of the oncoming train, buried itself in the bulkhead, solid once more."

"So how come it didn't break?" asked Remo.

"It is made of some metal or substance that is highly flexible yet strong. I have not yet identified it."

Remo shrugged. "At least we got some of his arsenal."

"By the way, I cleaned the battery contacts in the dead *katana*. It is working again. So be careful."

Chiun addressed Smith. "Emperor, might we be allowed time to ourselves?"

"Yes. Just remain within the building."

Tucking the blades under one arm, Chiun said, "Come, Remo. I have much to teach you before we confront the dastardly *ronin* once more."

"Teach me what?"

"The art of the *katana*."

Remo blinked. "What happened to 'weapons sully the purity of the art'?"

"You have no blades to call your own. And there is no time to grow proper Knives of Eternity."

"So you're going to drag me into sword fighting?" Remo said doubtfully.

"It is a dubious exercise, I know. But to fight a ghost, one must employ arcane methods. To fight a ghost with a short-fingered accomplice such as yourself is folly."

Remo thought about that. "I think I've been insulted."

"Come."

Remo folded his arms. "Not a chance. You always taught me to disdain swords, so I'm abstaining."

"You cannot abstain when the honor of the House is at stake!" Chiun flared. He clenched his fists before him.

"Tough. I've taken enough guff for one day. I'm abstaining."

Chiun whirled on Smith. "Emperor, talk sense to this wayward one."

"Remo, please." Smith didn't look up. He continued tapping his illuminated keyboard.

Remo looked at Chiun and purred, "What'll you trade me for cooperating?"

Chiun's eyes narrowed. "What do you wish in trade?" he asked thinly.

Remo glanced at the big steamer trunk with the lapis lazuli phoenixes resting on the office divan. "A peek inside."

"That will not release you from carrying it with you if I so command," Chiun said quickly.

"Damn. I changed my mind. Trade you for permanent release from lugging duty."

"Too late!" Chiun crowed. "You have stated your heart's desire. Learn the art of the *katana* and I will allow you a peek. But only one."

"Guess you got me."

"Yes. I have you. Now, make haste. And bring my precious trunk."

Hefting the awkward box on his shoulder, Remo followed the Master of Sinanju from Harold Smith's office. On his way out the door, he gave the steamer trunk a surreptitious shake.

The sound made him think of uncooked rice grain, but the box was too light to be full of grains. Toothpicks maybe. Or Rice Krispies. He gave the box another shake. That was definitely a Rice Krispies sound. Therefore, it was not Rice Krispies. There was no reason Chiun would have him lug Rice Krispies all over the place. Rocks, yes. Not rice in any form.

Stepping on the waiting elevator, Remo figured he'd learn the truth soon enough.

AN HOUR LATER, Remo was grinning from ear to ear.

Under Chiun's tutelage, he had learned the Wheel Stroke, the Clearer Stroke, the Pear Splitter and other samurai sword techniques.

"Hey, I'm pretty good at this," Remo said as he deflected Chiun's blade for the third time.

"Too good," spat Chiun, withdrawing.

"How's it possible to be too good?"

They were in the spacious Folcroft gymnasium. It was here that Remo had first met Chiun and where he had received his earliest Sinanju training.

Chiun frowned as deeply as Remo grinned.

"You may have some Japanese blood polluting your veins," Chiun said.

"Not a chance."

"You are such a mongrel, how are we to know?"

Remo grinned. "I'm good. That's all there is to it."

"You had an excellent teacher."

Remo saw his opening and took it. "I did, didn't I?"

And Chiun struggled so hard to hide his pleasure at the unexpected compliment that his wrinkled face twitched like a cobweb in a breeze.

"It may be we are ready to meet the *ronin* in combat," Chiun allowed, his voice stiffening to keep the unseemly warmth from it.

"I know I am. But what about you? *En garde!*"

And Remo lunged.

Chiun floated into the approaching stroke, *katana* gripped in two hands. It came up, clashed, parried and spanked both sides of the black blade four times before Remo could complete his thrust.

Fluttering out of the way, the Master of Sinanju said, "Remember who is Master and who is not."

Remo stared at his still-quivering sword blade. "Point taken," he said in a suddenly small voice.

They laid the blades aside.

"I wonder who this guy Batsuka is?" Remo asked after a while.

"A *ronin*."

"If he works for Nishitsu, doesn't that make him a samurai? I mean, he's not really masterless if he works for a corporation, is he?"

Chiun frowned in thought. "He does not wear the crest of his clan on his shoulder. Therefore, he is *ronin*, not samurai."

"Of course he doesn't. He's a saboteur. What's he gonna do? Wear the corporate logo?"

Chiun caressed his wispy beard. "I do not understand."

"It's simple. If he wears the logo, that points directly to Nishitsu. He can't exactly do that, so he leaves it off. Still and all, he is a samurai."

"We do not know this," Chiun said stiffly.

"Every step of the way, he used Nishitsu products."

"He is Japanese. He is comfortable with things Japanese. It is very Japanese to be that way."

"I guess that makes sense," Remo admitted. "Still wonder who he is really. Samurai died out a long time ago."

Chiun's eyes suddenly narrowed. Reaching into one sleeve, he produced the metal bulldozer plate found at the crash site in Mystic, Connecticut. His eyes went to the company symbol, four disks in a circle.

"This is the crest of Shogun Nishi," he muttered.

"Are you going back to that?"

"The crest of Nishi is the sign of Hideo, which is a limb of Nishitsu. Do you not see the significance, Remo? The sons of Nishi must be the shoguns of Nishitsu!"

"I don't think modern corporations have shoguns, Little Father."

"There is more to this than meets the eye," Chiun said slowly. His fists began to clench and unclench. He looked at his broken nail, and his wispy beard trembled.

"It all makes sense now," he said in a low, bitter voice.

"To everyone except me," Remo muttered. "I'll bet when we nail this guy he turns out to be an unemployed chop-socky actor or something."

24

For Furio Batsuka, the first step to becoming a samurai involved being beheaded.

The correct term was *kubi kiri*. In medieval times one's head was literally separated from his neck. But this was modern Japan. And Furio worked for a modern Japanese multinational corporation.

After the so-called Bubble Economy had collapsed, many things were different. Events formerly undreamed of became commonplace. There was crime and unemployment, bank failures and earthquakes. Some called it Japan's Blue Period.

In modern Japan to be laid off was the same as experiencing true *kubi kiri*. Especially if one were a batter for the Osaka Blowfish.

"I am beheaded?" he had blurted when the team manager broke the bad news to him over green tea, inadvertently using the ironic term.

"You play too aggressive. Too American."

"I play to win."

"It is not always necessary to win. Sometimes a draw is good."

Furio nodded, but not in agreement. Then the manager spoke the words that changed his life.

"The shogun is interested in you. See him tomorrow."

THE SHOGUN WAS Kozo Nishitsu, president of Nishitsu Industrial Electrical Corporation. Furio found himself bowing before him early the next morning behind closed doors.

The shogun spoke without pleasantries. "I would like you to go to America. To play with a farm team we own. Eventually with the Mariners."

Furio could not believe his good fortune. To play U.S. ball!

"Gladly," he said.

"But first you must be trained. For though you will work with the Mariner organization, you will remain in our employ."

"A spy?"

"A saboteur. I have watched your aggression. I like it. It is worthy of *bushi*."

And Furio bowed before the deep compliment. The shogun's ancestor's were fierce warriors. The code of *Bushido* was their way.

"I agree," said Furio Batsuka.

IN THE RESEARCH-and-development wing, white-coated Nishitsu technicians measured him and then showed him a faceless dummy dressed in classic black samurai armor. On one shoulder rode the four moons of the Nishitsu Corporation.

"I am honored," he told them.

The sharp voice of Kozo Nishitsu snapped, "You will be honored once you have earned the right to don this armor."

And so his training began. He was presented to an old man whose name he was never told. This man trained him in the ways of the warrior. He learned the *katana* and its sixteen strokes. Archery. Spear fight-

ing. The war fan. Jujitsu. But most of all, he learned
the code of *Bushido,* which made Furio *bushi*—a
warrior.

After nearly a year the old *sensei* brought him again
before the armor he coveted. Tears were in his eyes as
the shogun spoke.

"The samurai are thought dead. No more. You are
the first in generations. I congratulate you, Batsuka-
san."

"I am proud."

"But because this is the modern world, you will
wear modern armor," the shogun continued.

Sober-faced technicians dressed him. The many
layers fit him like gloves for the various parts of his
body.

The shogun said, "Years ago our superconductor
research enabled us to devise a flexible suit that would
alter the molecular vibrations of the human body so
that a man could walk silently and safely like a spirit,
and like a spirit, pass through solids. We called this
the Goblin Suit. That prototype was stolen from us by
Russian agents. But we have created a new suit, which
you see before you. We call it the Black Goblin."

When the helmet was placed upon his head, the
tinted, face-concealing visor dropping into place,
Furio Batsuka felt weighted down by generations of
pride.

Then someone turned the rheostat at his shoulder.
The heaviness vanished. He felt light, like a cherry
blossom. And the second phase of his training began.

Furio learned to walk through walls without fear.
To place his feet so that he did not fall into the earth
forever. And most frightening, to travel through tele-

phone fiber-optic cable like fast smoke through endless straws.

They presented him with modern versions of the *katana* and other samurai weapons, too, and showed him how to employ their wondrous metal-cleaving blades and phantom properties.

When these things had been learned, too, the shogun told him of his mission. "You will go to America to play ball and undermine their rail system."

"Hai!" Furio barked, bowing his head sharply.

"You will kill many innocents."

"I am a samurai. I obey my shogun."

"You will live in an alien land."

"I am a samurai. I will do anything for my shogun. And to play American ball."

"Well spoken. Now, there is one last thing."

And as Furio stood at attention, the shogun stepped over and removed the four-moon corporate seal from his armored shoulder.

"Why . . . ?"

"You cannot be captured except by misadventure or malfunction. But you may be seen. You cannot be linked to us."

"But I am a samurai. You have made of me a lowly *ronin.*"

"When you return, your *katana* red with American blood, you will be a samurai once more," the shogun promised.

And behind his tinted faceplate, Furio Batsuka wept in secret. He had been a samurai for less than a day.

Still, it could have been worse. At least he had a job.

25

The morning newspaper lay folded on Harold Smith's desk until after 11:00 a.m., its black headline screaming at him: RAIL MELTDOWN!

Smith had only glanced at the front page when his secretary laid it on his desk hours before. He was too busy trolling the net. The paper was of little value anyway. Printed in the middle of the night with hours-old information, it was already half a day behind the steady stream of bulletins moving on the wires.

A knock at the door caused Smith to withdraw his fingers from the capacity keyboard. Instantly the flat, illuminated keys went dark, fading into the black glass desktop, showing no trace that the desk harbored electronic secrets.

"Come in," said Smith.

The door opened, and Mrs. Mikulka poked her blue-haired head in. "Lunch, Dr. Smith?"

"Yes. The usual. And black coffee."

The door closed.

When Mrs. Mikulka returned, she laid the aqua particleboard tray on Smith's desk. He spread the newspaper on the desk. It was impossible to use the computer and eat. But the paper had one advantage. It was low tech.

So Smith ate and skimmed.

The news was as stale as he expected. The Amtrak derailments received extensive play. Congressional leaders were calling for the entire system to be shut down and abolished. There was a short but vague item on a hazardous-material situation in Nebraska that was obviously the ill-fated MX missile train. Smith made a mental note to deal with that problem later.

Under the fold was the beginning of an editorial that caught his eye. It was headlined U.S. RAIL SYSTEM TOO OLD?

Smith read along. Analysis always interested him.

It was dry stuff. Exactly the kind he preferred. The editorial writer crisply summarized the current state of the U.S. rail infrastructure and pronounced it dangerously unsafe on account of its age.

Modern, state-of-the-art diesels run on rail beds first laid down during the Garfield administration. The fact is steel-wheel technology is a product of the eighteenth century. The recent rash of rail accidents testifies to the dilapidated state of our once-great rail transportation system.

The future lies in bullet trains and magnetic-levitation technology. Clean, capable of speeds rivaling air travel, they are revolutionizing rail transportation around the world. Other nations have them. Why doesn't the U.S.?

The answer is simple. Conversion costs. With thousands of miles of track too run-down to upgrade economically, the only way the U.S. rail system can enter the twenty-first century is through a wholesale replacement of the existing

trackage infrastructure. But those costs out-
weigh the savings of maglev by a factor of more
than ten to one. The result—an impossible situation. The U.S. cannot implement maglev trains
because of existing rail conditions. And it can't
replace the tracks. Thus, the federal Maglev Initiative has been on the slow track for decades.

With this current spate of disasters, can the
United States afford *not* to replace its rail network? Ask the Japanese, who are anxious to sell
its maglev systems. Or the Germans, who have
one of their own. Then ask if America, clinging
to its historical love of old-style trains, can afford to lose its freight lines, as well as the dying
passenger-rail system?

Smith blinked as he absorbed the last paragraph.
"Maglev," he whispered.
Clearing his desktop, Smith brought his system up.
He typed in the search command, then input,
"Magnetic levitation."
Scrolling up came a long string of items. He
skimmed them.
In under ten minutes he had absorbed the state of
magnetic-levitation technology. It was first developed in the U.S. in the 1970s, but had been abandoned when a combination of cost and technical
difficulties—solved since then—had made it imprac-
tical to implement. The Japanese and the Germans
virtually controlled the field now, thanks to new ad-
vances in superconductor research.
Digging deeper, Smith pulled up the names of the
Japanese firms that were in the forefront of maglev
development.

He got only one: Nishitsu.

Keying off that, he asked the computer to pull up everything it could find on Nishitsu's maglev progress.

The first item might have hit him between the eyes. He leaned back in his chair.

An AP wire story only two days old, it told of the upcoming Rail Expo '96—to be held in Denver, Colorado—where new train technology from around the world would be on display to the public and industry alike. It was sponsored by an international consortium that included Nishitsu Industrial Electrical Corporation.

Smith frowned. He had heard of air shows where new technology was displayed, but not comparable rail shows.

Initiating a search, he attempted to learn more. There was no more. Then he realized the expo was already taking place. Today was the opening day.

Smith found a contact number and called it.

"Rair Expo '96," a chipper female voice said. It was obviously Japanese.

"Yes. I have just read about your function. Is is possible to fax me additional information?"

"Of course."

"Good." Smith gave her the number, then hung up.

The corner fax machine began beeping and whirring five minutes later. Smith pulled out the sheets as they came out one at a time.

There seemed nothing unusual about the information until the last sheet rolled out.

Smith was trained to pick out individual words or word strings of interest from large blocks of text. It was a speed-reading ability that had served him in good stead down through the years at CURE.

So it was not unusual that the instant his eyes fell on the last page, they jumped on two words that were uppermost in his mind. A name.

Furio Batsuka.

Eyes wide, Smith returned to his desk. He was reading as he fell into his cracked-leather executive chair.

Furio Batsuka, major-league slugger, formerly with the Osaka Blowfish, would be signing autographs all three days.

"My God!" said Harold Smith. "Could it be?"

HAROLD SMITH'S FACE was stark white when he burst into the Folcroft gymnasium.

"I have found the Nishitsu *ronin,*" he said.

"Where?" said Remo.

"He is signing autographs at the Rail Expo in Denver."

"Oh, that. That's where K.C. was headed."

"Who is K.C.?" asked Smith.

"A sensitive soul," said Chiun.

"A rail nut," said Remo.

Smith said, "According to what I have, Furio Batsuka is his real name. He is a Japanese baseball player who was released from the Osaka Blowfish four years ago. He came to this country and was signed up by a minor-league team. A year ago he joined the Seattle Mariners as a batter."

"Can't be the same Batsuka," said Remo.

"The Osaka Blowfish were sponsored by the Nishitsu company. And Nishitsu owns an interest in the Mariners. Remo, you follow baseball. Why didn't you recognize Batsuka's name?"

Remo grunted. "I haven't paid much attention since the strike."

"Ah-hah," said Chiun. "This explains the inexplicable."

"It does?" said Remo and Smith together.

"Yes. When I first encountered this fiend, he employed a fighting stance I did not recognize as Japanese."

"What stance?"

Chiun demonstrated by laying his *katana* blade across his shoulder and taking practice swings at an imaginary opponent.

"That's a batting stance, all right," said Remo.

"My God!" said Smith. "It all fits. I last tracked the *ronin* to Denver. That is where he is now. Signing autographs."

"That still doesn't explain what this is all about."

"I believe I have that answer, as well," said Smith.

They looked at him.

"For years now, the Japanese have wanted to sell the U.S. high-speed bullet and magnetic-levitation trains. But our rail systems are either incompatible or unsuitable for the conversion. It would all have to be replaced. From scratch. They're trying to convince us that our rail system is falling apart."

Chiun hissed, "The philistines! Let them tear up their own rails."

"They have. And now they enjoy bullet trains and maglev systems we can never hope to inaugurate as long as we cling to old steel-wheel technology."

"Well, that explains one thing that's been bothering me," said Remo.

Smith said, "Yes?"

"Now I know why K.C. left Melvis crying in his beer."

Smith looked confused.

"Never mind," said Remo. "Okay, I'll buy it. I guess we head to Denver, huh?"

"Yes," said Harold Smith in a grim, tight voice. "You go to Denver."

Chiun lifted a vengeful fist to the high ceiling. "The fiend will never harm our gracious engines again, O Emperor. Place your trust in us."

"Remo," said Smith.

"Yeah?"

"See that Batsuka is disposed of quietly. And make certain the Nishitsu people understand our deep displeasure with events."

A stricken expression crossed Chiun's wizened face. His beard trembled in shock. "They will be allowed to retain their heads?"

"Be discreet," repeated Smith.

"They get to keep their heads," said Remo. "Sorry."

The International Rail Exposition for 1996 was destined to be the largest, most ambitious assemblage of railroad rolling stock ever put together in one spot.

An outdoor fairground in the high mountain air of Denver, Colorado, was the site. Trains old and new, ranging from museum pieces to factory-pristine prototypes had been trucked and airlifted in for the event.

Gleaming passenger diesel-electrics stood on static display beside mighty Hudson Locomotives. There were Big Boys and U-Boats and Alcos, Baldwin diesels and Budliners. Narrow-gauge curiosities dwarfed by Challenger 4-6-6-4s and other titans of the steam age.

Farther in the fenced-off fairground stood the prototypes and the late-model diesels on longer lengths of trackage. They shuttled back and forth, like dumb, throbbing beasts of burden. GM Big Macs. French TGV's. German ICE trains. Swedish X-2000s. Russian diesels and all the latest in bullet trains and magnetic-levitation technology, bright in stealth livery or manufacturer's colors.

Beyond that impressive array, candy-striped flea-market tents were set up, displaying railroad paraphernalia ranging from massive coffee-table books to videotapes and memorabilia from lines lost to man but still remembered fondly by rail fans—all being snapped up by attendees, who milled about wearing the stunned, beatific expressions normally associated with religious fanatics.

Melvis O. Cupper wore one of those expressions. He was in hog heaven from the moment he paid his twenty-five dollar, one-day admission and walked through the wonderland of Mallets and Big Boys, taking his Stetson off in mute respect to the inert iron gods of steam he loved so dearly.

By the time he got to the dealers' area, he was primed to buy. And buy he did.

Three hours of picking over knicknack tables had filled his arms with treasure and emptied his wallet. He groaned under the weight of the two-place reproduction-Hiawatha table setting, the LeHigh Valley video collection, a *Texas Eagle* calendar and assorted plastic-model kits. He was happy; he was content. He had everything an honest rail fan could ever want.

Except one absent article.

K. C. Crockett.

Melvis had tried to shove K.C. out of his mind, but strain as he might, he couldn't uncouple her from his heart. That was the long and short of it.

Even with new derailments occurring hourly, and the NTSB shorthanded during this, the traditional vacation month, Melvis had reached his limit.

He'd called in sick, hopped a flight to Denver and practiced what he was going to say the next time he laid eyes on his heart's desire.

There was just one hitch in the rope.

There was no sign of K.C. anywhere. Lot of clues, though.

Whenever a flashbulb exploded, Melvis whirled, his eyes tracking the after-burn. Many times he barreled through the surging crowd, stepping on toes and muttering "Pardon me" until he felt like a weak-bladdered penitent at a Baptist revival meet.

But no K.C. gal.

It was as hard to take as sand in the journal box. But Melvis had come a long way, and giving up wasn't in his nature.

"Sure hope she didn't take up with that fool Air Force major," he grumbled as he set down his booty and availed himself of some cool bottled water.

Fanning himself with his hat, Melvis scanned the sea of heads. His chest expanded to see so many rail fans gathered in one spot. These were God's people, he reflected. There weren't truer or more-natural souls trampling God's good green footstool.

"If only I can rope K.C.," he muttered, "I'll be content with my lot in life."

His eyes, scanning the giant outdoor pavilions, rested on the largest of them all. A banner was hung across the entrance: MAGLEV. RIDE THE FUTURE OF RAIL NOW.

"If she's here, she's in that heathen den of iniquity," Melvis muttered. He swallowed hard. "Guess I just gotta steel myself and sashay into the lion's den," he said, picking up his packages.

Melvis strode toward the sign, his knees growing weak, his heart starting to trip-hammer.

"Steel wheels are my life," he told himself. "But if I gotta eat a little cold crow to catch me a rail-friendly wife, well, I'm man enough to do that, I reckon."

AT THE RAIL EXPO entrance, the Master of Sinanju refused to get in line.

"I am Reigning Master," he told Remo. "I will not stand in line with the common peasantry."

Remo looked at him. "So I have to?"

"No, you do not have to. But I will not stand in line."

"This is a co-equal partnership," Remo argued.

"If it is a co-equal partnership," Chiun retorted, "why I am burdened with these?" And he raised the pair of *katana* blades wrapped in butcher paper to disguise them.

"Because you insisted," Remo shot back.

In the end, Remo stood in line and, when the line finally reached the ticket booth, he waved Chiun to cut in front of him.

At Remo's back a commotion started up.

"Hey! That's not fair!" the customer behind him complained.

"I'm not with him," Remo said.

"You let him cut in front of you."

"No. He cut in front of me. I just didn't stop him."

When Chiun reached the head of the line, he came face-to-face with a slick-haired Japanese ticket taker in a tuxedo.

Their eyes met, and the ticket taker started to say something.

"Pay this *Nihonjinwa,* Remo," said Chiun, marching through the entrance gate.

Remo dug into a pocket.

"You are with him?" the ticket taker said thinly.

"Only as far as the grave," muttered Remo, handing over a fifty-dollar bill. "What time does Bat-sucker show up?" he asked.

"Batsuka-san due at one," he was told.

"I can hardly wait."

Inside, Remo found Chiun standing in the shadow of a giant black locomotive.

"Come on."

"What is the hurry?" asked Chiun, examining the wheels.

"We're on an assignment."

"Does that mean we cannot stop to smell the steam?"

"We can smell the steam after we bust the *ronin*."

Chiun looked up with appealing hazel eyes. "Promise?"

"Scout's honor," sighed Remo.

They walked on. Chiun carried his hands in his silvery kimono sleeves, where his broken nail would go unnoticed.

"Keep your eyes peeled for the Nishitsu booth or whatever it is. That's where Batsucker will be."

"You have peeled-eye duty," Chiun sniffed. "I am entrusted with the *katanas*, and so with the honor of the House."

They moved through the shifting sea of humanity like two needles passing through coarse-woven fabric on a moving loom. Even people not watching where they were going managed to miss bumping into them.

Remo got Chiun past the old-steam-engines section without too much delay.

Chiun's frown deepened.

"What's wrong?" asked Remo.

"I did not see my heart's desire."

"What's that?"

"A Mikado 2-8-2."

"I think they'll be kinda scarce here."

"I see trains from other nations. Why is the pride of the Kyong-Ji Line absent?"

"After this is over, you can write your congressman," Remo said dryly.

The flea-market tents were the most congested. Chiun insisted upon stopping at every table to ask if they had heard of the Kyong-Ji Line.

Of course, no one had. So the Master of Sinanju took it upon himself to explain it, finishing with a triumphant, "I rode her mighty Mikado 2-8-2 engine in my youngest days."

Soon Chiun had picked up a train of his own, a train of people wearing engineer caps and rail-fan buttons.

Chiun willingly signed autographs for any who asked. He posed for pictures. He charged all but the children under seven years, because they had been admitted free.

To kill time, Remo decided to case the Nishitsu display.

THE NISHITSU PAVILION was the largest of all, Remo discovered when he reached the far end of the Rail Expo grounds. It looked more like a miniature theme park with its own monorail system, except the monorail was flush to the ground at an open side of the pavilion. Something sat on the track, but it was shrouded in blue parachute silk on which the four-moons-in-a-disk logo was emblazoned.

Two Japanese men in royal blue blazers greeted Remo at the entrance. They bowed their heads in his direction and handed him Nishitsu business cards from a big fishbowl of cards.

"Preased that you come to Nishitsu dispray," one said as the other offered his card.

"Thanks," Remo said.

"You have card for us?" one asked.

"Sure." And Remo extracted his wallet, going through his set of ID cards until he found an appropriate one.

One Japanese looked at the name, blinked and took a stab at it. "Remo..."

"Llewell. That's with four *l*s."

"Rrewerr."

"Llewell. Try touching the roof of your mouth with your tongue on the *l*s."

The other struggled with it, his voice sounding as if he had a mouthful of peanut butter. "Rrewerr."

"Keep practicing," Remo said, brushing past them. "I'll be back to check on your progress."

Inside the pavilion, more Japanese suits were milling about, talking up the wonders of magnetic levitation, passing out pamphlets, photocopied newspaper articles and other items designed to tout the benefits of maglev and the horrors of steel-wheel and rail technology. Blowups of past U.S. rail disasters—some dating back to the steam age—stood beside artists' conceptions of pristine maglev trains whizzing safely through farmland and cities.

One greeter drifted up to Remo and bowed once. "You have heard of magrev?" he asked.

"Sure. Make rove, not war."

The Japanese looked blank, so Remo asked, "Batsucker here yet?"

"Batsuka-san wirr arrive shortry. Wirr sign autographs for nominar sum and talk of magrev. You have heard of magrev?"

"You asked me that already. Actually I'm a steel-wheel kinda guy."

The man shook his head violently. "Sterr-wherr technorogy no good. Backward. Trains jump track. Many die. Not good. Come, I show you future of train."

Remo allowed himself to be led through a maze of booths and audiovisual displays. One booth was empty but bore a standing sign.

> Seattle Mariners Slugger
> Furio Batsuka
> Autographs Only $55.00

"He's charging for autographs?" Remo said.

"Yes. Is very American, yes?"

"Tell that to the irate fans who skipped the All-Star Game."

The Japanese looked blank again, so Remo let it pass. They went to the side of the pavilion that opened to fresh air and blue sky.

The maglev engine sat on an aluminum guideway that belted around in a semicircle. The parachute silk was being pulled off in preparation for a demonstration trial. The engine gleamed white, a manta ray of a thing with an airflow body that sprouted two small, angled fins from its back. There was one passenger car attached, also white as toothpaste.

"There," the Japanese said proudly. "Magrev train."

Remo shook his head sadly. "It'll never fly."

"No. No. Fins for stabirity, not fright. In Japan magrev train convey persons as fast as airprane. Safer than airprane. Arso creaner. No porrution. No unsafe rairs."

"That's 'rails.'"

"Yes, I say that. Rairs."

"What time did you say Batsucker was due?" asked Remo.

"Batsuka-san due ten minute. You wait. He wirr exprain magrev for you. Must go."

And the Nishitsu shill hurried off.

Noticing the time, Remo decided to go find the Master of Sinanju and get the showdown on the road. He had heard enough. Nishitsu was pushing its magnetic-levitation trains.

MELVIS CUPPER WAS GREETED by two bowing Japanese. At the entrance to the Nishitsu pavilion, one offered his card.

Automatically Melvis offered his back.

They looked at the card and read the words National Transportation Safety Board. Then exchanged nervous glances.

"You here to see Batsuka-san?" one asked.

"Who?"

"Furio Batsuka, Seattre Mariners srugger. You know, *basuboru?*"

Melvis got bug-eyed. "The guy they call Typhoon Batsuka? He's here?"

"Yes."

"Dang, he's about the only thing in baseball worth spit these days. Point me the dang way."

"Not here yet. Soon."

"Thank you kindly," said Melvis, tipping his hat.

THE LIMOUSINE FERRYING Furio Batsuka pulled up at the rear entrance to the Nishitsu pavilion at exactly two minutes to one. He stepped out, wearing a bland expression and his white Mariners uniform.

Nishitsu employees bowed him into the immense pavilion. Security teams with ear microphones formed a flying wedge and protected him all the way to the autograph booth where he was to appear.

It was all very smooth, extremely efficient—and very, very Japanese.

Furio had missed such efficiency during his mission in America. But soon he would return to Osaka. Yes. Very soon.

There was already a line, he saw as he took the chair and a Nishitsu salaryman picked up a microphone and began announcing his arrival in English and Japanese.

It went with Japanese efficiency. They came up, mouthed crude banalities and handed over crisp dollar bills. Furio signed whatever was offered, charging an extra ten dollars if an eight-by-ten glossy was requested.

It amazed him still, even after three years in America. He was paid a handsome salary, and the very people whose ticket purchases paid his salary willingly exchanged good money for his signature.

It was no wonder, he had long ago concluded, that American baseball was slowly dying.

That and the fact they played it so clumsily. Everyone knew the perfect baseball game was one fought to a draw.

The sixth man in line had a booming, twangy voice that brought Furio out of his reverie.

"Hidy. Name's Cupper. Melvis O. And I'm a right big fan."

The face looked familiar. Then Furio noticed the black letters stenciled on the crown of the white cowboy hat.

NTSB.

I have seen this man before, was his first thought.

His second was *I have seen this man in Nebraska only yesterday.* And the blood in his veins turned to ice.

"You wish autograph?" he said, steadying himself.

"Sure."

And the NTSB man who should not have been there plucked an eight-by-ten glossy from the stack and laid it before him.

"What is name again?" Furio asked, silver ink pen poised over his own naked face.

"Like I said, Cupper. Melvis O. The *O*'s for Orvis."

A girlish voice suddenly squealed, "Melvis! Is that you?"

Melvis Cupper heard the voice he ached to hear and swallowed hard as his legs got all rubbery.

"K.C.?"

It was her, all right, sashaying up in her hip-hugging dungarees and Casey Jones cap. She hadn't changed a lick. That seemed like a right proper opening line, so Melvis availed himself of it.

"You ain't changed a lick."

"Shucks, Melvis. It's only been a day. What did you expect? Wrinkles?" She had her hands on her hips and a skeptical look on her oval face.

"What I expected is what I'm seeing," Melvis said. "K.C. gal, I came all this way to see you." He thrust out a hand, saying, "Here."

K.C.'s eyes flew wide. "Is this what I see?"

"Dang straight. It's the nose herald off an old Chicago & Northwestern F-unit. I just bought it. Thought it had your name all over it."

She was hugging the nose herald to her bosom as she said, "Oh, Melvis. I don't know what to say."

"Then let me do the talkin', K.C., I know you think I'm the lowest thing this side of the Red River and a ball-hog to boot from the way I got short with you back in Cornhusker territory, but I can change."

"Melvis, what are you trying to say?"

"I'm talkin' about a lash-up. You and me. Engine and coal car. Rolling inseparable down the main line of life."

"Shucks, Melvis. I don't rightly know what to say."

"Then say yes."

"Will you take a ride in a maglev train with me while I think about it?"

"That's a hard thing for me to do, bein' a confirmed steel-wheeler like I am," Melvis muttered.

"Well, either you can or you can't."

"One second. Let me say goodbye to my good Jap buddy, Batsuka."

But when Melvis looked back to the booth, Furio Batsuka was gone. So was his security entourage.

And Melvis was suddenly aware of all the disgruntled people milling about. One glance from K.C.'s Conrail blue eyes, and everyone else in the universe faded into the background again. The corners of his grin were nipping at his earlobes.

FURIO BATSUKA didn't understand what was going on, but he could take no chances. While the two Americans were busy with their crazy courtship talk, he had his security team usher him out of the pavilion and back into the waiting company limousine.

The limo roared back to the hotel. In the back he punched up a long-distance number on the cell phone.

"*Moshi moshi.*"

"There is a problem," Furio said quickly. "I think my cover has been blown."

The voice of Kozo Nishitsu at the other end became low and furious.

REMO FOUND the Master of Sinanju regaling a group of children with tales of the Kyong-Ji Line.

"There you are," Remo said. "Come on. Get a move on. Batsucker's due any second."

Chiun laid his long-nailed hands on the heads of two boys, saying, "Remember always—Korean steam is the most noble and pure steam of all."

They waved him goodbye, calling him Uncle Chiun.

"Batsucker's not going to be armored up, so this should be a piece of cake," Remo told Chiun as they moved through the crowd.

"It is time for the reckoning that has waited since the days of Kang."

"I thought you were off that ghost-*ronin* kick?"

"We fight the Nishi clan. There is no doubt of this. Take your *katana*, Remo."

Accepting the paper-wrapped blade, Remo led the way, Chiun following determinedly.

At the pavilion entrance, they were met by two stiff-faced Japanese greeters.

"You have heard of magrev?" one asked.

"We danced this dippy dance already," Remo said.

"One side, *jokebare!*" Chiun hissed.

"*Senjin!*" spat one greeter.

"*Chanko!*" snarled another.

At that, Chiun stripped his *katana* of its butcher paper camouflage and sliced their neckties off at the knot.

Faces whitening, the pair stepped aside.

"What's a *jokebare?*" asked Remo as they ducked into the Nishitsu pavilion.

"The worst thing you can call a *Nihonjinwa,*" spat Chiun.

Inside, Remo and Chiun found the autograph booth empty and a number of baseball and rail fans jostling about.

Remo collared one. "Where's Batsuka?"

"Ran off. Hardly gave six autographs. I tell you, these ball players have just got too big for their durn britches."

"Come on, Little Father. Something's wrong."

Moving in the direction indicated, they got barely twenty feet when they ran into Melvis Cupper and K. C. Crockett, walking arm in arm.

"Look, Remo!" squeaked Chiun. "It is Melvis and K.C. Reunited."

"What are you two doing here?" Remo asked.

"I came to make amends," Melvis said. "We're on our way to ride the maglev, poisonous as that thought may be to a true-blue wheel-and-rail man like myself."

K.C. jabbed him in the ribs, saying, "Watch your mouth, Melvis. Remember that you are on probation."

"Sorry, K.C. What about you two fellas?"

"We're looking for Furio Batsuka," said Remo.

"Hell, you just missed him. I was just talkin' to him, turned my back a minute and he'd lit out slick as greased lightning."

"He saw you?" Remo asked sharply.

"Sure. Walked right up and introduced myself proper."

"Damn. He must have recognized you."

"What's that again?"

"Forget it," said Remo, hurrying on.

THE PAVILION REAR-EXIT door was open, and Remo and Chiun went through it.

Two husky security men with earphones were standing with hands down, clasping wrists in what Remo recognized as the semiofficial bodyguard stance.

"Where's Batsucker?" Remo demanded.

"Are you with Nishitsu?" one asked in impeccable English.

"Are you?" Chiun countered.

"Yes."

"Good," said Remo, taking one by the neck and the other by the throat. "Listen carefully, I'm looking for Furio Batsucker and I am in a very violent rush."

"His name Batsuka," the second man said thickly.

"Thank you for the elocution lesson." And Remo squeezed.

The one whose throat was caught developed a new coloration while the one Remo had by the neck heard the distant sound of his cervical vertebrae grinding.

Both suddenly changed allegiance.

"Hotel. Limo," one gurgled.

"Denver Hirton. That way," the other wheezed, pointing.

"I could use your car keys."

They couldn't get their hands into their pockets fast enough. Remo picked the set with the Mercedes key ring because he was in a Mercedes mood. Then he squeezed their necks to clamp off the last, sluggish blood flow to the brain. They made a sleepy pile.

"Much obliged," said Remo.

The Master of Sinanju pointedly stepped on their faces as he walked over them.

Soon they were burning rubber out of the parking lot.

IN HIS HOTEL ROOM Furio Batsuka was talking into the portable cell phone he had carried up from the limousine.

"Leave Denver immediately," the shogun was saying from distant Japan.

"*Hai.*"

"Do not drive or fly. And above all, do not go by rail."

"There is only one other path," he breathed.

"That is the path you must take."

"I understand."

"Pick up where you left off. The U.S. media are doing our jobs for us. We must keep up the pressure. Let Nishitsu Denver promote the product. Now go."

Furio hung up. He had stripped off his Mariners uniform as he talked. For the last time, he knew. Now he stood nearly nude in the G-string undergarment of the samurai.

But he was not a samurai, he thought as he belted on the *shigati* and *obi* foundation garments. He was only a *ronin*. Forbidden to wear the crest of his clan as he performed his work in an alien land.

The armor went on layer upon layer. When it was in place, he donned the Nishitsu-brand nickel-cadmium battery-pack belt that powered the Nishitsu vibrating exoskeleton.

The last element was the folding tatami-style helmet. Furio covered his head, the tinted face shield dropping into place. He had taken great care never to be seen. But he wore a famous face and could take no chances even in a large, barbarian nation such as this, where white men saw a Japanese face rather than an individual one.

Going to the closet, he extracted his weapon bag. The loss of two *katana*s was humbling but not critical. He extracted a heavy battle-ax, thinking this is the proper tool to bring down a trestle bridge.

Attired in the electronic armor that made him more invincible than the mightiest samurai of old, Furio Batsuka dialed a number in Mobile, Alabama.

"Moshi moshi," a voice replied guardedly.

"Emergency transmission to come. Stand by."

"Hai," the well-trained technician said, instantly hanging up.

THERE WAS a cellular phone in the Mercedes's front seat, and Remo had Chiun dial it they as raced through the streets of downtown Denver.

Chiun held it to Remo's face when Harold Smith came on the line.

"Smitty. We just missed Batsuka. He got spooked. He's headed for the Denver Hilton. Odds are he's taking the fastest way out of town."

"One moment," said Smith.

The line hummed. Then Smith returned.

"Remo, I just phoned the Hilton. Batsuka is registered in room 14-D."

"We're almost there," Remo said, screeching through a turn.

"Hold the line."

Smith returned shortly. "Remo, a call was just made to Mobile, Alabama, from room 14-D of the Denver Hilton."

"We missed him!"

"Assume nothing. Check the room. If he has not escaped, there may be something I can do on this end."

"What do you mean?"

But Smith had hung up.

Chiun tossed the phone out the window while Remo went into a turn with the gas pedal pressed flat to the floorboards.

FURIO BATSUKA CHECKED his armor. It was very heavy when both armor and wearer were in what was called solid state. He'd been told that the original Goblin Suit had been white and fit the skin like vinyl. The fiber-optic cables were mounted externally and shone with racing golden lights when the suit was activated. This had proved insufficient for stealth assignments.

Furio would rather be a *ronin* than a goblin, if that were the only choice.

Battle-ax in hand, he reached his mailed fist toward the room telephone. It was time to be on his way. His finger moved toward the Redial button.

Furio heard the hotel-room door smash in with a sound like splintering thunder.

Turning, he saw them. The strange pair from Nebraska. One obviously Korean, the other the white with the thick wrists.

And to his surprise, each brandished one of his Nishitsu electronic *katana*s.

In that moment of shock, Furio Batsuka knew he had been exposed. He also knew he had time to activate his armor or hit Redial, but not both.

They came at him from two sides. A practical approach. He raised his *ono*. It was the heavier weapon. They had no chance even if there were two of them. He reached for the shoulder rheostat that would activate his armor.

It happened so fast Furio Batsuka had trouble comprehending it.

A fluttery swish came from one side. The Korean.

Then his battle-ax fell to the floor with a muffled clank.

Furio looked down.

It lay on the rug amid a splash of blood. Around it lay tiny sausagelike objects that seemed very familiar. He recognized them. Then understood that he was looking at his own fingers. The blood pumping from the newly made stumps of his right hand confirmed that stupefying conclusion.

Furio Batsuka had trained and trained for combat. He was a samurai. He was not going to be defeated by anything less than another samurai. And, of course, there were none.

He activated the armor. The lightness came over his body, and he strode to the telephone.

They danced around him, swinging and slashing furiously. Or at least the whirling dervish of a Korean was furious. He went for Furio's head, his ankles, his neck. His Wheel Stroke was quite adroit, amazingly.

The other showed inferior grace. But appeared to have mastered the Scarf Sweep. Furio could almost hear the blade bite through his neck longitudinally.

It was an impasse. As long as he remained in his spectralized state, he could not dial. But neither could he be harmed.

Folding his arms to show his lack of fear, Furio stood resolute.

The blood dripping from his fingers, he noticed, went through the rug without staining. It was a very interesting phenomenon.

They circled him.

"It's all over, Batsuka," the white said. "We're on to you."

"Fingerless *ronin*," the other shrieked, "you will pay for your temerity. For I am the Master of Sinanju!"

Furio Batsuka heard the word *Sinanju*. Sinanju? What was it he had heard about a Sinanju? The name sounded Japanese, but the old man gave it a Korean pronunciation. It could be Korean. But Furio could not recall where he had heard of it. A lesser martial art, he thought. There was so many. Anyone could learn kung fu or karate and those other inferior arts.

But in the modern word, there was only one practicing samurai. And his name was Furio Batsuka.

Eventually the old Korean grew tired of the aimless slashing of air. He stopped.

The white stepped around behind him.

Furio decided to ignore him. They could not harm him. And as long as he didn't bleed to death, he was all right.

"You have been exposed, *ronin* without a face. Your shame is great. Your humiliation is complete."

And kneeling briefly, he picked up Furio Batsuka's fingers and began throwing them in his face in the ancient gesture of contempt.

Furio stiffened. This was the supreme insult. It must be avenged. More importantly he could not allow his samurai fingers to be so desecrated. There was still time to sew them back on.

The idea struck him with unsurpassed brilliance.

There were telephones in other rooms. He could go to them.

And so he turned his back on the annoying pair and melted through the wall as if it were soggy rice paper.

Furio emerged on the other side with ease.

If they behaved logically, they would follow him in. Then he could simply step back, collect his fingers and fax himself to Mobile, Alabama.

The difficulty was, they didn't follow. Furio waited.

Were they struck dumb by his feat of electronic magic? No, they had seen him operate before. It could not be that.

Curious, Furio returned to the connecting wall and shoved his helmeted head through as if into a waterfall curtain.

They stood waiting for him. Or rather, the Korean did.

And he was holding Furio's five fingers in his hands. As Furio watched, he began breaking them like bread sticks.

Eyes widening with horror, Furio started back into the other room.

The initial sensation was of a blow. But of course no blow could harm him in this dematerialized state.

But he looked down anyway.

He was half in and half out of the wall. He could see as far down as his black breastplate. The pain was beneath that. Easing forward, he saw himself coming out of the wall—then saw the ebony hilt of a *katana* protruding from a seam in his samurai armor.

Furio Batsuka blinked.

How could this be? he thought.

Then he realized that the blade was in its dematerialized state, too.

I have been stabbed by my own blade, he thought. He recognized the thrust. An elegant Thunder Stroke. But who?

And down on the floor crouched the white with an expression on his cruel face that said *Gotcha.*

Instinct took over then. Furio staggered back into the other room. There the unguarded telephone waited.

He dared not look down. The blade had pierced him through the side, but perhaps the wound was not assuredly fatal. His clan would not allow their only samurai to expire. Not after such exemplary service.

Reaching the phone, Furio deactivated the armor. The weight of it oppressed him. And a sharp twinge convulsed his pierced belly. Through his pain, he stabbed out the number by memory. His eyes began tearing. For the blade was still in his belly.

The line rang once, the connection opened. Escape was his. And if his ancestors were with him, so was life.

Reaching for the shoulder-mounted rheostat, which would retune his molecules into a electronic state that would cause the open line to draw him in, Furio heard a voice.

"Batter up."

His eyes veered to the sound. It came from the door, which was open. The white stood there, one hand completing a sweeping motion. The fingers were splayed, the hand empty.

And before him, turning with a silent speed, was the other *katana*, making no sound, not cutting, therefore harmless to all things except Furio Batsuka in his current molecular state.

At that moment, the familiar suck and roar of the fiber-optic cable ingesting his spectralized atoms came, and he exulted, "I am safe now."

THE *KATANA* TURNED solid and bounced off the far wall. Remo went to pick it up, passing through the spot where Furio Batsuka had stood a moment before. His body had been sucked into the phone receiver like black liquid tar into a pipe.

Chiun hurried in, hazel eyes darting about.

He beheld his pupil picking up the *katana*. And rolling on the rug before him was the black *ronin*'s helmet of Furio Batsuka, the head still inside.

"Where is the rest of him?" Chiun asked, nudging the helmet to a stop. Instantly the rug started discoloring around it.

Remo pointed to a telephone receiver dangling from a desk.

"Went into the phone. Guess we got him, huh?"

"You only vanquished the head."

Remo grinned. "Half a *ronin* is better than none."

Reaching down, the Master of Sinanju picked up the helmet. He separated head from helmet and held the head up by its hair.

"What are you doing?" Remo asked.

"Some times the head does not die at once."

It looked that way here. The eyes were jerking and rolling about in their sockets. The mouth sagged, shut, then sagged again as muscular strength drained away.

"Looks like he's trying to say something," Remo said.

"Can you hear me, cur of Nishi?" Chiun asked. "I spit upon you."

The eyes suddenly got organized. They seemed to fall into focus on the Master of Sinanju's angry face.

The mouth struggled, then gaped all the way open, as if in surprise.

Chiun spit into the mouth.

FURIO BATSUKA FOUND himself looking into the face of the old Korean. His first thought was *How did he beat me to Mobile?*

His second was *I am taller that he. Why does he seem as tall as I?*

Then the room spun and spun, and Furio Batsuka saw the window glass zooming at him, shatter, and enjoyed an exhilarating view of the Denver skyline before his dead head dropped into an open Dumpster, where squirming maggots soon made a temporary home.

BACK AT THE HOTEL Remo picked up the telephone and heard a rush of static. He said, *"moshi moshi,"* and getting no response, hung up.

"Better check in with Smith," suggested Remo.

Harold Smith's voice was ghastly when Remo got him on the line.

"I assume you were successful?" he croaked thickly.

"How do you assume that?" wondered Remo.

"Because I had all outgoing telephone calls from the Denver Hilton rerouted to my office and I have a headless samurai warrior lying on my desktop," Smith said jerkily.

"Nice catch," said Remo.

Chiun was stamping about in circles, waving the trophy battle-ax in frustration. "It is *ronin!* Why can you two not get this straight?"

Harold Smith said, "Have you learned Nishitsu's true objective?"

"Yeah. They're pushing the horror of steel wheels on rail on one hand and the joys of magnetic levitation on the other. I think that says it all."

"They cannot be allowed to enjoy the fruits of their scheme."

"We could have some fun with their demonstration model," suggested Remo.

"Do so." Smith hung up.

Remo hung up. "Okay, Little Father. Once we tie up the loose ends, we're done."

Chiun tossed the battle-ax on the bed, but Remo recovered it. He had the remaining *katana* in hand.

"Can't leave these lying around to give the maid ideas."

They left the room.

"What is this thing called anyway?" Remo asked Chiun, hefting the ax.

"It is an *ono*. A battle-ax."

"That explains Yoko," Remo said as the elevator door opened to admit them.

27

The white-coated Nishitsu demonstration team stood before the waiting maglev engine and its single car, extolling the virtues of magnetic-levitation transportation.

Melvis Cupper heard the words, but he was like a Baptist at a Hindu widow-burning ceremony. He understood the reasoning; he just flat out did not believe in the procedure.

"Magnetic revitation is the future. Magnetic revitation is superior to arr other rair technorogies. The many viorent derairments America now experiencing proves that ord technorogy is no ronger good for America. Nishitsu magrev is the future for America. If this demonstration convinces you, write congressmen and senators. Write White House Terr them you want safe rair transporation, not train wrecks."

"Man, he is layin' it on thick, ain't he?" Melvis muttered.

K.C. punched him playfully. "Hush, Mel. Open your mind, not just your ears."

"Now it is time to board the *Nishitsu Express* to future," the corporate spokesman said.

The door hummed open, and they began boarding.

"Man, I hope I got the stomach for this," Melvis said.

K.C. said, "I won't force you, Melvis. You gotta take this step on your own."

Melvis's face scrunched up. "Oh, Lord, give me the strength. What I do, I do for love and not out of disrespect for rail and country."

Closing his eyes, Melvis allowed himself to be guided onto the humming car. He felt like Jonah in more ways than one.

"You can open them now," K.C. prompted.

Melvis did.

It was like being inside a pneumatic tube, he decided. All slicked up, plush, polished and featureless. The seats hardly looked like seats. And they were facing every which way.

"Prease take seats," a crisp Japanese voice said over the intercom.

Melvis waved K.C. into a seat and sat beside her. The car soon filled up.

Melvis noticed his knees were knocking together. He wasn't sure if it was because he had found true love or because he was letting himself be carried off by heathen rail technology.

A sudden increase in the humming warned him the brief trip was about to start.

"Magrev operates on principre of opposing porarity," the intercom voice continued.

"What'd he say?" Melvis asked.

"Polarity," said K.C.

"Sounded like *porarity*."

"The train is rifted off the guideway, and froats. Rinier synchronous motor provide forward propursion."

"Boy, this is way over my head," Melvis lamented. "I'm hearin' words I never did hear before."

K.C. slapped him on the top of the head. Melvis grinned. He liked his women playful.

"We go now," the intercom voice said.

At the last moment, before the doors could shut, two familiar figures jumped aboard.

"Well looky, K.C. gal. There's our good buddies."

"Hi, y'all," K.C. said.

"Sorry there ain't a seat," Melvis said. "Everybody seems to be goin' our way."

"We don't mind standing," said Remo.

"Surprised to see you astride this beast, old-timer," Melvis told Chiun.

"Hush," said Chiun. "I am attempting to think like an elephant."

"Is that a fact?"

Melvis noticed Remo seemed to be doing the same thing.

They closed their eyes. And with a whine, the maglev train engaged.

They felt the lift. A forward bump. And *crash!* the car dropped back into the guideway. Smoke began pouring from floor vents. Somewhere an electrical short began sparking.

"What happened?" K.C. wailed.

"Off train. Off train," the suddenly frantic intercom voice said. "Marfunction. Off train, prease."

They evacuated the car the way salt leaves a shaker.

White-faced Nishitsu technicians scrambled into the car, wielding dry-chemical extinguishers. They began throwing foam and white chemical everywhere in their panic.

"What happened?" K.C. said, aghast. "Why didn't it go?"

Melvis looked over to Remo and Chiun.

Chiun winked. Melvis winked back.

"If I were writing that up, gal, I'd call it an act of God. Pure and simple."

K.C. melted into tears.

Melvis saw this and, taking her by the shoulders, turned her around. He lifted her head up by the chin.

"Gal, you gotta get this maglev stuff out of your pretty head. Maybe maglev will get going someday. Maybe not. But I know one thing. I hanker to hitch my caboose to your train."

"You think we're gauge-compatible?"

"If we ain't, we'll make some changes. I plumb adore you, and that's that. What do you say to a lash-up?"

K.C. threw her arms around his neck, crying, "Melvis, when you talk that way, my boiler gets cooking like something unnatural. I am yours forever and ever!"

"K.C., you and me are a-goin' to honeymoon on the Texas beer train, riding over some of the most traction-motor-fryin', coupler-knuckle-bustin' track in all of creation."

"Shucks, I ain't never made it on a train before."

"Your first time's always special."

Suddenly remembering they weren't alone, Melvis turned and gathered up a great big grin on his face. "You fellers hear? We're gettin' hitched."

But there was no sign of the pair.

"Well, four's company, anyhow," said Melvis. "Let's go feast our eyes on some real U.S. of A. locomotives."

On their way out they noticed a ruckus at the front of the maglev engine.

Someone had plunged a sword and a battle-ax into the nose of the engine—right through the four-moon Nishitsu corporate symbol.

Melvis recognized the ebony handle of the sword.

Flashing his NTSB ID card, he bulled his way through and took possession of the sword saying, "Nice of them boys to remember this here *tanaka*'s NTSB evidence."

And tucking it under one arm, he offered K.C. the other and they strode off into the rest of their lives, grinning.

BACK AT FOLCROFT the Master of Sinanju surrendered the Nishitsu *ronin*'s helmet with great ceremony.

"The dread foe is no more, O Emperor."

"Er, thank you," said Smith, gingerly examining the helmet for its expected contents. Finding none, he looked up quizzically.

"Chiun tossed it into a Dumpster," said Remo.

"The honor of my House is restored," Chiun said stiffly.

"Where is the rest of the samurai?" Remo asked.

Chiun flared. "*Ronin!* I give you the correct term, and you throw it away like the peel of a banana."

Smith cleared his throat. "Actually Remo is correct, Master Chiun. The samurai was unquestionably a Nishitsu corporate employee. Therefore, he was truly a samurai."

"Impossible. The clans have been scattered to the winds."

"Not so," said Smith. "Several modern Japanese companies are in fact descended from old samurai clans."

"What is this!"

"I have been researching Nishitsu in depth. Its owners trace their lineage back to the Nishi clan. One of their subsidiary brands uses the old clan badge as its corporate logo."

Chiun made two angry fists. "Then our work is undone."

Smith nodded. "Although this is the first time Nitshitsu has used their electronic technology against U.S. interests, you will recall the former head of Nishitsu was responsible for the vicious military attack on Yuma, Arizona, several years ago. This was explained away at the time as the work of single deranged mind."

"I never bought that," said Remo.

"Neither did I," said Smith. "But now the company has shown its true colors, we are obligated to discourage them from thinking they can strike at U.S. interests with impunity."

Chiun bowed. "We will be pleased to steal into occupied Japan to settle the scores of your house and ours."

"Little Father, Japan isn't occupied anymore."

"It is occupied by Japanese, is it not?"

"Touché," said Remo. A thought struck him. "One thing I still don't get. That cattle-car derailment a year ago. Was it just a coincidence that I happened to be in the area?"

"It would appear so," said Smith.

Remo grunted. "If I kept my eyes open, I might have run into Batsucker last year. A lot of lives might have been saved."

"It matters only that we have emerged triumphant," said Chiun. "Not when."

"So, where did you stash the body, Smitty?"

"The basement coal furnace."

Remo laughed. "Don't forget to stir the ashes before you throw them out."

"I will get back to you on this assignment, Remo," said Smith, looking uncomfortable.

"No problem," said Remo. "Chiun and I have an appointment with a box full of mystery."

IN THE FOLCROFT GYM Remo stood over the silver trunk with the lapis lazuli phoenixes.

"Okay, open it."

Chiun hesitated. "I have told you this box contains sloth and shame."

"Over and over."

Chiun fixed Remo with his thinning hazel gaze. "*Your* sloth and *my* shame."

"Never owned a sloth in my entire life. And what do you have to be ashamed of?"

"For as long as I have known the greatness in you, Remo Williams, I have filled this box with the leavings of your stubbornness, your indolence, your—"

"Did you say leaves? This box is full of freaking leaves?"

"No. I said leavings."

"Well, open it."

Chiun frowned deeply. Then, bending, he inserted a long fingernail into the lock and twisted it. The lock clicked. The lid loosened.

"Here it comes," said Remo.

"Once this lid is lifted, your shame will be visible even to my ancestors, who are your ancestors."

"I can take it."

Abruptly Chiun flung the lid upward. Stepping back, he covered his face with his sleeves, saying, "I cannot bear to look."

"Well, I can," said Remo. He knelt.

The box was chock-full. The contents looked like excelsior, except it was a dull white. Old rice and dirty glass shards came to mind next. But the material was none of these things.

Carefully Remo grabbed up a handful. "These look like—"

"Yes!"

"I don't believe it!"

"Yes. They are yours. Do not deny it."

"You've been saving my fingernail *clippings?*"

"Since the first time you refused my entreaties to do the correct thing," said Chiun.

"All these years?" Remo roared.

"And now even the great Masters in the Void know," Chiun lamented.

Remo looked at the box with a stunned expression. Chiun peered out from behind one sleeve.

"It is not too late, you know," he said hopefully.

"I am *not* growing my nails like yours."

"Then all my sacrifices have been in vain," Chiun said sadly, his silk-draperied arms dropping like silvery wings. His head hung low. His eyes sneaked a look up past his sparse fluttering lashes.

Digging into a pocket, Remo pulled out Chiun's broken nail, which he had been carrying since Mystic. "Whose shame is greater, yours or mine?" he asked.

"Mine has been avenged," Chiun returned stiffly.

"What say we take our shame and bury them both for good?"

Chiun made wrinkles along the top of his bald skull. "This is a reasonable suggestion."

"Good," said Remo, tossing Chiun's long nail into the pile and closing the lid. He hoisted the trunk onto one shoulder.

"But remember," Chiun warned, "even when the box is empty, you have not been excused from lugging duty."

"My caboose," grunted Remo.

**Blazing a perilous trail through
the heart of darkness**

JAMES AXLER

Eclipse at Noon

The nuclear exchange that ripped apart the world destroyed a way
of life thousands of years in the making. Now, generations after the
nuclear blight, Ryan Cawdor and his band of warrior survivalists
try to reclaim the hostile land, led by an undimmed vision of a
better future.

It's winner take all in the Deathlands.

Take
4 explosive books
plus a
mystery bonus
FREE

Mail to: Gold Eagle Reader Service
3010 Walden Ave.
·P.O. Box 1394
Buffalo, NY 14240-1394

YEAH! Rush me 4 FREE Gold Eagle novels and my FREE mystery gift.
Then send me 4 brand-new novels every other month as they come off
the presses. Bill me at the low price of just $15.80* for each shipment—
a saving of 15% off the cover prices for all four books! There is NO extra
charge for postage and handling! There is no minimum number of books I
must buy. I can always cancel at any time simply by returning a shipment
at your cost or by returning any shipping statement marked "cancel." Even
if I never buy another book from Gold Eagle, the 4 free books and surprise
gift are mine to keep forever.

164 BPM A3U3

Name	(PLEASE PRINT)	
Address		Apt. No.
City	State	Zip

Signature (If under 18, parent or guardian must sign)

* Terms and prices subject to change without notice. Sales tax applicable in
NY. This offer is limited to one order per household and not valid to
present subscribers. Offer not available in Canada.

AO-00